For I

I hope you enjoy it!

love Sophie xx

To See The Light Return

To See The Light Return

a Brexitopian novel

Sophie Galleymore Bird

Published by Tablo

Table of Contents

DEDICATION AND DISCLAIMER

Dedicated to the most patient man I know, my partner Gifford, and to the memory of my mother, Frances, with all my love.

★

This is a work of fiction. The only things in it that are true are the bunker, Brexit and climate change. Any similarity to people or places is entirely coincidental. Any factual inaccuracies are entirely my fault.

PROLOGUE

I blame the Queen. If she hadn't died, if she'd clung on and outlived her son, or bypassed him in the succession and passed the crown to the more tractable William, Charles wouldn't have been crowned King. He wouldn't have confirmed himself as an autocratic and eccentric despot in the minds of the British public, and the old-school farmers of Devon wouldn't have rebelled against him using his status – as both monarch and landowner – to push Parliament towards converting all agriculture to organic standards. He might as well have been trying to enforce Satanic Masses for the uproar it caused among a farming community still reeling from the trauma and divisions of Brexit.

I also blame UKIP, declaring they spoke for all despite imploding as a national political party once the odious Farago departed. If they hadn't stoked up trouble from their HQ in Torbay, whispering rebellion in the ears of our County and District Councillors – a lot of them farmers struggling to adapt to climate change and a public persuaded away from the mainstays of Devon agriculture, meat and dairy – it could all have blown over and reached a compromise that would have benefitted everyone. But no, both sides in the argument dug in and became increasingly entrenched and bitter.

What sounded like a joke, co-opting local passport and 'Republic of Devon' campaigns begun by Remainers, became an actual thing – Devolution for Devon, Take Back Our Land, Make Devon Great Again – with a referendum bought and paid for by UKIP and modelled on the secession of Cataluña from Spain. Cornwall and Scotland had been talking the talk for decades but stood back and watched as we went and took the plunge.

Despite the confident rhetoric of the campaign claims, and the warnings of recent history, it turned out the Devolvers had no plan for how to structure our governanace once we had seceded. We continued to be run by elected Councils, so one could argue we are effectively a Republic, but scratch any one of the Councillors, or our successive Mayors, and I think you'd find a Royalist not far beneath the surface. That is our abiding problem – there was no real shifting of power to the people. I wouldn't be surprised if our latest incumbent saw himself as a defacto King rather than a civic dignitary. He certainly likes to wear his chains of office at every opportunity; if a crown and sceptre were to be proposed, I do not think he would refuse them.

It was hard to see the difference at first, once Devolution was 'won'. The real changes came after Westminster pulled the army and navy bases out, and we lost the jobs and supply chains they sustained. Militia were called up from the local populace – and I mean local, because thousands of the people who had flocked here to live in our ugly new housing developments left before the ink was dry on Devon's Declaration of Independence and Secession – but there was no money to pay them. The unemployed were drafted – and there were many of those, myself included, because there were very few jobs left with fewer retirees to service. Any that stayed were too skint to leave and therefore too skint to pay for lattes, colonics and home care. There was a mass die-off within the first three years because public services fell apart.

Militia – armed with weapons traded illegally by the more enterprising of the departing army personnel – began patrolling our borders, looking for people entering or leaving without paying the tolls. Identifiable by their black uniforms, with a patch on the chest denoting the Devon flag (a black-bordered white cross on a green field the colour of mould), tales of abuses of power, both within their ranks and towards the populace, were rife but whispered.

I managed to escape the draft, being a lesbian and thus undesirable in public service; sexual freedoms were one of the first things to go. My wife and I had to stop expressing affection in public, had to pretend just to be housemates and hide our wedding bands.

Roads were blocked and began to deteriorate without central funding. Train services were axed, because we couldn't afford to maintain the tracks, or come to an agreement with the national network. Electricity supplies became erratic, because the National Grid wasn't allowed to maintain our part of the network without paying outrageous fees for the privilege. Solar panels were raided from solar farms and abandoned homes, by organised gangs from Somerset, or stolen from houses as their occupants slept. Everything broke, and stayed broken, because most of the expertise had left and there were no spare parts.

Our water and sewage systems broke down, abandoned by private companies with an eye on their bottom line rather than ours.

After that life became – literally – shit.

From the memoirs of Mrs Prendaghast

IN CASE THE SUN

For almost an hour, nothing passed him but the high summer sun, angling its beams through the laurel but casting little heat in this dark recess of overgrown woodland. Then two women walked by on foot, and ten minutes later a man with a heavily laden donkey, all pedlars headed away from the village's weekly market, picking their way carefully across deep ruts, crusts of manure and lumps of old asphalt. By then the high humidity had soaked Will's clothing, his knees were aching, and sharp bramble barbs were digging into his skin even through the tough weave of his trousers. He was shifting position, taking care to keep his head low, when he heard the approach of an engine, hacking and coughing its way up the steep incline. Aches forgotten, he hunched back down and drew a battered notebook and a stubby pencil out of the rucksack by his side.

Finding a blank space at the end of his notes, he peered through a screen of laurel and watched the car, a beat-up old Audi, come around the corner below his hiding place. Will scribbled the model of car in his notebook and squinted at the number plate, struggling to make it out through the mud; he could only note the first three digits. It would be below him any moment, the engine straining as the driver changed gears.

The driver's face was hidden by smears of mud and bird shit on the windscreen; it was a wonder they could see well enough to steer. Will picked up a handful of dirt and threw it over the edge of the bank so it scattered across the car's bonnet. The car lurched as the driver reacted, the pale blur behind the glass twitching towards Will's hiding place just long enough to be recognised.

Mayor Spight himself. Will wrote down the name in his careful print. No passengers. The Audi continued its way up the hill, vomiting black smoke out of the rattling exhaust pipe. It stank of burned bacon.

Will relaxed and settled back against a tree stump, preparing to wait and log Spight's return. A sharp pain on his neck told him a horsefly had found a way through his protective scarf and was feasting on his blood. He slapped at it and the small body fell into his lap. He checked to be sure he had killed it.

A robin alighted nearby and cocked its head, watching him through a black and beady eye. Will threw the small corpse towards it and the robin accepted the offering, snatching it up and flying away. The sun disappeared behind thick grey cloud and rain began to fall, drops finding their way through the dense canopy and splashing on to his head. Will pulled his jacket tight around his skinny frame. It promised to be a long and chilly afternoon.

*

Dorcas staggered through the door with another heaped basin and slapped it down on the tray table beside the bed, the weight of its descent toppling her centre of gravity. She half-fell, half-slid into a chair and mopped at her forehead with her sleeve. In her bed on the other side of the tiny room, Alise was already wolfing down the contents of her own over-sized bowl, humming happily to herself.

Primrose eyed the food and farted. It was barely audible

and failed to ease her cramped digestion. She didn't blush. She was long past blushing.

'You've got to be joking, I've only just finished breakfast!'

'Too bad, got to make your quota and you've only a couple more days to go.'

Wearily, Primrose heaved herself up on her elbows and tried to get comfortable, pulling limply at pillows.

'Hear, you let me do that, you concentrate on them calories.' Dorcas shoved her forward, or as far forward as her belly would allow, and fussed with the pillows. Once she was satisfied they were flumped enough, Primrose was pushed back and the tray table wheeled over her lap. 'Now girl, you get stuck in.'

Primrose sighed, picked up the fork and stared glumly at the pile of glistening off-cuts from pork chops, bacon fat, remnants from slices of white bread, burger chunks, bits of pasta and left-over curry that filled the basin. Cunningly hidden were a few of the things Dorcas knew she loved; roast potatoes, sausages, nubs of cheese.

Dorcas saw her expression and wheedled, 'Get that lot down and I'll bring you some chocolate with your bedtime pudding and hot milk.'

Chocolate. Creamy, sweet, melting chocolate.

Primrose shovelled a bit of pork fat onto her fork and into her mouth. Dorcas poured out a drink from the bottle on the bedside table and handed it to her. Sweet fizz bubbled up and made everything taste the same.

On the other side of the room, Alise belched.

'What about when one of them dies?'

'Ever heard of foie gras?' Primrose could almost hear Dorcas's sly wink. 'It'll go down a storm across the water.'

Shrieks of laughter met this remark, and cries of, 'You are terrible.'

A shudder rippled slowly across her body and made the old bedsprings creak. They thought she couldn't hear them joking, Dorcas and Ivy, the new girl taken on to help look after them, folding sheets in the corridor outside the room. Or – and the thought made Primrose sweat more than the food she was failing to digest or the humid air in the room – they knew and didn't care. Who cares if the livestock can hear the farmer whetting the knife?

Well, she cared.

It hadn't been like this when she first came to the farm. She was more mobile then and wouldn't have stood for it. Now standing for anything had become a struggle and she had to lie down all the time, rolled from side to side to have her sores treated. On a good day. If Dorcas was busy she forgot, and Primrose was left in a peculiar state of numb agony from the places where her arse and back rubbed against rough sheets.

When she first arrived, she was served actual meals, served up as separate courses, on different plates, like in some fancy hotel from an old magazine. But as demand grew and Dorcas took on more 'guests', she started to complain about all the washing up, and began serving their food in basins, then the larger washing up bowls, everything thrown in together like swill. On days Primrose really couldn't eat any more, when her system backed up and she vomited helplessly over herself and the bedclothes, Dorcas screamed about the mess, but mostly about the waste of good food, threatening that she should make her eat it again. If Primrose cried, Dorcas said she should let her starve, her family as well. Once she calmed down, she brought extra helpings of gritty ice cream to soothe Primrose's throat, patted her on the head.

That night, after Alise finished masturbating and lay snoring and grunting in her sleep, Primrose had violent spasms of indigestion. She cried out for Dorcas, who was either out or downstairs in the kitchen with the CD player on, or just pretending she couldn't hear. Primrose had heard Dorcas through the door, complaining about it, so she knew some of the others would let go in the bed sometimes, the effort of getting to the bathroom or onto a pot just too much for them. I'm not quite there yet, thought Primrose, I can't lie here and shit myself.

She peered over the side of the bed, leaning as far as she dared without tipping out, but couldn't see the pot. Agnes or Ivy hadn't brought it back. She would have to go to the bathroom, three doors down.

It had been over a week since she left her room, and the last time she got properly out of bed was to sit in the chair while Dorcas stripped the sheets and sprayed the mattress with disinfectant: 'Just in case.' For a moment, remembering that, the girl felt like shitting herself just to spite the old cow; a flood of anger gave her the energy to move, slow and lumbering, inching across the mattress to the side of the bed and heaving herself over it, onto feet and knees and hips that protested at the strain.

After putting in a handful of sawdust and replacing the lid over the stinking contents of the communal bucket, Primrose shuffled back out into the corridor in her worn slippers, and along to the head of the stairs. The house was silent, not even a sound from the kitchen where the night nurses – guards really – could usually be heard complaining about their luck at cards as Dorcas quietly and expertly stacked the deck.

It wasn't until Primrose was making her slow way back to

bed that the thought occurred to her, a thought that had tried
to surface before, that fear had pushed down before it could
emerge fully. She didn't have to stay here. Some of the others
had signed contracts but she had been too young when she
first arrived, and Dorcas had neglected the paperwork when
she turned sixteen; legally, Primrose could leave. She stood at
the top of the stairs, let the idea take shape.

It was terrifying. What would she do then? Where could
she go? Her parents wouldn't take her back, they would return
her to Dorcas for the sake of their weekly stipend and their
pride in doing their bit. She wobbled, literally, and had to hang
on to the banister for support.

But she hated it here. Not just the force feeding and
farming, but the boredom, the lack of privacy. The loneliness,
the discomfort; the knowledge there would never be anything
else other than maybe a new book or magazine for her to read.
An ex-librarian, reading was about the only occupation Dorcas
encouraged besides jigsaw puzzles or cards, reasoning that it
was unlikely to consume too many calories. Her library had
been the last in Devon, closing when Dorcas became farm
Matron. Most others shut down before Devolution, victim of
austerity cuts according to her old teacher, Mrs Prendaghast.
Just another thing from history to Primrose's generation;
another thing they couldn't have.

Much of what she read mystified her, particularly the pre-
Devolution magazines. The 'real-life' stories were so shocking;
lurid and violent. Was that really how people behaved back
then? And the apparently famous people in the pictures looked
so odd: both sexes with shiny faces that looked like they had
been inflated, the women with skinny bodies and huge boobs
or bottoms. Or they were fat, like her, in which case they were
ashamed, or 'fighting the flab', or ridiculed for not being

ashamed.

Which made Primrose feel really bad, like she should feel guilty about her weight, though she had no control over it. She realised not much had changed. The staff, the occasional visitors, all looked at her like there was something wrong with her.

It could be like that, out there, if she left. Should she take the chance?

If she stood here much longer she would either unnerve herself completely, or else a night guard would come and bully her back to bed. Once there it would be too hard to climb out again and she would stay, getting fatter and fatter until she couldn't move if she wanted to. One day they would cart her out on a stretcher that would need six men to carry it, for disposal, like she'd seen happen before.

She had to go now, while she almost had the nerve. There was no point going back to her room to get anything, she'd worn nothing but voluminous gowns or nightdresses for years, and luckily today was a nightdress day so at least her bum wouldn't be hanging out of a hospital gown. She'd just have to hope her slippers would hold up, and her fat would keep her insulated if it was cold tonight.

Gripping the banister, she carefully lowered herself onto the next step, then one more, making it down to the ground floor in only a few minutes, her heart palpitating so her breath came high and thready and she had to rest at the bottom. Now there was only the hallway and the front door between her and freedom.

For one horrible moment, she thought the front door was locked, but after a moment's panic she realised it was bolted. The bolt was high up and she had to lean her bulk against the door to slide it open but she managed it quietly and there was no sound from the kitchen to show anyone had noticed anything.

Outside the air was damp but not too cold. After the stuffiness of her room and the house, its freshness was shocking. There was no moon and plenty of cloud, and no one to see her as she made her slow way down the stone steps, where she was soon screened from the house by a dense laurel hedge flanking the drive. She had no firm plan or direction in mind. It was so long since she had left the house her memories of the village of Bodingleigh were fragmented, but she had grown up knowing where the fat farm was – everyone knew – and had a rough idea of how to find the school and the schoolhouse next door. Mrs Prendaghast had always been kind to her; Primrose hoped she might take her in.

The surface of the drive was pitted, eroded by decades of heavy rain channelling itself down the hill, but the road beyond was worse and her progress slowed even more as she struggled to keep her balance on the ruts. Her slippers kept coming off and it was an effort to stoop and pull them out of clods of mud, then slip them back on her sore feet. She was sweating and breathing hard even though she was going downhill, and the dark and quiet were so unfamiliar, after all these years of being indoors, that she was terrified.

It began to rain, pattering drops giving way to a steady downpour; soon her nightdress was plastered to her and she was shivering.

For half an hour, she had no company but the trees – whispering overhead as the breeze built up – and the occasional scuttling of something small fleeing from her, making her jump. But she kept going, gritting her teeth against the pain in her joints and chafing of her thighs, her wet nightdress clinging to her shins and making it even harder for her to walk. She lost her slippers in the dark and was too miserable to go back to look for them.

She made it perhaps half a mile before she heard a car engine approaching behind her. The sides of the lane banked steeply; there was nowhere for her to hide before headlights swung around the bend and she was trapped in their glare, blind. The car slowed wheezily beside her and a window stuttered down.

'And where do you think you're going, Missy?' Dorcas's tone was light, but Primrose could hear the anger underneath, sliding like knives under silk, ready to tear her head off. 'You get yourself in this car, Primrose, or I won't be held responsible for what happens to you.'

Defeated, hanging her head, the girl stumbled around the bonnet to the passenger side and fell into the seat, the car's suspension complaining loudly as it dipped.

As she executed a clumsy reverse back up the hill, to make a five-point turn at the entrance to the drive, Dorcas berated Primrose at length. The girl was too sick with shame and disappointment to do more than hang her head and cry into her lap, and so she missed the note of fear behind the anger.

'What were you thinking? Making me waste all this fuel finding you, selfish cow … and after all I've done for you, keeping you all these years, useless lump … You'd best hope Mr Spight doesn't hear about this or we'll both be…'

Frowning, Dorcas clamped her mouth shut, remaining silent throughout the time it took to get them back to the fat farm and up the stairs to Primrose's room, hauling the girl mercilessly behind her and ignoring her whimpers. None of the other inmates appeared to see what was going on but Primrose could sense them behind the closed doors lining the corridor and imagined them straining their ears, agog at her attempted escape. Would they think she was mad, or secretly thrill at the thought of freedom? A momentary euphoria lifted her, but then it occurred to her that if Dorcas really wanted to punish her she could tamper with the anaesthetic. Leave her conscious throughout the 'procedure' and during the painful recovery period. Euphoria shrivelled and tears resumed as she clambered back into bed, her bleeding and filthy feet staining the sheets. Alise snored on, oblivious to the dramas being enacted in the waking world.

*

It wasn't in his mission briefing – he was there to record the comings and goings of cars out of Bodingleigh, and this car only came and went again before it even got to the village – so Will wasn't sure whether to make a note of the poor fat girl and the Matron from the farm, but he decided it was better to note too much than too little. He couldn't see to write very well, as his torch was shielded, but he noted the car, the route and time, and Dorcas, and when she mentioned the girl's name he started, then noted that down too.

Little Primrose. She and Will been in the same class at school back before he'd gone to Cornwall, had even hung out and held hands. He never would have recognised her in the pale, shaking obese girl in the soaked nightgown, cowering before tiny, raging Dorcas.

It was nearly the end of his shift. He would take the information to the Major, see if he felt it was important and should be included in their report.

He'd heard Primrose staggering down the lane before the car came and scooped her up, seen a smudge of something pale in the darkness, but pedestrians were not of interest to the Major, even late-night ones dressed in nightgowns. Will supposed she must have been trying to escape the farm. As the car reversed laboriously up the road, he felt a pang of regret that he had not helped the girl he remembered as sweet and kind. Even if she was – albeit reluctantly – one of the enemy now. But the Major was very clear; Will wasn't to allow himself to be seen in case someone recognised him. His parents' views were well known and considered dangerously subversive and radical by Spight and his followers. Seeing Will once more might make people wonder why he had returned and was hanging about in the woods next to the fat farm.

*

Primrose hadn't been due for harvesting for another two days. Clearly her escape attempt had brought it forward; when she woke after fitful sleep, old Dr Harrow was already in her room, a vague presence in the pre-dawn light.

Alise and her bed were absent, rolled out and into another room so the gurney blocking the corridor could be manoeuvred through the door and the other girl wouldn't be freaked out by witnessing the procedure. It would be her own turn soon enough. Dr Harrow turned towards Primrose when he heard her grunt of surprise, pulling on surgical gloves with a loud snap. His face – even through its gnarls and wrinkles – smoothed into the mask she was becoming used to seeing on the faces of the few people she met these days. The polite blankness that masked their shock. She wasn't sure which was preferable, that or outright revulsion.

Last year, Dorcas had allowed in a field trip from the village school, organised by the Mayor. The children, most of them too young to remember Primrose, had stared at her as if they were at one of the old zoos she'd read about; not horrified but brimming over with questions and wide-eyed fascination. 'Do you get to eat cake *every* day?' and 'I bet you never have to eat vegetables.''Is it true you're so greedy you'd eat your own shit?' This last from Hector Junior, the snot-nosed ten-year-old grandson of the Mayor; he had the same narrow gaze and high, domed forehead.

Of all of them, he would be the only one to benefit directly from the farm. All fuel that wasn't sent direct to Spight was supposed to be kept for emergency heating and to run the old fire truck and few remaining ambulances, but it was an open secret that it was also bestowed as 'special grants' of generator rations, as tractor fuel for favoured farmers, and to run Spight's private fleet. She'd seen the Mayor and his family from the farm's windows, driving past in one of the few cars in the village still running, and wondered if she was the one supplying the fat it ran on.

Mrs Prendaghast hadn't been with the class; that day they were in the care of Mrs Harrow, the Doctor's wife, leader of the Door Knockers, and the only person Primrose knew who resembled the women in old magazines, with shiny, stretched skin that failed to make her appear younger. Primrose had been sorry not to see the teacher's friendly face, sure she would, at the very least, have sent Junior out of the room for asking that rude question. Someone told her later that Mrs Prendaghast had refused to come, saying she would not be party to such disgusting practices. It was the first time it had occurred to Primrose that what was happening to her wasn't sanctioned by all the villagers.

'I hear you gave Dorcas some trouble last night, hmmm?' It wasn't a real question, Dr Harrow never really spoke to any of his patients, just made these little pronouncements, so she didn't bother to reply. He drew the trolley of instruments over to the bed, its wheels squealing and bumping over the uneven floor. Primrose's gut contracted with fright, but at least there was a full hypodermic there, glinting on the green cloth next to the dull rubber of the hose attached to the much bigger needle he used for the liposuction. They weren't going to punish her. Or at least not now.

Dr Harrow picked up her arm as if it was a side of beef, deftly swabbed inside her elbow and slid the hypodermic needle under her skin.

'Count down from twenty,' he instructed and, habituated to obedience, she began.

'Twenty, nineteen, eighteen, seventeen, sixtee ... four...'

The room went dark.

⋆

The entrance to the bunker was so well disguised it took a while for Will to find it; someone must have rearranged the bramble bushes that hid the entrance when they went in or came out. Stumbling around in the soft grey light slowly permeating the woodland, he was so tired he could barely stand. As visibility improved, he recognised the shape of a fallen tree and turned himself slightly west. There, that darker hollow, that was it.

Ducking around the bramble screen, shivering as droplets of water shook free and fell inside his collar, he found the metal of the door under his hands and felt for the lock. The key was on a string around his neck and meant he had to stand awkwardly with his cheek pressed up against the cold, wet steel and fumble until he heard the lock click. Before he pushed the heavy door open he paused, looking and listening to check there was no one about that shouldn't be. A few sleepy birds were calling and beginning the morning's chorus, but otherwise the woods were quiet.

Beyond the door, a tunnel had been dug into the bank, extending about five metres and lined with rough concrete; the floor was packed dirt and covered with a drift of leaves. Crouching, as the roof was less than five and a half feet high and he'd recently had another growth spurt that took him to over six foot, Will rearranged the brambles before he closed the door behind him. When he heard it clunk he relocked it and shuffled along to the inner door. This also was locked. He rapped on its wooden surface with the code knock and waited.

The air that greeted him as the door swung open was warm and stale, tainted with the funk of unwashed males and fumes from the foul pipe the Major held in his hand. He insisted he be allowed to smoke it inside, pointing out that he couldn't very well do so outside, in case someone smelled it and investigated.

The Major looked like he hadn't slept either, his face lined with fatigue, and grey-streaked black hair standing up in tufts. He stepped back and gestured Will inside.

'Come in, I've just boiled some water, you can make yourself useful and brew some tea before you turn in.' The Major resumed his seat at the small table in the centre of the room as Will ducked through the low door.

Somebody must have been cooking recently because he could also smell hot fat. He hadn't eaten anything except some dried apple since he started his shift and his stomach rumbled even though the reek was unappealing. He removed his jacket and the woolen hat he'd used to cover his pale hair, draping them over a chairback to dry.

'What's for breakfast?'

'Eggs. Mal pinched 'em from the farm coop before he came off watch yesterday. Bit of bread left.'

Will crossed the cramped and windowless room to the camping stove, set on an old door propped on plastic crates. As he passed, he nodded a greeting to Mal, an agent a year or two younger than his own eighteen years, who was sitting on a foldaway bed in the corner. A plate with smears of egg yolk was held on his lap.

'When's the next supply run? We're getting low if we're down to stealing eggs.'

'Nothing low about it, eggs is premium grub,' Mal mumbled through a yawn. 'Busy night?'

'Nothing past one o'clock, except a girl did a runner from the farm. Primrose ... used to know her from school, before.' Maybe they had eggs, but they were down to the last few teabags. Will pulled one out of the box and dropped it in the stained teapot.

'A runner eh?' The Major looked interested. 'She get out?'

'Nah, Dorcas came and scooped her up before she got to the village. Poor cow could hardly walk she was so fat. Don't know where she thought she was going.'

'Back to her family?'

'Doubt it, they're the reason she's there in the first place.' Will hadn't known the rest of the family well, but he did remember Primrose's parents and siblings looking better fed, and wearing smarter clothes, after she was 'selected' for the fat farm; her dad had a promotion at the more conventional farm he laboured at, owned by Mayor Spight. Soon after that, Will's own parents had taken him and his sisters away, crossing the Tamar to reach Cornwall by boat one night, seeking sanctuary with his mum's sister and her family in Saltash.

They had been founder members of the radical Archimedes' Society for the Creation of Renewable Energy for the West, a group of concerned citizens seeking to use Devon's remaining solar, wind and hydro infrastructure to supply electricity direct to the populace. Tolerated by the County Council at their inception, tensions had grown as their project looked to be on the brink of successfully hooking up what remained of an old solar farm. Accusations were made in a heated Council meeting that SCREW could not be trusted, that they were in league with external forces to control Devon's energy supplies. SCREW's representative countered by saying they were dedicated to preventing the Mayor and his allies from using energy scarcity to control the population.

Incensed, Spight proposed that SCREW be disbanded; the motion was carried unanimously, and calls were made for mass arrests. Worried for their children, Will's parents had decided to get out while they still could, along with many others. Once settled in Cornwall, and with the support of their new community, SCREW had reformed as an activist group dedicated to putting power in the hands of the people of Devon.

'Ah, well, it's academic now, but it's useful to know there's someone up there,' the Major gestured in the direction of the fat farm, 'who wants out. Could be an ally.'

'Maybe. Don't see what use she'd be,' Will said dismissively. 'She's the enemy anyway,' he laughed.

BANG! The Major's fist hit the table, bringing a sifting of dust from overhead and startling Will so badly he almost dropped the pan of hot water he had taken off the hob. 'Don't EVER let me hear you say that!' the Major shouted. 'She's been sold like cattle by her parents, she didn't choose what happened to her!' He continued in a more moderate tone.

'What we're doing here – it's for her and all the others on the farm, and all those other poor sods down in that village and all over this benighted county, and don't you ever forget it. They've been lied to and tricked, and they are not "the enemy".'

Will blinked, ashamed. But it was hard being in a war and knowing that if any of the … opposition … came across him, they would have far fewer qualms about treating him as an enemy of their state.

The Major's face had softened. 'Not that some of them aren't bloody hostile,' he said in a kinder tone. 'Now, get yourself something to eat and have some rest. There's plenty to be doing tonight.'

Still red-faced and embarrassed, Will busied himself making the pot of tea, using the one fresh teabag and supplementing it with a couple of used ones. Once it was brewed he added powdered milk and handed a cup silently to the Major – who accepted it as if nothing had just happened – and poured some into a clean thermos for Mal, who was putting on his waterproofs, preparing to take the next watch. Hopefully the bed he had just vacated would still be warm when Will climbed into it.

Before doing anything about food, he would have to treat his horsefly bite and check himself over for ticks. Parasites were having another bumper summer and it didn't pay to be careless. He could still remember the long drawn out death from Lyme disease one of his mates had endured back at basic training, having not checked himself over thoroughly after an exercise in long grass. Wearily, Will began removing his shirt.

★

Another chilly morning despite the season. Thick cloud obscured the sun and shielded Bodingleigh from its ferocious heat. Mrs Prendaghast applied a combined sunscreen and insect repellent procured from an itinerant hedgewitch, before dressing for warmth; but in layers, in case the sun emerged later. Once equipped for the vagaries of the day's weather, she went downstairs to the kitchen.

The room lay in shadow, curtains drawn against the damp of the night before, but she didn't bother opening them. If the sun did come out while she was in class, to beat through the single-paned and cracked glazing, the room would become uncomfortably warm. Neither did she begin the laborious process of lighting the stove to heat water. She hadn't the energy to empty it out and the ash bucket was already full. She would need to ask one of the older children to take it across the village to the communal composting area; it was too much for her knees these days.

Besides, her wood store was low, and she wasn't due another allocation for two weeks. Perhaps she could quietly borrow a few logs from the school's well-stocked store, again with some help. Unless Spight Jr was in class, and snitched to his grandfather. If that happened her next allocation would be docked as punishment. Probably best not to risk it.

She sighed and, using one hand to prop her weight against her knees to support her back, stooped down to start laying kindling in the open fireplace. She'd light the fire tonight, unless the sun had warmed the stone of the cottage, and make do with a couple of slices of bread and butter and some milk for breakfast. At least the classroom would be warm. Mr Spight had increased the weekly ration of fuel that came to the school around the same time his grandson started there.

Hector Spight Jr was indeed in class that morning, though he was late. Mrs Prendaghast had already marked him as absent and was setting out the work for the morning on the chalkboard, when he announced his arrival by throwing his bag loudly down beside his desk. The bang it made was familiar, she didn't jump or turn around but continued writing, the tiny nub of chalk squeaking and setting her teeth on edge. Her sleeve was falling away from her arm. She hoped now wouldn't be one of those times Hector started making snide comments about the intricate but faded tattoos spiralling up from her wrist, her daily reminder of a life pre-Devolution.

'Good morning, Hector, thank you for joining us. Please sit down and take out your notebook and pens so we can get started.' She turned to face the class, wiping chalk dust from her hands, giving the children a pleasant smile dredged from somewhere deep.

Hector grunted and scraped his chair out from under the desk, slumping down into it and punching the younger boy next to him in the arm. Mrs Prendaghast pretended not to see. Some battles were not worth fighting, and it hadn't been a hard punch. For Hector, it was almost friendly.

'Now then class, this morning we will be working on arithmetic. Between morning break and lunch, we will work on your spelling. Those of you who don't have to go home this afternoon can have some free time for reading or drawing. Your page assignments are written on the board.' It would be only a handful of children staying after lunch, though the class was not large to begin with; only twenty-six children from the village and surrounding farms were of an age and aptitude that the Council – or rather Mayor Spight – considered likely to benefit from a formal education. Though what was formal about it Mrs Prendaghast was at a loss to say. There was no real curriculum, no measuring of achievement beyond the grades she gave them, and no qualifications at the end of it. They came to her from the ages of five to fourteen, and she did her best by them within the constraints set by her employer.

That meant no history unless it was about the Empire before it imploded, and with a heavy emphasis on World War II because, as the Mayor was keen on quoting, it had been Britain's finest hour.

The running order of monarchs was acceptable up to and including the reign of Queen Elizabeth II – though the Battle of Hastings was a sore point – and there was absolutely nothing to be said about philosophy, creative writing, languages, alternative models of economics, or sciences beyond the proper application of agricultural chemicals. Nothing containing the C words of climate change. Preferably nothing written pre-twentieth century, when the rot set in with gender politics and uppity foreigners. No mention of any authors outside of the British Isles, as that would imply foreigners were on the same footing and of equal worth and intelligence.

Teaching a wide range of ages was challenging; she used to get around that by allowing the older and more able students to mentor the others, helping them to overcome their frustrations at the slow pace of learning, and encouraging them to study the school's meagre library during the hours they weren't out working for their families, the farms or the village.

But that had all changed. Though he had been a sweet little boy when he first arrived, since turning eight Spight's grandson seemed to live to disrupt – she suspected it was the only reason he bothered to turn up. That or the possibility that, like everyone else, he was afraid of his grandfather.

Of course, she'd have more students if they didn't keep getting sold off to the fat farm by their parents or called up to join the militia to fight the civil war rumbling along the county borders. Or else just disappearing, which happened from time to time. At least those who vanished might have made it out of Devon and be enjoying a happier life elsewhere. She sighed, watched the children's heads bent over their ancient textbooks, and looked at the clock. Ten past nine. It would be a long morning.

ABSOLUTE BLACKNESS
SETTLED ALL AROUND

He didn't know how long he had been sleeping, as the light in the room was unchanged when he awoke. Will fumbled his father's wristwatch off the crate standing on its end by the cot to make a bedside table, which told him it was two o'clock in the afternoon and he'd been asleep for five hours. The Major wouldn't expect him to be up for another hour, but he felt rested, if stiff from having spent last night's watch cramped in one position for so long.

The room was empty, but he could hear a faint murmur of voices coming from the radio room next door. He didn't have clearance to go in there without an invitation or an emergency, so he allowed himself another five minutes of rest while he speculated what the Major might have for him to do that night. The pattern of his shifts hadn't changed for two weeks straight – lurk, observe, take notes of not very much. So far as he could see, nothing had happened in that time that would mean the mission was closer to being completed.

Hopefully, whatever it was would get him out of the bunker, and not just for observation duty. It was hard going being in such confined and windowless quarters for longer than it took to eat, sleep and, occasionally, wash. The small complex buried in the gardens of Bodingleigh House had been built during World War II as a failsafe in case of a successful invasion and had not been designed for comfort. The radio operators stationed in the grand, mock-Gothic manor house would have decamped to the bunker to carry out covert acts of communication and sabotage, in concert with others stationed at strategic points around the country, and thus achieved victory.

Perhaps because it had never been called into use, it had fallen out of public awareness in the village. It was Will who had rediscovered it, having crashed through an open escape hatch while trespassing to climb trees, in the weeks before his parents took him away. Until he passed on news of its existence, SCREW had a much riskier plan to use an abandoned barn on the estate. The bunker was perfect for their needs; despite a century of neglect, it remained largely intact.

Will first learned about World War II from old Mrs P's lessons. From what he had read in the tattered books in her classroom, shared with unruly neighbours and their sharp elbows, he could be excused for thinking that history had ended then. For one thing, fashions in Devon had barely changed. The men and women in the old black-and-white photos looked indistinguishable from the adults he saw every day, men dressed in homespun woollens and women in home-sewn dresses and imported nylon housecoats.

It wasn't until he arrived in Saltash that he realised anyone could wear another colour besides black, navy or brown, and not until he entered basic training as soon as he turned sixteen that he discovered what winning the war had meant in terms of losing the battle with the climate before anyone outside of a scientific and industrial elite even knew there was a battle to be fought. In classes in old Nissen huts, together with the rest of SCREW's newest volunteers, he had learned another story: of how a frugal generation, brought up under rationing and brutalised by horrors that had to be borne with a stiff upper lip, had been rejected by their children. How a habit of empire had persisted as the old order was remade and maps redrawn, and globalised markets had metastasised the canker of extreme neo-liberalism across the world and turned a diverse planetary ecology into one malignant shopping centre dominated by multinationals.

He had to admit – to himself, he wouldn't dare say it to anyone else – to being jealous that he hadn't been alive in a time when you could order anything you wanted, so long as you had cash or access to credit, and have it delivered to you the next day. The way it was described, it sounded like magic. It seemed so unfair, for his generation, that they were lucky to get a new, scratchy home-knitted sweater or socks for Christmas or birthdays and had to work so hard. Life was much better in Cornwall – and, he was told, the rest of the country – than it had been in Devon. It was still harder for generations born since the turn of the millennium than it had been for the previous two.

It was harder to admit, even to himself, that he was still a bit seduced by the glamour of the wartime story absorbed in childhood. The simple narrative of good versus evil, played out in the black-and-white films watched on the school projector, using a generator reserved for special occasions only, held the warm glow of nostalgia and the comfort of certainty. But then he would remember where the fuel for the generator came from, and how the Nazi regime used the fat of slaughtered concentration-camp victims, and feel a bit sick that harvesting still happened, even if the victims were now living.

The bunker was far enough underground to be soundproof. Escape tunnels and hatches in case of discovery, ventilation ducts and tubes containing wiring, riddled the surrounding hillside in a complicated circulatory system. It also had a very basic toilet and shower supplied by a tank fed with rainwater. All of this was news to Will, who had been primarily interested in the fact he had a secret place to go to be sure of being alone and had told none of his friends or family about his discovery. His sisters were a pain, and his parents too caught up in their dispute with the Council; home had been a place of fraught conversations held in low voices behind closed doors. And then weeks later he was gone, and memories of the bunker had faded in the excitement of new impressions and experiences. It wasn't until after finishing training and volunteering to be posted back to Bodingleigh that he remembered the bunker and realised how useful it could be to SCREW.

It also had its original radio room. Devoid of equipment, it did retain a full set of switch panels, reconnected once the Major had broken into an abandoned military museum in Dartmouth and appropriated the kit they would need to keep in touch with other cells of activists while they coordinated strategy. The upper echelons of the resistance had satellite phones, but they were expensive and could be more easily monitored and tracked. Radio was safer.

With nothing to do but wait, Will made himself useful by putting a pan of water on the cooker to boil. By the time the door to the radio room opened the tea was brewed, using up another precious tea bag. The liquid he poured out was barely brown, but tea-making was more of a symbolic act in the bunker.

The Major came out carrying a folder, closing the door carefully behind him. He stretched and rubbed his neck, running his hand through already untidy hair. He was wearing the unofficial uniform of all SCREW activists – tough black jacket and trousers with plenty of pockets, without insignia.

From a distance they could be mistaken for militia.

'Ah, Will, good.' He accepted the mug Will offered him and yawned. 'We'll be having a briefing in half an hour. I'd get yourself something to eat while you can, you're going to be busy tonight.'

Through the closed door, Will could hear a female voice speaking, relaying information up the line. His stomach fluttered; he was far too excited to eat.

The woman who emerged from the radio room half an hour later was unknown to Will, though her face tugged at his memory. The Major introduced her as Mrs Mason, which Will assumed wasn't her real name. She was short, in her thirties and pretty, with long dark hair coiled on top of her head, dressed in a knee-length housedress and a nondescript and lumpy cardigan; if he'd seen her outside of this setting he would have pegged her as a wife and mother, happy in the home. Possibly a Door Knocker; not a resistance fighter. Until she raised her eyes from the notepad she handed to the Major and he was caught in a steely gaze that sliced to his core. He was sure she could tell what he had been thinking. His own eyes dropped as he mumbled a greeting.

They gathered around the central table. The Major cleared away old mugs and plates, grabbed a map from the stack tottering on shelves to his side and unrolled it, reclaiming a couple of mugs to hold it down. While he was sorting out his papers, the code knock sounded on the door.

'Ah, good, bang on time. Let them in, Will.'

These faces were more familiar. Tom, Dick and Harriet, code names the Major seemed to find amusing; two young men and a younger girl Will had trained with in Cornwall, who had connections locally and had been hidden by sympathisers in neighbouring villages. They crowded in and removed damp outer layers, adding to the moist fug in the air.

'Right, gather round, no time for chit-chat. We can do tea and biccies when you're briefed. Will, I'm relying on you to brief Mal. He'll be our liaison here tomorrow night, fielding communications, but he's on watch now.'

Four young faces gazed at the Major expectantly. Mrs Mason clearly knew what was coming. She leaned back a bit and it looked like she was fanning away some of the closeness in the air.

'We've been working towards this for years, ever since Spight started farming our people for fuel, hoarding food and using it to control the county, clinging to obsolete ways of thinking – exploiting weakness, greed and irrational fears to keep everyone under his thumb. Well, tomorrow's the night we start the fight back, and you five are key to our success ...'

*

In her dreams she is light, floating. Faint breezes blow, wafting her here and there, not letting her touch the ground for more than a moment at a time. Warmth suffuses her, a bubble of laughter forms in her belly and ...

Pain. All of her hurt. Light stabbed through her closed eyelids, but she couldn't turn away, held immobile by pain. Primrose's eyes blinked open and she squinted in the bright sunlight falling through the window.

She'd survived then. She didn't know whether to be disappointed or relieved. Sooner or later, she was sure, she would slip away while she lay there on a slab like a beached whale and they sucked up all that was useful of her, her departure unnoticed as they gathered all the blubber and carried it off to turn it into fuel.

But not today.

She was lying in an awkward position, halfway down the bed. Maybe Dorcas hadn't had the help she needed to prop her up. The girl moved her arms, preparing to lever herself upright, but it provoked an additional rip of agony and she fell back awkwardly. She looked down and saw grubby bandages wrapped around both arms, from wrist to shoulder. More bandages wrapped her body, from her chest down to where she disappeared beneath the sheet. Pulling the sheet up, she saw bandages continuing all the way down her legs.

Underneath the bandages there seemed to be a lot less of her. And what was left, all of it, hurt.

They'd taken it all. Not just her stomach, which she'd expected, but legs and arms, hips, bum and boobs. She felt her face, wincing as she moved her arms. Even her chins were gone.

Primrose screamed with shock.

'Hurts, don't it?' Alise was sitting up in her own bed, munching on home-made shortbread, dressed in one of the enormous surgical gowns Dorcas had requisitioned from a hospital, that made it less of a chore for her staff to wash the inmates. It gaped, and crumbs dropped into her ample cleavage. She plucked them out and licked them daintily from her finger. 'You'd think we'd get used to it, but hurts like a bitch every time.'

'What's all the commotion about?' Dorcas bustled through the door, red-faced from running up the stairs.

Grief and agony clogged Primrose's throat; she couldn't speak. The best she could manage was a wail.

'It hurts,' Alise explained, using a thumb to indicate Primrose.

'Well, there's no need to make such a fuss! Of course it'll be
a bit uncomfortable for a while. I'll go get something to help,
and we'll start some compression going when I have a minute.
Then I'll get you something to eat. You've been out for two
days, you must be starved.'
    Uncomfortable? Was she crazy? Slumped and twisted,
feeling diminished, all Primrose could do was weep.

Groomed for the farm from a young age, Primrose had been
picked out from her six siblings as the one who might fulfil her
parents' ambitions to escape the poverty that blighted their
neighbours, the village, the whole of the devolved county of
Devon. Distracted by constant, gnawing hunger, made worse
by the hours of housework she did every afternoon, Primrose
didn't notice at first that her portions at dinner had become
larger; that she was the only one to get extra treats of dripping,
biscuits or honey in her tea, or was offered the bits and pieces
left over from preparing meals with her mother.
    It was one of her brothers who pointed it out, pinching the
ample flesh of her upper arm and hissing into her ear how
unfair it was, what had she done to deserve it, fat cow? It was
mortifying to realise, looking into the eyes of the others
scrunched up in the bed they all shared, that they all felt the
same way. Next day she'd asked her parents to work in the
fields with the others and had refused a special treat of sugar. A
week later she was here at the farm. She was eleven years old.
    Five years later and here she was still, wheezing and
shuffling along the landing towards the bathroom and the
bucket, tripped out on poppy juice for the pain. Somewhere
downstairs she could hear music playing. Her tormentors were
down there, having a laugh and listening to music playing on
machinery paid for by her rendered fat, while she was suffering

to keep it playing a little longer, and to fuel the cars driven by a select few. How could this be fair? How could she ever have thought it was fair?

★

The buckets were heavy and banged against her shins as Dorcas backed cautiously through the door to the cellar, pivoting on the spot to be sure of not taking a tumble down the steep stone steps that led from the kitchen. She gave soft grunts of effort at each tread, taking care not to spill any of the buckets' contents. The fat was solid at room temperature, but could still leave a slimy mess, treacherous underfoot.

The smell from the rendering room had permeated the stairwell and she wrinkled her nose in disgust, taking shallow breaths. At the bottom of the stairs was a screen made up of old strips of plastic, to keep flies and other insects out, and here she turned and backed through. It was stiflingly hot on the other side; Agnes had already lit the stove and was warming the pan they would use to melt down the fat Dorcas was delivering. Tiny vents high in the wall were inadequate to remove all the smoke escaping the chimney and the room was slightly hazed.

'Right girl, you get this lot started, I've another bucket to bring down.'

Carrying buckets was more menial work than Dorcas liked her girls to see her do. It was important to her that she maintain her status as someone above that sort of thing, but Ivy was off with the flu and Spight was complaining he didn't have enough fuel to get the next supply run in to the village, so needs must. And she hated the rendering room and its smells and smoke. Better to do the donkey work than stir the blubber as it rendered down to oil.

Dorcas poured the blood-threaded lumps of yellow, waxy fat out of the buckets and into the pan, scraping out the residue with a metal spoon, then handed the spoon to Agnes, who started poking around and distributing it more evenly.

'Mind you don't let it burn,' Dorcas admonished her, before starting the journey back up the stairs, empty buckets banging carelessly together. 'I've got to go take care of our prize cow. She'll be shipped out soon enough and she's got to be fit to travel.'

*

The compression bandages were helping a bit. So was the poppy juice Dorcas had been trotting in with every four hours. It was helping so much that Primrose had spat the last dose into a water glass and hidden it on the windowsill, behind the curtain above her bed, keeping it for later. Because Primrose had a plan. She had to get out of here, and she had to do it tonight while everyone thought she was in too much pain to move. Hopefully, she could stash enough poppy juice to see her through the escape. She could still remember how difficult it had been walking the last time; at least this time, she might be in pain from the dozens of healing punctures in her flesh, but she wouldn't be carrying so much weight.

Clothes. She needed clothes. And shoes. Her own had been taken when she arrived, and even if she still had them they would no longer fit her. She had grown upwards as well as sideways over the last five years. She knew Dorcas kept a wardrobe of assorted garments and footwear on this corridor, for the rare occasions she took her livestock out of the farm to village events such as Christmas concerts or fêtes. That hadn't happened for at least a couple of years, since the drive for more and more fuel had become the new norm. But presumably the clothes were still there.

The first time she tried to have a look, pretending she needed to go to the toilet again, Agnes whisked out of a room at the end of the corridor and Primrose had to turn away quickly and pretend she was just on her way into the bathroom. She waited a good ten minutes before going back out, but Agnes was still there, dusting the staircase, and Primrose returned to her room frustrated. She waited another hour, then groaned, clutched her stomach and moaned that she had to go back to the loo. Alise looked at her with indifference and continued crunching her way through a bag of imported crisps, her reward for passing her weight gain target the day before. The rest of her booty – chocolate and a tin of biscuits – lay scattered over her blanket.

This time the corridor was empty. The wardrobe was past the bathroom, set back in an alcove. After checking there was still no one about, Primrose opened one of its two doors and was rewarded by the sight of coats and shoes. She grabbed a coat at random and a pair of shoes that looked like they should fit. The other door revealed shelves of folded clothes and a rail of dresses. Wanting loose garments that wouldn't aggravate her wounds, she grabbed a dress and what looked like a jumper. Too scared to take the time to look to see what else was there, or to check for fit, she closed both doors.

Now what? She couldn't take them back to the room while Alise was there and awake. The bathroom had a cupboard for storing the threadbare towels and sheets for this landing, and she headed there as fast as she could limp, burrowing in to the back, stashing the clothes where they would stay hidden until the next bed change, which shouldn't be for another few days unless everyone became incontinent at once. Heart beating wildly with elation, she closed the door and turned to find Agnes, come to retrieve the bucket.

'What are you doing in there?' Agnes was only a couple of years older than her, but she was looking at Primrose as if she had true seniority, rather than a job skivvying for Dorcas and carrying shit around. Primrose felt a blush rise up her neck and, in that moment, she hated the other girl.

'I was looking for sanitary towels, I think I'm about to come on,' Primrose improvised, amazed at her own ready response. She clutched at her belly to back up her story and winced as the pressure bore down on the punctures from the liposuction.

'We don't keep them in there, Dorcas has a store cupboard upstairs. And you don't go getting your own, you know we bring them to you.'

'I know, I'm sorry, I just didn't want to make a mess for you to have to clear up.' Primrose smiled ingratiatingly and started towards the door behind Agnes, stooped over and holding her belly.

'Surprised you can feel anything with all that medicine,' Agnes huffed, but she made way for Primrose and picked up the bucket. 'I'll bring you some pads in a minute, and a hot water bottle. Just got to deal with this.' Her nose wrinkled, and Primrose felt ashamed of the pulse of hatred she had felt a moment ago. Agnes was just as trapped as she was.

★

A cold wind was blowing in off the waters of Plymouth Sound. Clouds were clearing to reveal a new moon coming up in the eastern sky. Will's mum, a keen believer in astrology, would have seen it as auspicious at the beginning of their mission, and approved. Thinking of her, and his dad and his sisters, Will felt a moment of longing that made his heart clench. It had been months since he had seen or spoken to his family. Alone in the darkness, hoping his part in the events of the night would not be necessary, he felt afraid, scared he'd mess things up and let everyone down, even more scared of what would happen to him if he got caught. He tried to control his breathing, as he had been taught, to calm himself and focus on the present moment. It helped a bit.

Which was when he became aware he was hungry. All he had was a bag of last year's walnuts and a flask of water to see him through. In the end, there had been so many questions the night before there hadn't even been time for more than a couple of the home-made biscuits Mrs Mason had brought with her. Which she was now, presumably, eating with the Major while they waited for the boat. The hours between had been a rush of small missions, carrying information and equipment to other teams, with little time for more than a sandwich.

In the truck, before he and the others headed for their boats, the Major had roused his team by reminding them that Spight's grip was strong, but heavily dependent on three things. Inertia, and his control of goods coming in from outside Devon's borders accounted for two of them. The destruction of the road and rail bridges at Saltash, the mining of the A30 and A39, checkpoints at all minor roads crossing the borders and control of its ports and harbours, meant that very little came in that he didn't then disburse through an efficient system of bribes and cronyism. And – which was even more damaging according to the briefing seminars Will had fidgeted through – he controlled the types of goods imported, setting up trade deals with regressive fiefdoms such as the Real USA's

New Jersey, Ohio and Florida, as well as Poland, China and Saudi Arabia; choosing fossil fuels, junk food and substandard electronics built without guarantees or safeguards and thus needing frequent replacing. Crap that fulfilled an immediate want but no actual need.

With global demand for gimmicky rubbish at an historic low – as more socially developed states put the cooling of the planet above individual whims – these retrograde states were totally dependent on each other for trade.

The third thing Spight exploited was energy. With no access to cheap fuel, he had a monopoly on all energy supplies within the county. In the first few years after Devolution, thousands of trees and hedgerows had been cut down by people desperate to heat their homes during savage winters and cook their food year-round. Once he became Mayor, Spight had taken control of public woodlands and set up licensed groups to manage them (taking a share of the licence money), to ensure trees were planted as well as harvested: fast-growing varieties such as willow, hazel and sycamore. He befriended or threatened those with private woods, persuading them to allow similar groups on their land, in exchange for some of his imported goods. Everyone was entitled to a share, but allocations were controlled by patronage and favour, and anyone found with more than their allocation was at risk from a judicial system administering penalties that began with public shunning and escalated rapidly to summary execution.

Their Stage One mission tonight was to attack the first two things propping up Spight's regime. By intercepting the scheduled delivery, due in from New Jersey, they would hit Spight where he kept his feelings – in his pocket – and show him up as fallible. Once this had been achieved, Stage Two – drawing him out – would follow on naturally. From there, the

Major promised them, it was but a short step to Stage Three.

Will's part in all this was simple. As one of the youngest and least experienced of the team, he was to stay out of harm's way, and report back to Mal via walkie-talkie from his observation post, in shadows at the water's edge of the deep-water dock in Plymouth. If anyone came to disrupt the blockade he was to alert first Mal and then the Major, but to stay out of any violence that might ensue. He was secretly relieved by this. He was nervous enough without the fear of being obliged to get into a physical fight. Two years of fight training and six months of active deployment had not obliged him to hurt anyone, and the thought of doing so filled him with nausea.

The usual docking procedure was for incoming vessels to anchor inside the breakwater and wait for daylight, before unloading onto smaller boats that would come inshore to dock. It was unlikely any workers would arrive the night before a scheduled delivery run, but they couldn't be certain, and so the Major had detailed Will as lookout.

He was hidden from casual observers by a small wooden shack that had survived the developers, back in the day when Plymouth was undergoing its first makeover since the 1960s. At the turn of the millennium, Mrs P had told them in a history lesson – shortly before she was banned from teaching them modern history – there had been an attempt to boost the national economy by building new houses and roads, paid for by the taxpayer and making the owners of construction companies very rich, something she called corporate welfare.

When the global economy crashed in the early 2020s – as the reality of climate change bit and efforts were finally made to cut carbon emissions, as fossil-fuel giants fought back, countries disintegrated, and Devon devolved – everyone who had bought second homes in the city upped and left, along with thousands of university students who had been the source of much of the city's employment. There were few jobs for those that remained; more people left. Plymouth was a ghost of its former self, with rows of vacant houses and empty high-rise blocks of flats, and a bleak city centre of boarded up and burned out shops.

The docks, halfway through the process of becoming luxury waterside flats when the crash happened, still serviced some smaller cargo ships. The larger vessels were kept out by a harbour slowly filling up with silt. National government used to keep the harbour dredged to accommodate naval aircraft carriers and Trident submarines, but now the Kingdom was no longer United, there was no regional money to pick up the slack and Plymouth's imports by sea were under threat. Will wondered if Spight had a plan for when the cargo boats could no longer dock.

But that wasn't an issue tonight. The cargo ship coming at Spight's behest would be meeting their flotilla, out beyond the breakwater. The Major, Mrs Mason, Tom, Dick and Harriet, and a host of resistance activists from across Devon and Cornwall, were waiting in small boats, using up precious fuel, preparing to turn back the cargo vessel by whatever means necessary. Of course, it could all go horribly wrong. It was a cold night to be rammed and thrown into the sea. In the dark. Chopped up by propellers. Shot at. Drowned. Will shivered and his stomach churned. At least he was no longer hungry.

★

Two miles out to sea, the Major was unknowingly echoing Will's concerns for the safety of himself and the others, who remained invisible even when the slim crescent of the moon emerged from behind cloud to cast light upon the swell. There was a strict embargo on showing lights until their target was in sight. Bobbing around in a small fibreglass day sailing boat with Mrs Mason, as the moon disappeared, and absolute blackness settled all around him, they could have been on their own in the middle of the ocean, if it weren't for the sound of waves breaking on the boulders of the breakwater, and the occasional light on the horizon behind them.

If only .... The Major drew his thoughts back from that particular cliff edge and turned them in the direction of their mission. Which should be starting ... he began to check his watch and realised he couldn't see it in the dark. And couldn't show a light. Which meant he couldn't smoke his pipe. He held it loosely in one hand anyway.

Never mind, he thought, it couldn't be long now.

It felt like an age before lights appeared off their starboard bow, still way off in the distance as a ship rounded Rame Head. From its running lights, it was headed straight for them. Time to gear up.

He could hear a gentle snoring. Mrs M had fallen asleep. He nudged her and she snorted awake. 'Boat's on its way in,' he whispered.

'Why are we whispering, who's going to hear us?' Mrs M whispered back.

'There could be a lookout at the breakwater, sound carries.'

He could sense an eyebrow being raised, but she kept her opinion to herself.

'Papa Bear to Baby Bears, Papa Bear to Baby Bears, hold position and get ready for the approaching bowl, over,' the Major rasped into his walkie-talkie. Mrs M had chosen the call signs, designating herself Goldilocks. Her reasoning, that no one accidentally coming across their wavelength would take them seriously.

'Baby One to Papa Bear, received and understood, standing by, over,' came through the walkie-talkie. Tom and his team were in position.

'Baby Two to Papa Bear, received and understood, standing by, over.' So were Dick and his team.

'Baby Three to Papa Bear, received and understood, standing by, over.' This came through so close he heard Harriet's voice in stereo, both through the radio and from his left, nearby.

'Papa Bear to Baby Three, we're too bunched up, get yourself over to port. No engines, you'll need to row. Over.'

He could hear Harriet and her team cursing as they hunted in the bottom of their boat for their oars. A clatter of wood as the oars were slotted into rowlocks and then silence. He gave them a couple of minutes, then 'Papa Bear to Baby Three, give your position, over.'

'No idea Papa Bear, but we can't hear you any more. Er … Baby Three. Over.'

'Roger that.' It would have to do.

The lights of the oncoming boat were coming closer. The Major reckoned they had another five minutes until it would be upon them. Mrs Mason nudged his shoulder and passed him her hipflask and a piece of flapjack. While he sipped whisky and ate, he heard her going over their weapons, dry-firing to check the mechanisms were in good working order, before loading them with the few bullets they had. Guns were still fairly easy to come by. Ammunition was harder to find.

HER MOONSTRUCK MOMENT

It had surely been hours. After sitting still for so long in intermittent rain and the chill wind coming in off the water he was freezing, despite his heavy wool jacket. At least the rain was passing over and clouds were clearing. The moon had crossed the midpoint of the sky and was heading for the western horizon. Will yawned and checked his watch by flashing his torch briefly. If Mrs Mason's information was correct, there was still about half an hour to go before the boat reached her and the Major. So, more waiting.

Hopefully he wouldn't have to be here much longer, or he might start glowing in the dark, irradiated by the abandoned Trident nuclear submarine facility at Devonport, two miles away from where he was sitting. Stories of what decades of accidents and inadequate storage of materials had done to the local population were legion all across the county. Will reckoned they were rubbish, but still, it made him uncomfortable to be there.

He slumped back against the shack. And heard a scuffing sound, nearby.

He tensed, listening hard.

It came again.

Will held his breath. Should he take a look around the corner of the building, and risk being seen, or wait for whatever it was to come around that corner, and definitely be seen? Whichever it was, he needed to get up. Getting to his feet as quietly as he could, he waited, nerves thrumming with tension.

It was too big to be an animal, unless it was a human-sized animal. A someone, or some *thing*, from Devonport …

The scuffing separated itself out into shuffling footsteps. Then came a scraping noise, a bang, and silence. A thud and, a few moments later, snoring reverberated through the wood he was leaning against. Shaking off his fear of Devonport, Will surmised he had heard someone coming home to sleep in the shack. Homelessness was endemic in the city. Most of the empty streets of houses had shutters screwed onto the doors and windows as property speculators bought them up and waited for the financial tide to turn. Some were squatted and many of those were crack houses offering the most basic and squalid shelter to addicts. These were controlled by gangs, who protected their own patches under their overlord Spight with a brutal regime of violence and intimidation.

From the resonance of the snores, Will decided he was safe enough. It didn't sound like the sleeper was going to be waking any time soon. He rested his back against the wall and yawned.

Other sounds roused him from a light doze.

These were simpler to decode. Sniggering, whispering, a harsh laugh. The sounds of young men out to do damage.

'Stupid fucker's left the door open, that's gonna make it easier.'

'Listen to 'im snore – like a pig!'

'Who's gorra light?'

The voices were young, male and drunk, their accents a mix of broad Devon and a hard, urban patois peculiar to Plymouth.

There were three of them. Will had done well in fight

training, but he knew he was outmatched. What on earth was he supposed to do now? The significance of what was being said wasn't really sinking in as he started to back away towards the chain link fence that delineated the dock. Surely the Major would understand if he carried out the rest of his mission from somewhere safer, with a reasonably clear view of the harbour.

There was the sound of flint being struck. A *whoosh* as something ignited.

'There you go, stinking dickwad!'

'Serve you right, pukin' all over me trainers.'

A *whump* as flames caught hold.

'F-u-c-k, look at it go!' The dirty, cobwebbed window in the wall Will had been leaning against was aglow with flickering light. High-pitched giggling, on the verge of hysteria, told him the lads were still there.

No no no no no. What was he supposed to do now?

'Shit, is that paint cans?'

'What? Where?'

'Back wall. We gotta go, they gonna blow the fuck out the place!'

Sounds of running feet and hoots of laughter.

Will was torn. He wanted to carry on backing away, he didn't want to run into the burning shack and pull out an unconscious drunk. Any minute now he would get word from the Major and he couldn't afford to be distracted.

But if he didn't, someone was going to die.

But he could die if the shed blew up in his face.

But he had a duty; he'd sworn to follow the ethics of the resistance, co-opted from the international Permaculture movement. Earth care, people care, future care. If this wasn't people care, what was?

The peeling paint on the back wall of the shack began to

blister.

Swearing loudly, Will ran around to the front, where roiling black smoke was pouring out of the open door. Pulling off his hat and holding it over his nose, he switched on his torch and ran inside, keeping low to avoid the worst of the smoke. The fire had taken hold in a pile of old overalls and cloths to one side of the shed and was spreading fast. Casting the beam of his torch around the interior, he could see the tins of paint, but no sign of the drunk.

A hacking cough over to his right. Will crouched, peered into the beam of the torch, and spotted an old man lying on another pile of rags and overalls on the other side to the fire.

Stuffing the hat in his pocket and holding his breath, Will darted further in, grabbed the old man under the arms and heaved him off his bed of rags. An explosion of sparks as the blazing pile tipped, and now the flames were creeping closer to the paint tins and the temperature in the shed was rising rapidly. The old man struggled as he started coming back to consciousness and, startled, Will dropped him on the cement floor, where he flailed around. His eyes opened and he wailed in fear as he saw the flames and clambered to his feet. Instead of running to the door and safety, he rushed back towards his bed.

'Nooo!' Will darted after him and grabbed him by the shoulder, pulling him back. The air in the shack was foul with smoke and he was spluttering and choking as he shouted, over the ever-increasing roar and hiss of the fire, 'We've got to get out of here!'

The old drunk swung back around and rummaged among the rags. Pulling out a rucksack, he started trying to put it on, weaving on his feet.

Shit! Will dived across and took the man out at the knees,

sending them both sprawling, then grabbed the fabric of his coat, and pulled with every ounce of strength he could summon. The old man clutched his rucksack to his chest but at least he didn't resist as Will inched him across the floor towards the door and safety.

The cool, damp night air that met them outside soothed Will's scorched face but made him cough as it met the smoke in his lungs. He managed to haul the drunk's dead weight another twenty yards before he collapsed onto his knees, hacking and choking. The old man seemed to have lapsed into unconsciousness again, but when Will forced himself to his feet to drag him further away, expecting the shack to explode at any moment, he fought back, slurring and shouting curses and insults that were too garbled to be coherent. Eventually Will gave up and dropped him, wiping the greasy feel of the coat onto his trousers and stumbling another dozen yards before collapsing onto his back and gasping for breath.

The shack was burning brightly, illuminating the whole of the dock. So much for the Major's instruction to remain invisible. He grabbed the walkie-talkie out of his pocket, but he must have damaged it when he took down the old man; nothing happened when he pressed the button.

Now what should he do?

Flaming paint cans shot skyward like comets, trailing fire, as the shack exploded.

★

Alise was snoring heavily. The rest of the house was quiet. It was time.

Primrose pulled back the bedclothes and swung her legs out of bed, wincing and suppressing a gasp of pain. The poppy

juice had worn off and she fumbled for the glass she had
stashed behind the curtain, giving in to the urge to numb
herself. The liquid was bitter but she choked it down and put
the glass back on the sill.

The corridor and landing were empty and dark, all the
candles burned out. Even though she could claim a need to go
to the bathroom she couldn't stop herself from scuttling
furtively down the corridor. Once there and with the door
wedged closed by a hand towel – there was no lock as Dorcas
didn't trust her charges not to hurt themselves either
deliberately or accidentally – she carefully removed the stacks
of linens from the cupboard and found the clothes she had
stashed. It was too risky to get dressed in the bathroom, in case
someone came in or spotted her before she got downstairs, so
she bundled the clothes under her nightgown and held them in
place over her stomach. Now she looked big again; unless
someone got close enough to realise who she was, and knew
she had just been harvested, she would look like just another
inmate.

There were sounds coming from the kitchen as she crept
down the stairs, and light showed under the door. It was
perversely reassuring, like a mouse knowing the cat was
elsewhere. As she took each step, she was concentrating so
hard on being quiet and avoiding the known creaks, she barely
registered that the trip down the stairs was far less difficult than
last time.

The door was bolted again. After drawing back the bolt –
her heart stuttering with fright in case someone came out of
the kitchen – she ducked into the downstairs cloakroom and
brought the clothes out from under her gown. Shivering from
fright more than cold, she pulled on the dress and found that it
was far too big, and an ugly shade of brown. The jumper was

hand knitted and also too big, hanging halfway down her thighs. Its bottle green clashed horribly with the brown. But they were clothes. The first clothes she had worn in years. The leather shoes were a tight fit, but she managed to loosen the laces to give her toes a bit more room. And the coat was wool and long enough to keep most of her legs covered. And it was black, which would be helpful if she had to hide.

The nightdress she left hanging on a peg among a rack of staff overalls.

The hallway remained silent and empty when she let herself out of the cloakroom. Nothing stirred as she pulled open the heavy front door and felt the cool night wind try to snatch it from her hand. Clinging on to the handle, horrifyingly aware of how weak she was, she stepped outside and pulled it shut behind her. There was a thud and a snick as it closed and the catch caught. She froze, ear pressed to the door to see if anyone was coming to investigate. Nothing.

Shaking, summoning her courage, she pushed herself away from the door and staggered down the stone steps. In contrast to her last escape attempt, there was a sliver of moon over the treetops, though dark rainclouds were massing to the west, and the cool westerly wind made her glad to have brought a coat. Buttoning it and holding it tight around herself, Primrose set off down the drive. The sound of stones crunching under her feet alarmed roosting rooks and pigeons into noisy flight, but no one came to investigate and she hastened on.

Weak though she was from inactivity, she was able to walk much faster now she wasn't carrying so much weight. The clothes itched, the shoes were rubbing against her bare feet, but her knees and hips were no longer screaming; if she hadn't had half an ear out for a car engine revving behind her she might even have found herself enjoying her mad, staggering

dash towards the village. Maybe it was the poppy juice that
was causing a bubble of exhilaration to form in her chest and
turning the night sounds that had terrified her last time into a
quiet chorus urging her on, but for a moment she felt
invincible, like the heroine in some old book, escaping from
the castle.

It took her half as long to reach the spot where Dorcas had
found her last time, and she barely noticed its significance as
she sped on her way. The final uphill slope to Gibbet Cross
slowed her considerably, as did the sight of the gallows, the
rotting wooden structure in the centre of a grass bank to the
north of the crossroads showing black against the night sky.
Excitement cooled and congealed into dread.

The last hanging – that she knew about anyway – had been
when she was about six years old. She had been forbidden to
attend, a fact for which she was grateful now, but she
remembered feeling cheated at the time. The corpse had been
left dangling from the gibbet as a warning, rotting until the
head parted from its body and the remains were removed, to
be thrown into a hole in the ground outside the churchyard
wall. Before that happened, she and some friends had sneaked
away after school one day and seen the corpse swaying in the
wind, face bloated, purple, crow-pecked. Her friend had dared
her to touch it. She had refused and been called a coward.
Stung, she brushed the dangling trouserleg, and screamed
when the wind pushed it and its stink towards her. Shrieking,
they had run back to the village and their chores.

Primrose hadn't known why the man had been hanged. She
had asked her dad and he said something about rustling, but
making noise seemed such a small crime for such a big
punishment.

The gibbet was empty now but still she didn't look fully at

it, hurrying past before turning left and away, feeling its
presence at her back and imagining the ghosts of its victims
dragging themselves along behind her, her spine crawling with
a shiver of horror until she turned a bend and the sensation
faded.

From there the going got easier; more effort had been
made to keep the approach to the village level underfoot, and
the gradient was less steep. As she reached the first,
tumbledown cottages, hidden behind hedges to her right, she
forced herself to slow down so she would be able to hear
anyone else out past curfew and find somewhere to hide.
Besides, she was starting to pant from exertion, and her legs
were feeling wobbly. A sudden fit of faintness forced her to
pause a moment, and skeins of colour danced across her vision.
Following them with her gaze, she looked up and became
mesmerised by the moon's lambent glow, its bright sickle
shape like a curved door into a better, brighter world.

A light drizzle began to fall and clouds stole across the
moon. Primrose shivered as cold wet drops pattered onto her
upraised face, remembering where she was and what she was
supposed to be doing. Even though it was darker without
moonlight, colours danced in her vision. She forced herself to
ignore them, and to think about the business of finding
somewhere to hide before dawn, preferably under cover,
preferably the schoolteacher's cottage. She started walking
again, grateful no one had come across her during her
moonstruck moment. With the collar of her coat up she was
confident she was now all but hidden in the dark, though her
bandaged legs glowed pale below the hem.

The village was laid out like an asymmetric ladder. The
road she was on would fork about a hundred yards down, with
narrow alleys connecting the two tines. The school and Mrs

Prendaghast's cottage were located on the second of these, in the heart of the small settlement. Forcing down nerves, Primrose walked as slowly as she could stand, choosing the left-hand lane that would take her down past the pub and the church. At this time of night, she thought this would be safer than going past people's homes, where someone might be wakeful and happen to look out of a window.

A clattering broke the silence and she froze. Eyes glinted at her from shadows by a fallen-down cottage. Before she could summon the wit to flee, something growled at her and slunk further into the dark. A dog. There were several feral packs that kept to the outskirts of villages and foraged at night. Thankfully it had been alone, or it might have taken her on.

Aside from the dog there was no one around, and no lights in any of the windows she passed. The pub was closed up tight, and the church next door loomed over the churchyard and village green. Heart in her mouth, wheezing and shaking now with exhaustion, Primrose crept down the lane that led to the school. Tucked round to the side of that was the cottage Mrs Prendaghast was permitted to live in. It, too, was dark. She didn't want to knock in case a neighbour heard, so she pushed at the door and tried the old-fashioned latch. The door was unbolted. Bless Mrs Prendaghast and her trusting heart.

Primrose pushed the door wide and slipped in. It was colder inside than out, but at least the wind was no longer whipping at her. Shutting the door quietly, she stood with her back to it while her eyes adjusted. She was in the small kitchen, with a table in front of her, an unlit range against the far wall and two closed doors across the other side of the room, one of which she knew would lead up to the bedroom and bathroom, though she had never been up there on her few visits as a child.

Over to her left was an old armchair and she headed for

that, sinking down gratefully, before jumping up with a stifled yelp as she sat on a bag of crochet hooks, knitting needles and wool. Moving the bag onto the floor, she settled herself into the lumpy seat, pulling a throw slung over the back across her knees and slipping off the uncomfortable shoes so she could draw her feet up under her. She would wait here a minute while she warmed up and her breathing steadied, then go upstairs to wake the teacher.

Closing her eyes, the fear and tension of the last few days slowly ebbed. A poppy-induced warmth suffused her limbs, making them relaxed and heavy. Five minutes after leaning back against the cushions, despite the throbbing of her feet, she was fast asleep.

★

The sudden flare of light on the Plymouth dockside did not bode well for their mission. Mrs Mason and the Major twisted round and watched the glow brightening the horizon and throwing the shadow of the breakwater lighthouse across choppy waves.

'Shit, what now?' The cargo ship was half a mile away and closing fast. The Major grabbed the radio. 'Papa Bear to Porridge, what the hell's happening over there? Over.'

Nothing but static.

'Papa Bear to Porridge, you OK? Over?' The explosion, when it came, could be felt even two miles away. The flash of light showed them the rest of their flotilla, spread out across the mouth of the breakwater, before it faded to leave them blinded by negative afterimages, and the shockwave of the rolling *BRROOOOM* knocked them flat in the bottom of the boat. The Major's hand banged against the gunwale of the boat and his pipe fell free from his hand, splashing soundlessly into the water.

'Shit, Will, what the hell is going on back there?' The Major was blinking furiously, trying to restore his night vision.

'We can't worry about that now, there's nothing we can do for him from here, and we're about to go live.' Mrs Mason's voice was firm and the Major was grateful she and her common sense were there with him. 'Now, reassure the team, I expect they're freaked out too.'

Right. He took a breath. 'Papa Bear to Baby Bears, Papa Bear to Baby Bears, it's time. Get your flares ready, start your engines, we'll sort out Porridge when we've secured the Bowl. Over and out.'

A chorus of 'Rogers' came back. The Major retrieved the flare gun from his duffel bag. Mrs Mason got ready with the loudhailer, before starting the ancient Mercury outboard engine and putting it in reverse so they could keep pace with the ship. Their guns sat between them on the bench.

Adrenaline was making his hands shake. He was fumbling with the flare. If he wasn't careful he'd light it, drop it and set fire to the boat. And if he took too long, the ship wouldn't have time to slow down or change course, and they risked being mown down and drowned, or minced. Mrs Mason seemed to know how he was feeling. He felt her hand grasp his sleeve and give his arm a reassuring squeeze.

'Come on Major, you've got this.'

'Yes, right.' He shook himself, looked at the freighter's position and calculated. He pushed the button on the radio. 'It's time,' he shouted, 'over.' Bracing himself to keep steady in the boat, he popped off the cap, took a breath and pulled the string. A pause, a few sparks, then a bright gash of red light erupted, forcing him to turn his head away. Instinct screamed at him to drop the flare, but he held on tight, raised his hand and waved it slowly above his head. To left and right, other flares blazed into life and the heaving seas reflected them back in glittering and shimmering fractals of light.

'AHOY! YOU MUST TURN BACK!' Mrs Mason bellowed beside him, her voice amplified by a battery-powered megaphone, deafening him. 'THERE'S BEEN AN INCIDENT AT THE DOCK, IT ISN'T SAFE FOR YOU TO STAY HERE.' Nice improvising.

The vessel was now looming above them, with no obvious signs of life on the illuminated bridge, or of it slowing down. Maybe they'd left it too late, maybe they wouldn't be able to keep up with the ship's speed and were about to be hit and the boat smashed. They were all wearing life jackets, but that wouldn't help them much against hypothermia or whirling propellers.

'AHOY,' Mrs Mason shouted, 'ACKNOWLEDGE AND CHANGE COURSE.'

'What's going on? Why's the dock on fire?' The twang of an American accent as a deep male voice boomed down from the ship's Tannoy.

'THERE'S BEEN A LEAK OF HAZARDOUS MATERIAL AT DEVONPORT DOCKYARD. WE'RE EXPECTING MORE FIRES AND WE'RE EVACUATING ALL RESIDENTS AND WORKERS. IT'S TOO DANGEROUS FOR YOU TO COME FURTHER INSHORE. WE CAN'T RISK IT, OR YOUR CARGO.' You go, girl. Everyone knew about the shonky state of the old nuclear facility. It was miles away from Millbay, but even if the skipper had enough local knowledge to be aware that, who would want to take the risk?

'We just crossed the fucken *Atlantic*, where you suggest we go?'

'NOT MY PROBLEM, SIR.'

'What you doin' out here 'stead of raising us on the radio?'

'ALL COMMUNICATIONS ARE DOWN, SIR, BECAUSE OF THE FIRE. NOW PLEASE, CHANGE COURSE.'

A long pause, then, 'Acknowledged, we'll anchor up outside Dartmouth. Tell your boss we'll be in touch 'bout his cargo.'

'ROGER THAT, SIR.'

The flares were beginning to sputter and diminish. They were also getting incredibly hot. The one in the Major's hand was starting to burn through his glove and he could hear curses of pain coming from the other boats. Changing hands just spread the pain. 'Shit!' He had to put it out before it did him some serious harm, or he dropped it in the dinghy and put a hole in it. Plunging his hand in the sea he doused the flare, dumped it beside him in the boat and sat back, panting as if he'd been running hard. To left and right, his troops were following his lead, and the fitful lights stuttered out.

He was elated. Though it was now pitch black, and despite the bright images dancing in negative before his eyes, he could see from the position of the running lights that the looming prow of the ship was turning ponderously to starboard and eastward.

They'd done it! They'd actually turned the ship away. Stage One was complete.

★

Will could see the flares come into life, throwing the silhouettes of the breakwater's lighthouse and fortress into sharp shadow. He could only imagine the exchange taking place between the occupants of the tiny boats and the cargo ship that could turn them all to kindling if it chose. The fire on the dockside couldn't have helped. But at least the worst damage to himself was some singed hair – he knew that because he could smell it – and scorched hands.

The drunk he had rescued was still out cold. The best Will could do for him was turn him over on his side so he wouldn't choke if he threw up, and cover him with his jacket, heavy with the night's rain. There was no sign of the boys who had set fire to the shack, and no one had come to investigate, but he had withdrawn into shadows by the fence, in case that changed and he had to leg it.

Nothing that had happened had been his fault, he knew that, but he still felt responsible for the disastrous fire. Thinking he'd completely screwed everything up was agonising, as he waited for some sign of how things were going for the rest of the team. After some few minutes that dragged by like aeons, the flares were extinguished abruptly and the horizon went suddenly dark. Did that mean they had succeeded, or that the ship had ploughed into the dinghies and sunk them all? He wouldn't know until he went to the rendezvous point. If no one turned up he'd be left with the knowledge that he'd caused the deaths of everyone in his unit, ruined the mission, and had no way of getting home. And where would home be? There would be no point in going back to the bunker. He could rejoin his parents in Cornwall, but would they want him when they heard what he'd done?

It would be a while before he knew either way, but there was no point hanging around at Millbay any longer, he might as well head for the pier. To get there he would have to climb back through the hole he had made in the chain-link fence and scuttle down Soap Street, a waterfront once bustling with industry and now full of half-built houses that had achieved dereliction before they'd even been finished.

The wind coming in off the sea was picking up and cut through Will's jumper. Once he moved away from the fire he would really feel the cold. He could do with his jacket and looked over at it longingly. Could he live with himself if he took it from a helpless old man? A sudden gust that tried to blow him off his feet told him he could try. After all, the old guy had the flames to keep him warm, and they wouldn't die down for a while yet. Of course, the poor sod would be in deep shit if the lads came back, but Will told himself they must be long gone.

He crouched down and took hold of a sleeve. The old man stirred and rolled onto his back, pinning the jacket beneath him. Will grabbed hold of it with both hands and pulled. Bloodshot eyes opened and stared blearily up at the sky. The old man looked confused. Will supposed he had every right to be – he'd gone to sleep in a shed and woken up out of doors, with a stranger looming over him, lit by fire.

'What … what's happening? What you doing?' The drunk's voice was high and quavering.

'I'm, uh, just taking my jacket.' Will grabbed the sleeve draped over the man's stomach and pulled.

'No, it's mine!' The sleeve was snatched out of Will's hands. For an old drunk, he was surprisingly strong.

'Er, no, it's mine. I put it over you after …' Will gestured vaguely towards the blaze. 'I pulled you out. Remember?'

The old man sat up and turned towards the source of heat and light. He turned back. Will wasn't expecting a rush of gratitude but the fury that distorted the man's features was startling.

'You set fire to my home!' Rage deserted him and tears leaked down the filthy, lined cheeks.

'No! That wasn't me. They said you'd puked on their shoes, three young guys. They ran away.'

'My home!' He started to sob, rocking back and forth.

Will didn't know what to do. He wanted his jacket but he could sacrifice that. He needed to leave, but how could he walk away from a defenceless old man, grieving for the roof that had protected him and his few possessions, now going up in roiling black smoke?

'Look, I've got to go. You can keep my jacket.'

The old man ignored him. Until Will stood up; then he began to wail louder and rock harder.

Shit! 'Look, you can come with me.' If he was still alive, the Major would kill him, but what else could Will do? 'Come on, get up.' The old man flinched when the boy stooped over him, cowering into himself. Will grabbed him under the armpits, leaning in to the stench of unwashed body and piss-stained clothes that enveloped him, strong enough to cut through the acrid smell of burning. Heaving him upright, he slung the old man's arm over his shoulder, tipping him off balance as Will was several inches taller. The jacket was slipping to the ground. Will grabbed it and threw it around both of them like a cape.

'Right, now, we got to go.'

'My things …'

The rucksack was lying where Will had dropped it. Bending awkwardly, he grabbed it. The old man snatched it away from him and hugged it to his chest, crooning softly.

Sighing, Will exerted gentle pressure and hobbled round to turn the two of them towards the fence. They lurched towards it in a zombie shuffle.

Progress towards the pier was slow. Will had to help his companion through the hole in the fence, bending him like a doll, desnagging him from the bits of wire that caught in his clothing. Every couple of minutes Will was asked where they were going, what was going on, who was he? After the first few times he responded with grunts, which didn't seem to bother the old man, who started up the same round of questions and lapsed eventually into an incoherent mumble.

Some of the ruined houses they inched past seemed to be inhabited. Lights flickered in windows and Will could hear voices. Shrill, drunken laughter erupted as they passed one house less dilapidated than others. That the old man had chosen to sleep alone in a shed when there were houses and companionship available here told Will he didn't want to hang around to meet the neighbours. Exerting slightly more pressure, he hurried them along, keeping to shadows wherever possible.

Hulks of sunken boats protruded out of the water, still tethered to the two concrete jetties set at right angles to the harbour wall. A long low warehouse ran along the length of the first one they came to. For a moment Will thought he could hear a child's crying coming from inside but put it down to gulls wheeling overhead, their white plumage tinged pink. It was not a reflection of the blaze; looking to the eastern horizon saw that dawn was beginning to break. It was time to get out of sight.

Behind the warehouse, a ramp led down to the water and rotting pontoons with slightly more serviceable boats moored to them. Some of these were used by fishers, smugglers or drug runners. Will chose the first pontoon, canted at a steep angle by the dropping tide. The old man seemed fearful and held back, but Will persisted, keen to get out of sight, and hustled him down it, making encouraging noises, until eventually letting go and snarling in frustration, 'Right, stay here then. I'm off.' The old man clung to him fearfully and cried and Will felt ashamed. 'Come on then, it's not much further.'

The two of them staggered down sideways, stepping with difficulty over missing planks. The pontoon at the bottom ran along the harbour wall towards the jetty at the end and a row of empty berths; the rendezvous point. When they reached the first of these Will slumped down on to the rotten boards, completely spent. All he could do now was wait.

★

Two of the flotilla had returned to Cornwall, crossing the perilous straits of the Hamoaze to reach the Rame peninsula and Saltash. The remaining boats headed back to Plymouth, cutting their engines and rowing the last few hundred metres in silence. By the time they reached the pontoons the Major was exhausted, but at least the exercise had kept him warm. Sitting still for so long, waiting for the ship, had chilled him to the bone.

There had been no time to celebrate out on the water, and they couldn't afford to do so now, but he allowed himself a small smile as he considered the success of the night, tempered by concern for Will, and the urgent need to get back to their vehicles. The sun would soon be fully over the horizon and people would be about.

The nose of the boat bumped up against the dock and he stood, the bowline in his hand and stiffness in every limb, trying to summon the energy to jump out and tie up.

'Here Major, pass that to me.' Will appeared out of shadows cast by the dock and leaned over from the pontoon, hand extended.

'Will! We thought something terrible had happened when
we saw the fire.' The Major passed him the line and Will
looped it around a cleat, pulling the boat in tight.

'I'm so sorry, there was nothing I could do to stop it ...'

'Stroke of genius boy, just what we needed to get the
Captain to change course. Mrs Mason improvised on it.
Genius.'

'Oh, well ...' Relief washed over Will's face. He offered a
hand to the Major, who clasped it in his own so Will could
haul him up onto the pontoon, where he stood bowed with
weariness. Mrs Mason allowed herself to be helped up too.
Younger crew had already tied up and disembarked and stood
by in silent clusters. Dick, the closest, smacked Will in the arm
to signal pleasure that he was still alive.

The pontoon swayed underfoot, and now the Major felt
seasick. He'd been fine on the water. 'Right, well done
everyone. Mission accomplished, and now it's time to get out
of here. Back to the vehicles. Dick, you lead. The rest of you,
keep an eye out for locals but do not engage unless it looks like
they're going to interfere, or get on to radios or phones. It's
going to be clear what we've been up to soon enough, but it
would be good to get out of here first.'

Dick led his team along the pontoon towards the harbour
wall, where it turned a sharp left. Will, the Major and Mrs
Mason took up the rear. Will fell in next to the Major.

'Er, Major ...' He kept his voice low.

'Yes Will.'

'I had a bit of a problem.'

'Yes, look forward to hearing your report when we're back
in the truck.'

'I mean, there's someone ...'

They were reaching the turn. A sharp wailing erupted,

causing consternation at the front.

'What the hell?' The Major picked up his pace so he was at the head of the procession, taking care not to push anyone into the oily waters as he passed. Someone was cowering in the corner of the dock, arms over his head. The Major reached down and yanked one elbow. The filthy, lined face of an old man emerged from between hunched shoulders.

'Please!' Will reached across and offered his hand to the wailing man, who grasped it. The Major didn't know whether to be more astonished by that or the sudden appearance of a stranger in their midst.

'Major.' Will's tone was pleading. 'He's harmless. He was in the shack that burned down – it was set alight by lads trying to kill him. I pulled him out and then he wouldn't stay on his own. He's scared they'll come after him again. We can't leave him here!'

This was all they needed. But clouds were rolling in threatening rain, he was cold and he needed a bed, even if it was only a cot with one thin blanket. Every moment he delayed took them closer to the threat of reprisals from locals loyal to Spight.

'Bugger it. OK, he can come with us, but he's your responsibility and he won't be able to stay long, it's too risky. We'll sort something out later.' The Major watched with distaste as, helped by Will, the old man stood, swaying more than the pontoon warranted. The sour smell of cheap booze and unwashed skin reached him. 'When he's sober.'

EVER-MORE TWISTED AND DARK

It didn't stop with Cataluña and Devon. Before the actual and metaphorical walls went up around the county we were hearing of other nation states breaking up, the most notable and bloodiest being the USA.

Details are hazy, because not much was reported by mainstream media (considered too incendiary, probably. By then all national governments were living in terror of us revolting peasants and we got our news from social media, which wasn't a reliable or neutral source of information, but most of us felt that way about governments and mainstream media by then), but as far as I can piece together now, with a faltering memory, it was shortly after Trump declared himself President for Life, and the ensuing riots, that the worst ever wildfires struck. The Paris Agreement and global trade wars had meant restricted markets for the coal mines Trump had reopened, so he could prance around in a hard hat and fulfil an election promise that meant ecological Armageddon. Coal mountains lay in huge, unsaleable piles all over the heartland of the country, and ignited during an extended drought.

The piles burned for weeks, fouling the air with black plumes of toxic smoke that killed thousands too poor or old to get out fast enough. Many of those that did escape had terrible respiratory damage and didn't have private medical insurance or access to restricted public health provision. They died too. Overall, tens of thousands of US citizens were killed by the fires and their aftermath.

It was horrifying to watch, until the videos were pulled offline as unrest mounted.

As the ashes and tempers cooled, while Trump was whooping it up at one of his golf courses, an interim cross-House alliance took over the White House, with the support of much but by no means all, of the population. Those who didn't agree resumed rioting and Washington became a war zone, the NRA arming anyone who could pay for a gun. Trump was offered refuge in New Jersey and fled there with his family. The US fell apart as Trump-supporting states seceded in disgust and rallied behind the orange one, now such an old man it is reasonable to suppose he was suffering from dementia, as well as narcissism and delusions of grandeur.

The good that came out of it was the final demise of the fossil economy, at least for most of the world. Big corporates bucked but really it was their death throes. The economy tanked, but at least this time it was the rich feeling it. The rest of us, who'd been fucked over by the politics of austerity for so long, didn't notice it so much. We really were 'all in it together' at last. I was working crappy cafe jobs, having given up my teaching degree as the costs of tuition spiralled. The money was terrible, but demand was reliable and living costs low, as I was back home in Bodingleigh, living with my parents and my wife. Then Devon decided to devolve, and everything went down the pan.

My wife and I had no money and nowhere to go so we stayed, and I stayed after she and my parents died in the flu pandemic of 2027. Thousands died that year, as they had in the years before. Medical supplies were non-existent, and the antibiotics dropped in humanitarian relief efforts by our neighbours turned out to be useless against the new superbugs. Since then we have become dependent on expensive imported drugs, or on hedgewitches and their ancient lore; but hedgewitches are persecuted by Spight as ungodly, and transactions with them must be carried out in secret.

I stayed on in my parents' house until it fell down a decade or so later. By then I had been asked to take over teaching at the village school, and Spight offered me the schoolhouse. I was too desperate for a dry roof to say no.

I think he thought I ceased to be a lesbian once my wife had died. In his mind, I was no longer a corrupting influence and so was safe to be around children again.

As far as I know now, with the limited access to world news that I have (mainly snatched moments of gossip with Gloria or Flora, who are, of course, much better informed), the Trump dynasty is still doing its best to screw everyone over in the name of liberty, aka free markets for its goods and services, with Trump Jr's grandson in charge of a loose federation of states calling itself the Real USA, governed – if you can call it that – from New Jersey and spreading south and west like a tumour. The remainder of the country has joined with the rest of the world in trying to decarbonise its economy, cleaning up and cooling down our planet's air and oceans. I believe much of the UK is trying to do the same, but here in little ol' Devon we are holding to the old ways.

This is what I would like to be teaching in modern history. But no, I have to regurgitate a Spight-approved syllabus about the British Empire, the so-called Enlightenment, Industrial Revolution and WWII, as if any of that can be taught without the context of what it led to: the carving up of poor countries for exploitation by the rich, environmental degradation, a dangerously warming planet and the resulting, repugnant saga of resource wars and displaced peoples that fed grotesque acts of xenophobia and genocide.

From the memoirs of Mrs Prendaghast

★

Mayor Spight's grand house stood in the heart of Bodingleigh. Once the local Lodge, there had been some raised eyebrows when he comandeered it after his departure from the fat farm, where he had lived with his family from the inception of fat tithing until the birth of his grandson. But as most of the local Freemasons had died out, and Spight was Grand Master of those that remained, there was no real opposition. Three storeys of granite, it dominated the small square in which it sat and cast long shadows on sunny days. Devon flags flew during daylight hours, fluttering from flagpoles that jutted out above the ground floor windows. Successive storms had left these ragged and Spight was awaiting the arrival of bolts of cloth to have new ones made up.

News of the successful blockade reached the house and Mayor Spight later than it might have done, there having been a period of 'You do it', 'No, *you* do it,' among his subordinates as reports started to come in from Plymouth. It was the task of the luckless Bob to wake him and deliver the information that he would have to wait somewhat longer for his cloth and the rest of the ship's cargo.

'Why wasn't I informed immediately?' he snarled, furious at being woken and further enraged when he learned the reason.

'What is it Hector?' Gloria Spight rolled over in bed, shading her eyes from the light spilling through the door.

'Shut up and go back to sleep, you useless cow.'

Used to being spoken to in such a way, his wife rolled away from him. Spight threw back the covers and fumbled for his slippers and dressing gown. He could hear wind rattling the windows as he tied the sash of his gown.

'Right, let's go sort out this shit storm.'

But there was not a lot he could sort out, or could have done if he'd been woken sooner. The cargo ship carrying containers of favours promised to subordinates and cronies had been turned away and was making for Dartmouth. Its skipper, Dwight, had been in touch to say the agreed terms were no longer valid and they would need to meet to negotiate a new deal. If he could agree that, he would have to arrange for his goods to be unloaded in Dartmouth and brought in piecemeal, which would cost a fortune given the state of the roads and the lack of sufficient boats. If he couldn't, it would do untold damage to his finances, his reputation and his power base.

'Fuck!' Spight sat in his kitchen, light twinkling off his sweaty forehead and the shiny new chrome appliances arrayed along the worktops, the reality of the situation percolating his sleep-fuddled mind. How to deal with this and turn it to his advantage, or at least not let it escalate?

'Call a public meeting,' he told Bob, who hovered nervously at his shoulder, careful to stay out of Spight's line of sight but aggravating him nonetheless.

'A meeting?'

'Yes, a fucking meeting. You deaf?'

'Er, when would you like me to arrange it for?'

'Tomorrow. No, tonight, let's not give the bastards time to spread their slander. Six o'clock. Might as well get a full day's work out of all the lazy fuckers. Village hall. No, the church.'

'Yes, Mr Spight, I'll see to it. I'd better go and see about setting that up.' Bob moved towards the open door leading to the hallway.

'Yes, you better fucking had. I'm off back to bed.'

Spight didn't make it upstairs. The churning of his mind

proved to have a detrimental effect on his digestion and made it impossible to contemplate going back to sleep; when Bob returned at eight o'clock, Spight was still in his dressing gown and seated at the kitchen table, the notes of several drafts of his speech for that evening spread across its surface, most of the text crossed out with angry black lines. Mrs Spight was washing up breakfast dishes with a carefully neutral expression. One of her cheeks was red and slightly swollen, the result of a burned slice of breakfast toast earning her husband's disapproval.

'Well?' Spight's temper had not improved since venting his frustrations on his wife.

'The farms are going to let all their workers know, I've got the Door Knockers out. Also, posters up around the village and runners about to go out with more copies.'

Not many houses had their own phone; landline cables, mobile phone masts and fibre broadband cabinets had been quietly sabotaged soon after Captain Spight of the militia became Mayor Spight, for 'reasons of security'. A select number of households were allowed access to an intranet. Access to the worldwide web was restricted to Spight and a very few of his most trusted lieutenants across Devon. As a result, an accelerated grapevine had to be used to impart local news that had to travel at the speed of gossip. The Door Knockers were mostly older women, who could be relied upon to call on their neighbours. Some of the less respectful of Spight's men referred to them as Knockers, but never in his hearing. Spight abhorred vulgarity in others.

'Right. Good. I'll want recordings made. After tonight we'll get the runners out to spread our side of the story.'

'Yes, Sir, I've made sure Dug'll be there to tape you.'

'Well then, I'd better get dressed.'

'What do you want me to do, Sir?'

'Make yourself useful. Help the missus there with the washing up. Then we need to work out how we're going to get my goods back – who we need to grease and who we can just kick up the arse.'

The order to wash up was a deliberate insult to his underling. Spight despised men who undertook 'women's' work. Bob enraged him further with a quiet, 'Yes, Mr Spight.'

'Don't just suck dick, get on with it.' Spight stormed from the room and thumped his way upstairs.

★

She must have forgotten to wind up her old alarm clock, because it was already a quarter past eight when she woke. She had to be in the classroom in half an hour. Cursing, Mrs Prendaghast fought herself free from the blankets and peered out of the window. No wonder she had slept in; it was so murky it was hard to tell it was morning, rain streaming down the cracked panes. Her notebook had fallen to the floor from where she had left it on the bedspread after writing in it the night before. She picked it up and stuffed it back under a pillow.

No time to light the stove to heat water for a wash, which would make it two days in a row. She really would have to make more of an effort tonight. But then she remembered the parlous state of her wood store. Bugger. Hopefully Hector Ji would bunk off today so she could borrow some logs from the school.

Five minutes later she was dressed and standing in the dimness of her kitchen, clattering plates and rummaging for bread. An odd noise made her look round. A stray cat maybe.

There was a tabby living in a ramshackle shed next door and sometimes it snuck in when she wasn't looking, though it usually made its presence felt by climbing on her bed in the night and waking her up for cuddles, with wet fur and cold paws. She looked around but couldn't see the cat. But something was there, moving in the shadows across the room; a human form unfolding itself from her chair.

Mrs Prendaghast shrieked and dropped the bread knife. It clattered off the table and fell to the floor. She stooped down with a groan, snatched it up and held it out in front of her like a short sword.

'Who's that? What are you doing in my house?'

A soft, shaky girl's voice replied, 'Sorry, Mrs Prendaghast. It's me, Primrose.'

'Primrose? From the farm? What on earth are you doing here?'

'I ran away from the farm, I couldn't go home, I couldn't think where else to go.' The voice was wobbling.

Mrs Prendaghast put down the knife. This was going to make life very complicated. If not downright dangerous. What could she do but say, 'Oh, you poor thing. Come here.' She moved around the table and opened her arms wide. Primrose flew into them.

The girl towered over her. She had grown much taller in the last five years. But she wasn't fat. When Primrose sat back down in the chair and Mrs Prendaghast drew the curtains on a window that didn't face onto the street she could see why. Bandages covered the girl's arms where she'd pushed up the sleeves of the hideous jumper she was wearing, and also wrapped her legs below the baggy dress. It explained the rather lumpy element of their hug.

The teacher knew what the fat farm did, everyone did, but

seeing the proof shocked and sickened her.

Primrose was describing her escape, breathless and giddy now with relief. She must be light-headed after the night's adventure and in need of some breakfast. Which reminded Mrs Prendaghast she was due in school any moment. A quick glance at the clock told her she only had a few minutes. She cut the girl short as she was describing her run to the village.

'Primrose, I'm sorry but it's a school day, I have to go to the classroom.'

The girl's face fell. 'Do you want me to leave?'

'Of course not, don't be silly. You can stay here while I'm in class, and afterwards we'll make a plan. We've just time for a quick breakfast and then you go up and have a proper sleep in my bed. Just make sure no one sees you or we'll both be in trouble.'

When she locked up and hurried next door to the schoolhouse she found her class waiting, huddling together in the rain in the small and weed-strewn playground. There was no Hector, which was a small blessing. Mrs Prendaghast was so distracted by the knowledge she had a fugitive in her house that she kept making small mistakes that he would have pounced on mercilessly. The rest of her class were either less unkind or just didn't care enough to notice her absence of mind. Then at a quarter past ten, the door banged open and Hector appeared in the doorway. Mrs Prendaghast's heart sank as her pupils looked up from their books and turned to see who it was.

'Public meeting tonight, at the church, Mrs P. Six o'clock. The rest of you, make sure your parents are there. Can't stay, I have to go round the farms.' Looking self-important, Spight Jr strutted back out of the classroom.

Well, what was all that about? She had a horrible feeling it had something to do with her guest.

Half an hour before the official break for lunch, experiencing a growing sense of disquiet at leaving Primrose alone for so long, she allowed them all to choose something from the small store of books at the back of the room and told them to read until it was time to go home. She would see some of them for an hour or two after lunch, while the older children were put to chores for their parents, but it would be easy enough to set them some work and leave them to it. The murmur of voices began even before she closed the door on them, but for once she didn't turn to admonish them.

There was no sign of Primrose in the kitchen when she returned. A quick look upstairs showed her the girl fully dressed and asleep on top of her bed, curled up under a crocheted blanket. Leaving her undisturbed, Mrs Prendaghast lit the stove, hoping she would have a chance to scavenge some logs later, and started preparing vegetables to make soup. Vegetables were one thing the village still had in abundance for most of the year; those that coped with unpredictable weather anyway. Many of the villagers had gardens large enough for their own plots, and those that didn't made use of allotments at the top of the hill by the vicarage, keeping poultry as well as growing produce. As fresh vegetables were difficult to import from overseas, now there was no access to air freight and the boats came so infrequently, Mr Spight had no interest in them and this was one necessity he did not tax or control. He did, however, run a profitable sideline in exotics like avocados and lemons.

With a tiny, north-facing garden, and a bad back that no longer permitted much cultivating of her allotment, Mrs Prendaghast was often gifted with surplus by the parents of her pupils, stored carefully in the extension that housed the downstairs loo, that no longer worked and was cold enough to keep things fresh for weeks before she had to start making batches of preserves. This early in an erratic growing season, supplies of everything were running low, but she could supplement old onions, carrots, squash and potatoes with some nettles, growing abundantly outside the back door. Villagers were sniffy about eating weeds, but she knew that so long as she could find a few nettles she would never starve.

Half an hour later soup was bubbling on the stove's hot plate and an appetising aroma was permeating the cottage. Primrose came down the stairs, yawning and wrapped in the blanket.

'Wow, that smells amazing.' She stood awkwardly by the table. Mrs Prendaghast steered her towards the only armchair and told her to sit.

'It's just vegetable soup, but it's warming, and good for you.'

'Vegetables … can't remember the last time I ate any of those.' Primrose didn't look too keen about reacquainting herself. 'Not real ones anyway. Plenty of chips.' Now she smiled. Then frowned, as she thought about what eating so many chips had led to. She fidgeted with the bandages on her arms.

Mrs Prendaghast started cutting the last of the loaf and tried to remember if she had enough flour to bake more. 'We'll have to sort out those bandages later. How long should they be kept on for?'

'A few days. It's only until the cuts scab properly.'

'Well, we'll have a look at you. I'm sure I've got an old sheet or something I can cut up.'

'I'm really grateful, Mrs Prendaghast, for the soup, and the sleep. I really don't want to get you into trouble.' Primrose

looked at her with big brown eyes. She had grown into a pretty
girl, despite the dirt, straggly hair and terrible clothes. Things
would go badly for her if she was found here; bad things
happened to pretty girls in Devon.

'You let me worry about that. Now here, make yourself
useful and butter this bread.'

While they were eating, Mrs Prendaghast tried to establish
if the girl had any other family besides parents and siblings,
who might take her in or help her leave the county. Primrose
remembered aunts and an uncle nearby, but had never been
close to any of them, and the last she had heard, before she was
sent away, they all had more mouths to feed than they could
handle and would be too dependent on Spight's favour to risk
his wrath by helping her.

'There's no rush,' Mrs Prendaghast said, with a sinking
feeling that she was getting her old self into some serious
trouble. 'You can stay here as long as you need to.'

Gratitude suffused Primrose's face. Mrs Prendaghast tried
to shake off a sense of doom.

*

When Hector Jr had finished his rounds of the local farms,
ordering everyone he met to attend the public meeting, he was
soaking with sweat from pedalling hard on his bicycle over the
broken roads and green lanes that ranged the rolling hills, and
had a raging thirst. The rain had stopped, and the sun still lay
hidden by thick cloud, but the temperature was rising, and
humidity had made him break out in a sweat before he even
got on his bike. If only they'd let him take a car, but he was still
too young to drive according to his grandfather, whose
opinion was the only one that counted. Which didn't mean

Junior hadn't been practising in secret, in the part of the village hall car park that hadn't been adopted as a fly tipping spot for old white goods. That old suck up Bob showed him how, whenever he'd managed to scrounge – or siphon – some fuel from one of his grandfather's fleet, and grandfather was out of the parish on business.

Junior couldn't wait to take his proper place at his grandfather's side. Only another year or so and he'd be able to become the true heir apparent. His dad, Fred, fancied himself in that role, but he wasn't blood, only married to Junior's mum, and Junior knew Hector Sr had no real respect for Fred, just a need for the man's loyalty, and brutish nature from time to time. Junior himself, though he feared his dad when the man was in a rage, had no real respect for him. Not that he didn't punch out anyone else who showed his father disrespect. Like that time he'd twatted one of the boys in his class when he'd caught him taking the piss out of Fred's rolling gait and thickset arms, held out to the sides, like a chimp's. He knew about chimps from antique issues of National Geographic kept in his grandfather's library, where he had also seen pictures of black women with their boobs hanging out.

He thought about that now as he sat with his back against a gate and took a swig from a plastic bottle of cola. Not Coke, they'd run out of that a couple of weeks ago, but it was imported cola, and still better than any shit water that just came off the roof or out of the ground, like any old dweeb could boil and drink. He'd enjoyed punching that kid, and kind of hoped he'd get a chance to do it again. He'd also liked looking at the boobs.

The only place he still needed to go was the fat farm. Mrs Harrow, chief Knocker, might have spoken to Dorcas already, but he liked to go and laugh at the fat kids if he got the chance, though Dorcas would block him if she could. She said it put them off their feed if he made them feel bad about eating so much, and that made it harder for her to meet her quotas. But she might not be there. And anyway, this was preferable to being in school, which was where his mum would send him if he went back too early. Junior did respect his mum. She was the only woman he respected, but he wasn't afraid of her in the same way he was of his dad. She had never hit him. But then she didn't need to. She had a way of looking at him that chilled him to his marrow when she was displeased.

Sometimes he thought she didn't like him much, and that hurt, but not enough to stop him doing the things she didn't like. He just made more of an effort to hide aspects of his behaviour from her that he didn't care if other people saw.

Horseflies were gathering around him, drawn by his sweat. He batted at them but there were too many to dodge for long. He would have to outpace them and hope they fell behind. Time to move on.

The final stretch of lane up to the farm was steep and gullied. He had to push his bike, sweat that had cooled while he rested making him cold and clammy before it began to break out afresh. His grip on the handlebars slipped as the weight of the bike tried to take him back down the hill and he was gasping by the time he reached the driveway. And hot again. Here it was level enough that he could get back on the bike, and he pedalled carefully along the rutted gravel.

The house was very grand, even covered in ivy and with its grey granite rusted with orange lichen and beslimed by the green mildew that thrived in the damp air of Devon, staining everything. Hector knew his family had lived there until shortly after he was born, and rather wished they still did. It had towers and turrets, and looked a bit like a castle. Entering it always made him feel important.

The wooden front door was closed. Rather than knock and risk Dorcas answering, he dismounted and pushed his bike around to the kitchen door, where he might be able to scrounge something to eat. It was open. Propping his bike against the stone wall, he slipped inside.

The kitchen was full of steam and held a rank stench of hot fat that quelled his appetite, until he saw a rack of brownies on one of the work surfaces. He rammed one into his mouth and slipped another into his pocket as he headed for a closed door that he knew would take him to the stairs up to the rooms the fatties lived in. Before he could reach it, it opened and Agnes, Dorcas's skivvy came in. She stopped dead when she saw him. Her hands were taken up with buckets, covered with lids but still emitting a miasma fouler than the stink of fat.

'What are you doing here?' she demanded.

Hector saw her eyes flick to and take in the crumbs around his mouth, her thin face twisting into a scowl. He took exception to her tone and bristled. Who was she to question him, the grandson of her Mayor? 'I've been sent here by Grandpa.' He brushed off the crumbs.

'Why?' She looked scared now. That was more like it.

'Public meeting tonight. Six o'clock in the church. Be sure and tell your *mistress*.' He took care to stress the last word and gave a meaningful nod towards the buckets she was carrying. 'I guess you'll be too busy wiping bums and emptying out slops.'

'A meeting? Why's there a meeting?' Agnes put down the buckets and wiped her hands on the grubby apron she was wearing, wringing the rough fabric nervously.

'What's it to you? Where is she anyway?'

'What?'

Why was this pasty girl panicking? Hectic spots of colour

appeared in her otherwise pale cheeks. 'Dor-cas.' He enunciated the syllables v-e-r-y s-l-o-w-l-y as if she was a bit stupid. She probably was, who else would do the sort of work she did?

'Oh! Dorcas! That's fine. She's out, taking care of some business, you know.'

He didn't know. Frankly he didn't care. He weighed up his chances of getting through the door and going upstairs, decided it wasn't worth the bother and turned away. Just to make the point of how important he was, he grabbed another brownie on his way out.

His mission accomplished, Hector relaxed and sauntered on foot down the drive, steering his bike with one hand. The second brownie was tasting good, and it and the third in his pocket meant he didn't need to rush home to eat his tea before the meeting, which would be in – he checked his cheap wind-up watch, a present from Fred – three hours. What to do between now and then? Rather than go back to the village, and either school or chores, he decided to take a bit of time to reacquaint himself with the woods that lay between the fat farm and the lane. There was a gate a few dozen yards further on, well out of sight of the house. Leaving his bike hidden in the hedge that flanked it, he climbed over.

Local legend had it that the house and grounds had been a private estate back in the dark ages of two centuries ago, and remained so until the last big world war, when all the men of the area had gone off to fight and the government had commandeered the house. There had been no one to tend the laurel hedges and they had grown wild. After the war, the house had been left to decay, the gardens to become more overgrown. The owners had already moved to what used to be the United States, now the Federated States of America and the smaller and more bullish breakaway Real USA that exported to his grandfather and, by extension, Devon. This was almost as much about world affairs as Hector Jr knew, and he was allowed to know more than the other kids in his class, because he could listen in on his grandfather's conversations, whereas they had to listen to their stupid peasant parents talk about … well, whatever it was stupid peasants talked about.

The place had lain empty for a few decades, the woodland becoming ever-more twisted and dark as laurel grew, blew over, rerooted and grew again. An incomer family had bought it and restored the house towards the end of the previous century, but they left after Devolution.

'Those that blow in, blow out again,' was the way Hector Sr had put it one night, as he drank imported bourbon with Bob and Fred, and his grandson kept quiet hoping to be ignored so he could score a rare late night. Junior understood that Senior was referring to the sorts of people who lived in a place while it suited them, and then left when things got tough and it came time to do the work of making a place fit for decent folk to live in. People who couldn't stick, who didn't have roots in a place like he, Hector Spight Sr had.

Which meant that, when the idea first came up of having a fat farm, where biofuel could be harvested from idle berks who were no use otherwise, the empty and crumbling house had been the perfect location. No one knew who owned it anymore, but who cared? It was big enough and it was empty. Work parties had set about repairing windows and parts of the roof, Dorcas had been installed as a sort of Matron and his grandparents had moved into one of the wings with his mother.

The woods had been left largely undisturbed aside from some harvesting for the farm's boiler. The sorts of hand tools available couldn't handle the density of laurel, and locals were wary of burning it because of the cyanide it contained, and besides there were abundant other woodlands at the time. His grandfather had confided he had a secret special project, and the acres of laurel wilderness would yet serve a purpose, but in the meantime they had been left to run wild, so that now, ahead of him, he saw a dark tangle of black limbs through which no sun could shine. It was quiet in there. Small birds shunned the woods, finding no food to tempt them in. Rooks roosted in the top branches of some of the surviving trees, that stood tall enough to find light. He could hear them bickering and grawking above his head.

A small part of the wood had been cleared and reclaimed for growing produce for the farm, but there was no one tending the beds of straggly and beaten-down vegetables. Hector had the place to himself. He crawled and climbed his way across and along and under and over sinuous laurel trunks – smearing himself with green slime – to a stream. Walking down the stream was easier than climbing, so he followed this path of least resistance until he thought he was nearing the road and remembered he would have to make his way back to fetch his bike. He couldn't leave it there, even hidden as it was; someone might steal it. After all, that was how it had come into his possession.

If he cut across to his left, he would come out of the woods and on to a path that led up past the vegetable plots and back to the gate. It meant some wiggling through mud to get under tangles too complicated to climb over, and within a few minutes he was soaked through. As he crawled out and collapsed in a comparatively clear area, a familiar but unexpected smell drifted past his nose. He sniffed the air.

He could smell weed. He was sure of it.

Who on earth would be smoking grass out here?

He knew the smell well, having appropriated the stash of an older kid he had heard bragging about smoking it, who had in turn stolen it from his dad's store of home grown. Threatening the older kid that he'd tell his grandfather where he'd found it – the Mayor had very strict views on drugs that didn't come in imported bottles with pharmaceutical company stickers on them – Hector had spent a few weeks experimenting with different ways of smoking. Tobacco had been hard to come by so he had tried various herbs and implements, before deciding that he didn't actually like it very much, because it made him feel out of control, and worse, giggly.

The wind was southwesterly and the laurel limbs he would need to traverse were numerous. The safest bet was to retreat and work round to the west. Some tortuous minutes later he found himself close to the lane and turned left to flank the edge of the woods and work in that way. The smell had gone, but he didn't hurry, relying on years of experience of hunting game with his grandfather. Moving as quietly as he could, tucking and turning to avoid getting snagged, he found himself on the edge of a small clearing. Forced to stop, he took the opportunity to catch his breath, coming fast from the excitement of the hunt.

There was the smell again. Much stronger. Keeping as still as he could, he widened his gaze without moving his head. A brief flash of movement. Someone was squatting on the other side of the clearing, above the road, looking down into it. A hand went up to the face, and a moment later a puff of smoke appeared and drifted across to him.

When the face turned in profile he didn't recognise the boy, who wasn't much older than him. He had short hair, unlike most of the villagers, for whom keeping scissors sharp was a chore, and was dressed in dark clothes with lots of pockets, looking like one of the militia, but without the breastpatch of Devon colours. Now he was stubbing out and throwing away the butt of the joint he'd been smoking and getting up from his crouch. Hector froze in position, but the boy didn't see him or even look in his direction as he crossed the clearing to a clump of bushes, parted them, and disappeared.

★

The church was full when Mayor and Mrs Spight arrived with Fred, Bob having been sent ahead to make sure the heating had been turned on – a necessity even in summer as the eighteenth-century granite church was always numbingly cold – so the villagers would be reminded who looked after their creature comforts. Spight thought it as well to do so before he had to tell them of the delay to their allocations of tea, coffee, crisps, fizzy drinks, chocolate and other goods considered essential to a modern and meaningful life.

He had timed his departure from his house, just around the corner from the church, to be sure they arrived ten minutes late and he wouldn't have to wait for everyone to take their seats. His grandson had tried to disrupt his strict timetable with some story, bursting into the kitchen as he was having his tea, collapsing into a chair unbidden and panting hard across the table, which quite put the Mayor off his meat pie. He'd snapped at the boy, telling him to have a wash and change his filthy clothes, and come and talk to him later, when he'd calmed down. Junior had slunk off, glowering, but that was to be expected when he was so poorly disciplined by his parents. Spight knew he needed to spend more time with the boy before he became irredeemable, starting as soon as this crisis was over.

As he swept through the throng standing at the back of the nave, heading for the ornately carved pulpit in the chancel, the general hubbub of voices dropped off. Sunshine poured through the elaborate stained-glass windows, bathing his face as he marched towards the front and glinting off the gold of his Mayoral chain. By the time he got to the foot of the pulpit his congregation were silent, except for some small children, too young to be left at home in the care of siblings, who were quickly shushed. He didn't notice Mrs Spight choose not to sit in the seat reserved for her in the front pew and stay instead at the back, close to the door.

The vicar was waiting for him in front of an elaborately carved and gilded Gothic screen that stood before the apse, his face registering disapproval at the appropriation of his house of worship for a meeting about worldly affairs. Accordingly, he was not wearing vestments but his other uniform of sensible cardigan over sweater and misshapen trousers. But he couldn't refuse the use of the church, knowing his position to be precarious. The Church of England had no official standing within Devon. Already suffering from declining attendances and looking to be on the point of extinction at the time of Devolution, the vicar's posting had been controversial. He had come into the county as a missionary, eschewing more exotic locations for the damned souls of Britain's most apostate district, and his reception had been lukewarm. The Reverend knew that without the Mayor's support, the church roof would never have been fixed after slates were stolen for use elsewhere, and his sermons would have continued to be delivered to a dwindling number of aging faithful before becoming completely moribund as they died out.

A devout believer in the power of religion to enforce social cohesion – and in the subliminal authority imparted by perceived favour with the Reverend, and by extension, God – Spight was a regular church goer, and anyone wanting his favour was expected to attend services throughout the year. As a result, the vicar had enjoyed record attendances in recent years, and was kept busy with weddings, christenings and burials across the parish.

Spight climbed the pulpit steps, conscious that he would be backed by the light of God pouring through stained glass as he spoke, the thought putting a smile on his face as he turned and regarded the expectant faces raised to his. Such sheep. Somewhat shabby, careworn sheep after a long day of labour. It was a good thing they had him to shepherd them; the Good Lord alone knew what would happen if they didn't.

No reason had been given for the meeting and the air was thick with curiosity. Spight looked at his notes, already in place thanks to Bob, and removed them, tucking them into the inside pocket of his suit jacket. Time to improvise.

He took a moment to gather his thoughts, nodding to key supporters assembled in the pews, including Dorcas, passing over Mrs Prendaghast who was off to one side and looking grim, smiling at a mother with a baby in her arms. When he received a nod from one of his men, Dug, dressed smartly in militia uniform, to convey that the tape recorders were cued and ready to go, the Mayor conjured an expression of sorrow.

'Friends.' Was that a titter at the back? He fought back a scowl and made a mental note to check with Fred, standing by the doors, to see who had had the temerity to snigger. Concentrating on the effect he was trying to create, he didn't see his wife slip out of a side door, or Bob follow her a few minutes later. 'Friends and neighbours, I've called you here today to let you know that our enemies have struck.'

Murmuring broke out. 'A cowardly act of sabotage has temporarily delayed our scheduled delivery.' A rumbling of disquiet. 'But this will not be tolerated or allowed to undermine our right to determine how we live, or stop us winning the war. Our way of life, our very *existence*, has been under threat for years from those who would do us harm. From those who see us as a threat to their corrupt and decadent lives. Those who would chain us with their laws and rules, their ideologies, their jealousy of what we have achieved here.' A quiet swell of agreement.

'That you, decent hard-working men and women, toiling in our fields and factories to provide for your families – you who just want to raise your fine children and live law abiding, respectable lives filled with plenty – that you should be deprived and forced to suffer because of the actions of foreign, radical extremists, makes me mad. It's bad, it's wrong, and I won't rest until I, as your Mayor and, yes, I hope, your *friend*,' a meaningful glance in the direction of the titterer, 'can bring your hard-earned goods here, and hand them out to you personally. We shall prevail, and the saboteurs, our enemies, will be made to regret their actions. Let's keep Devon great!'

There were smatterings of applause, led by Fred and Dorcas, which built slowly as people realised he was done, and was now watching closely to see who was laggardly with their support. He made a cutting gesture to Dug, signalling that recording should stop before the swell of clapping died down. Pews wobbled and squeaked as people started to get up and leave, murmuring among themselves. He suspected they weren't convinced, but as long as he got their junk to them in the next couple of days no one would dare criticise him openly and his position would be safe.

He needed to begin negotiations for the delivery of the

cargo immediately, and in person. No one else could be trusted to handle it effectively and who knew how long it would take. Gloria would have to pack his bag as soon as they got home, while he made arrangements for getting to Dartmouth. Which was when he noticed that his wife wasn't there. Typical! Lazy cow, she'd probably gone home as soon as she could so she could sit on that fat arse and read the American fashion and lifestyle magazines he imported for her at vast expense.

Dorcas was standing by the door when he got there, after clasping hands and slapping backs all the way down the aisle. His face was aching from smiling. They left the church together and he steered her to stand by one of the headstones in the graveyard.

The westering sun was still out and the heat was blistering, raising instant beads of sweat on his face. He dabbed fastidiously at his forehead with a handkerchief, before placing it back in the top pocket of his suit jacket.

'I'm going to need all the fuel you've got in store,' he said without greeting. 'I'm heading down the river, and back, and then there'll be the transfer.'

'That shouldn't be a problem, we've done a fair bit of extracting and rendering in the last few days, getting everything ready.'

'Good, I'll send Fred back with you to collect the jerry cans, and I'll need you to do another harvest as soon as possible.'

Dorcas frowned. 'That might be a problem. Maybe a volunteer drive ...?'

He looked at the stream of people leaving the church. 'Not enough meat on that lot.' He grabbed the flesh of her upper arm and gave it a hard pinch through her cardigan. She winced. 'You, on the other hand ...'

'You can't be serious,' she said, shocked.

'Why not? We all need to do our bit in desperate times.'

'Desperate, are we?' Her eyes were flinty and her tone sarcastic. 'I thought this was just a temporary setback.'

Careful. He shouldn't have pushed it and vented his frustration on her. He could rely on Dorcas only so far. If she sensed weakness she'd be like a shark smelling blood in the water; she still hadn't forgiven him for ending their affair and moving out of his suite of rooms at the fat farm, ostensibly to provide a home for Flora and the newborn Junior but really to keep his image as a devout family man intact.

She had been furious, pointing out that most of his best ideas had come with the help of her research in the library, born out of their shared interest in Hitler and Nazi Germany. It was she who had first had the idea of extracting fat for biodiesel, and – though she didn't know it – she had also given him the inspiration for his special project.

He took a deep breath.

'It is temporary. But it's going to take a lot of fuel to get me to that ship and then to bring everything back upriver in small loads. If we can't get that from your lot, it's got to come from somewhere.'

'Well, I might just have a little stash. Put away for this sort of emergency.'

'How very cunning of you Dorcas.' He'd suspected as much but seethed inwardly to hear confirmation.

'I might be persuaded to free some up, for a consideration.'

'It isn't yours to bargain with! It belongs to the village!'

'It came from my allocation! I've been keeping some back and making do. Walking. Skimping on heating – that lot aren't going to miss it if the thermostat's set a degree or two lower, all the blubber on 'em!'

That had to be a lie. Dorcas wouldn't walk anywhere

willingly, and the farm was heated with timber from the grounds. But he couldn't call her on it. His teeth were almost grinding as he gritted out, 'What do you have in mind?'

'I hear you're bringing in some white goods – our dishwasher could do with replacing. Oh, and some new DVDs. The ones we've got are all starting to skip. And a new laptop would be nice too, to play them on.'

Extortion. No other word for it. But he needed that fuel. 'I'll see what I can do, I can't promise any ...'

Dorcas interrupted him. Spight was too taken aback to do more than gape. 'Then I can't guarantee I'll be able to lay my hands on those jerry cans. You know my memory isn't what it was, and I'll need some encouragement to go looking for them.'

This was taking too long, and making him look weak in the eyes of a woman he needed onside, however much that might rankle.

'Fine,' he all but snarled. 'Dishwasher, laptop.'

'And DVDs.'

He didn't dignify that with a response. 'Bob will give you a lift back to the farm. He can help you look, and load up. BOB!' No Bob appeared. Where was the man? 'Fred will go with you. FRED!'

His son-in-law put his head out of the church door.

'Sir?'

'Take Dorcas back to the farm and load up all the fuel you can find.' He sneered as he continued, 'Including her secret stash. Take it to the boat. I'll meet you there in two hours.'

'Yes, Sir.'

A DENSE NET OF SHADOWS

It was as though night had fallen early as they bumped and bounced their way up the heavily shaded and gloomy lanes in Fred's ancient Land Rover, headlights cutting out periodically from fraying electrics. Once at the farm, Dorcas settled Fred in the kitchen with some biscuits and a cup of tea while she rounded up Agnes and dragged Ivy, still snotty from her cold, out of her bed. The three of them huddled in the laundry room, out of range of listening ears.

'Right, Spight's cocked up, but it's going to do us some good. You get a new dishwasher out of it, my girl.' She looked at Agnes expectantly. The girl seemed underwhelmed. In fact, she seemed positively agitated. Dorcas sighed with exasperation. 'We've to give Fred all the fuel we have stashed, or at least what he can find. And we'll have to ramp up production to make up for it. We might even need to make a contribution ourselves. It'll be just like the good old days,' she wheedled, referring to the fat drives. Those had been before Agnes and Ivy had been born and they didn't look impressed by the idea. To be fair, both of them were too scrawny to be much good to her.

'Once we've loaded up, I need you to check the weight gain charts, and it might be an idea to get everyone together, let them know what we're expecting of them.'

'Do you think that's a good idea?' Agnes plucked at her apron.

'Of course, that's why I said it.'

'Yes Ma'am. Of course, sorry.' What was wrong with her? She wouldn't meet Dorcas's eyes. Oh, who cared? She had more important things to worry about. Like keeping back a few jerrycans from the eagle eyes of Fred. Who knew how valuable fuel might become while they were going through this little difficulty? And if the wood-fired boiler broke down they might need it themselves.

Fred had finished his tea and cleaned them out of biscuits. Dorcas put him to work hauling containers of human-derived biodiesel through what used to be the coal hole to the cellar, using a rope and pulley for the larger drums, with the help of Agnes and a sniffling Ivy. While he was busy, she hid a few cans in the back of what used to be the old garage and was now a store for tools, broken furniture awaiting fixing – her inmates were hard on springs – and old junk. When Fred was done with the recent harvest she led him to a small shed and showed him the half a dozen or so cans stashed there.

'That's it, and I'm happy to do my bit for Devon,' she declared.

'I'll have a quick look around if you don't mind, see if there are a few others you might have forgotten about.' Fred's tone was heavily ironic, and Dorcas resented it. How dare he take that tone with her? But if she refused it wouldn't look good. She followed him around as he poked around in cupboards and under tarpaulins in all the outbuildings clustered around the main house. When he got to the garage she tried to distract him with chatter, but he ignored her and rootled about, moving towards the back in a methodical sweep, or as methodical as possible with all the junk littering the floor.

'Aha, here we are,' he declared triumphantly, holding aloft one can. 'These will do nicely. I can see why you forgot about 'em, they were so well hidden you might think it were deliberate.'

'Well done Fred, I'd quite forgotten about those.' Inwardly she was seething as she signalled to Agnes to carry one to the Land Rover. Fred carried the other four, oblivious to their heavy weight. The back of the vehicle was now full. Spight would be happy.

Fred climbed up into the driver's seat. 'Right, I just got time to go meet him down the quayside. Ladies, a pleasure.' He tipped an imaginary hat at them. Dorcas forced herself to smile as he started the engine and crunched gears.

'Smug bastard,' she hissed, as the Land Rover sped away, spitting gravel before braking hard to avoid hitting the first of the potholes at speed. It proceeded down the drive at a more sedate pace.

By now it was eight o'clock and supper was an hour overdue, which was hardly going to help them get everyone back up to a farmable weight. Dorcas sent Agnes to break out the chip pan and set Ivy to peeling potatoes. Half an hour of hard graft later and they were ready to start dishing out eggs, chips and beans, the best they could do at short notice. Never mind, Agnes had baked earlier and there were brownies for pudding, and the last of the fizzy pop. Besides, she knew about the secret stashes in bedside cabinets.

'Why don't you go and have a bit of a sit down, Ma'am?' Agnes suggested as she sweated under a tray of plates with zinc covers, heading for the staircase. 'You must be knackered.'

'Don't be daft girl, it's all hands on deck until we get this lot fed. Surprised they haven't rioted.'

Dorcas bustled up the stairs under her own heavy load, sending Ivy up to the top floor, while she started at the west end of the first-floor corridor and Agnes started at the east. She was met with gratitude and a limited range of jokes along the

line of 'You get lost?' or 'Was about to start eating my own
hand!' Two more trips to the kitchen and there were just two
plates left, for Primrose and Alise. As she headed for their
room she collided with Agnes, who somehow tripped over the
hall carpet and knocked into her, sending both plates crashing
to a carpet already tapestried with old stains.

'Oh my god, I'm so sorry, I'll clean it up in a minute …'
Somehow Agnes had two more plates at the ready. She made
to slip past Dorcas, who blocked her, grabbed the plates and
nudged the door open with her hip.

'You best stop ordering me around, girly, and yes you will
clean it up.' She sailed into the room, deposited one plate in
the outstretched hands of Alise, and turned towards Primrose's
bed. Which was empty.

'Where's Primrose? Bathroom?'

'Nah, she split,' Alise mumbled around a mouthful of egg
and chips. Yolk dripped down her chin and into her cleavage.

For a moment Dorcas imagined Primrose literally splitting.
Maybe before she was harvested that would have been
possible. Then the real meaning hit home. She turned slowly,
still holding the plate. Agnes was standing in the doorway, eyes
wide, like a rabbit.

'Yeah, she must've snuck out last night some time,' Alise
continued helpfully. 'I was asleep. She were gone when I
woke.'

'How long have you known?' Dorcas asked Agnes, her tone
icy.

'Oh, she's known since breakfast.' Alise popped another
chip in her mouth and chewed noisily. 'If that food's going
begging, I'll eat it.'

But the plate was already sailing for Agnes's head. She
ducked and it smashed against the wall behind her, leaving

long smears of yolk as it fell in pieces to the floor.

★

Fred found Mr Spight and Bob on the quayside on the outskirts of the nearest town, downhill and to the east of the village. Longmarsh lay only five miles away from Bodingleigh but was inaccessible to many of the village's older inhabitants, the roads being all but impassable and the road so steep it was difficult to climb on foot. It had been this difficulty that had been used to justify the tithing of fat for fuel nearly twenty years before, when imports of petrol had become prohibitively expensive and a newly elected council leader, in the person of militia hero Captain Hector Spight, decried attempts to decarbonise their local economy as giving in to the ideological stranglehold from which they had chosen to devolve.

If they were to forge their own path and 'Make Devon Great Again', they needed oil, and it was up to everyone to do what they could to supply it, if only to show the rest of what had been the United Kingdom that Devon had what it took to go it alone. He had been first in the queue to donate at the inaugural tithe; Fred, in his twenties, newly promoted in the militia, worshipping both Councilman Spight and his daughter Flora, had been right behind him.

A year after becoming leader of the Council of Longmarsh and District, Mr Spight had become the elected Mayor of the whole of Devon and delivered on a pledge to convert all of the county's generators and remaining diesel cars to run on biodiesel. Although outside of his own district his grip was looser, and he was forced to share power with the rest of the Council, its members were – largely – hand-picked by him and co-opted without the bother and expense of actual elections, as natural wastage and the occasional scandal created empty seats. Mayor Spight had held office without interruption and his re-appointment next May was expected by a populace made cynical by the politics of the early twenty-first century and happy to have someone decisive in charge.

The quay lay alongside an old boathouse, pre-Devolution headquarters for a ferry service catering to a thriving tourist industry before visitors stopped coming. Since then the river had silted up; the flat-bottomed skiff Bob was preparing – while Spight made calls on his satellite phone to agree a rendezvous with the skipper – had a shallow draught that could get them all the way to Dartmouth, so long as they waited for the high point of the tide.

All of which was irrelevant to Fred as he pulled up in the Land Rover, because as soon as he reached them Spight told him he wasn't coming on this trip. He was to load up the fuel, stash what they couldn't fit in the boat in the old ticket office and go home. Bob would be steering, so Spight could continue coordinating the transfer of goods and payment by phone.

'Need to keep the boat light,' he explained tersely when Fred questioned his decision. 'Get on with it man, we need to be off.'

Fred had been looking forward to a trip on the water, a chance to feel significant in a town bigger than Longmarsh, and a possible quick fumble with a whore upstairs in the hotel while Spight was conducting business. It was only fitting that he, as the natural successor to the Mayor, should be the one to accompany him on important business. How come it was Bob – mousy, insignificant Bob – who was chosen to make the journey?

Fred's good mood, brought about by Spight trusting him to retrieve the fuel from the fat farm, curdled. He stumped from the Land Rover to the boat, and then the Land Rover to the boathouse, ignored by his father-in-law and avoided by Bob, who busied himself with filling the boat's fuel tank and stowing spare cans so they wouldn't upset the balance of the skiff.

Eventually Spight declared them ready and directed Fred to untie the boat and push them away from the quay. The sound of Bob's oars slapping the water mocked Fred, left alone on the waterside as the boat drifted off into the twilight. An owl hooted. Fred felt sure it was taking the piss.

His drive back to Bodingleigh was slow. There was no rush to return. His wife would be out do-gooding somewhere or bossing the Knockers around. He didn't care where, or who she was with; he'd stopped asking years before, and she'd stopped telling him some years before that. The only things keeping them together were the conventions of a small village, the will of her father, and Fred's ambitions to take over from him when the old man got too senile to carry on. Admittedly that still seemed some way off, but in the meantime there were, sometimes, perks to being Spight's son-in-law.

He fought to remember that when he got home to the three-storey house they all shared, after leaving the Land Rover in the car park up by the village hall. He hadn't had time to eat before the meeting, or after it, and there was no dinner left out for him, or plated up in the fridge they were privileged to be able to maintain. Mrs Spight had retired to her bedroom for the night and, as expected, there was no sign of his wife. Clearly the lazy cow had fucked off out without thinking to see to her husband's needs.

He was making himself a ham and cheese sandwich at the kitchen counter when his son came into the room.

'Where's Grandpa?' Hector Jr had been banned from the

public meeting, as had everyone under the age of sixteen, and had no idea what it had been about, though he'd tried to wheedle information out of Fred earlier. His father had no intention of making the little snot-nose happy. The boy was cocky enough.

'Out.'

'Obviously. When's he gonna be back?'

'Dunno.' Fred bit viciously into his sandwich. Taking the plate, he crossed to the table and sat heavily in a chair. He was tired from all the lugging of heavy containers and pissed off at being excluded from family business. It felt good to pass that on.

Hector drew out a chair and sat down opposite his father, who was astonished. Junior hadn't willingly spent time with him in years. He must want something. Fred remained silent, ate his sandwich and waited to see what that might be.

'I was up in the woods by the fat farm this morning, after telling everyone to go to the meeting, and I saw something.'

Fred grunted and stuffed in the last crust, leaned back and wondered if he wanted more to eat.

'I was having a poke about, and I saw someone, and then they just disappeared.'

Nope, he wasn't that hungry, but he could go a pint. Dismissing Junior's prattling as irrelevant fantasy, Fred checked his watch. There was still time to go down the pub for a few pints of cider. It would probably be packed after the meeting, and someone would be bound to buy him a drink in the hope of getting some inside info. It didn't matter that he didn't have any. A few noncommittal grunts and a knowing look should get him at least a couple of pints. Maybe a chaser of poteen. He pushed his chair back from the table and stood, leaving the plate for one of the women to clear up.

'Dad! Listen!' Junior smacked the table, a right chip off old Grandpa's block. Fred was so astonished he didn't even act on his first impulse to smack him one. 'This boy disappeared right in front of my eyes, so I poked around in the bushes where I'd seen him, and I found a door! There's some secret place in the woods, and there's people hiding in there.'

This was his moment to shine. With no Spight around to take control of the situation, Fred was free to take matters in hand and deal with what could turn out to be the worst crisis they'd had to face in years. He was delighted. After questioning his son closely, and with the help of an antique Ordnance Survey walker's map, he pinpointed the area where Hector had seen the youth disappearing to within a few square feet, wrote notes of his son's description of the spot in the margin, then called someone he could trust. It took a long time for the phone to be answered, and when it was he could hear pub noise in the background. Without giving details, in case this turned out to be a crock of shite, he arranged to meet Dug and Biff at the Land Rover in twenty minutes.

Junior was sent to bed, much to his disgust.

'You need me there to help you find it,' he pointed out.

'I need you out of the way. If things go bad and something happens to you, I'll cop it from your mum and granddad. Go to bed. I'll tell you about it in the morning.' Turning his back on his son, Fred started rummaging through kitchen drawers to find things he might need. A torch and spare batteries that had cost them a fortune in local produce, and a sock full of loose change that sometimes came in handy as a cosh. He didn't have a key to the gun cupboard.

Behind him, he heard Junior stomping up the stairs to his room.

*

As soon as his dad had left for the car park, Hector Jr sneaked back downstairs, still fully dressed. His mum was out, and Grandma was asleep and snoring in her room, but he snuck around the house anyway as he found his coat and shoes, in an emotional state ricocheting between excitement and resentment at being left behind, when he was the one who had found the secret hideout and knew where it was.

His bike was by the back door where he'd left it, and he wheeled it quietly up the alley at the rear of the house. There was still a trace of light in the sky, but the village lay shrouded, and he took care to keep to the shadows between the few streetlights. As he passed the school, he saw the warden approaching, come to snuff the candles and turn the streets dark. It must be eleven, curfew time. He hid behind a wall, the knowledge he was now officially breaking the rules – as well as disobeying his father – giving him a massive buzz.

He didn't want to get ahead of his dad and be caught, so he ducked into a derelict cul de sac above the village and crouched behind a grass bank, just in time to avoid being lit up by the headlights of the Land Rover as it swept out of the car park and turned left towards the lane. Now he'd have to peg it to catch up, or he'd miss all the action.

About half a mile from the fat farm driveway was a shortcut into the woods that he was sure his dad didn't know about, and there he left the road, dragging his bike up through a gap in the dense hedge and leaving it leaning up against a trunk. From here the hill climbed steeply, a dense tangle of laurel and ivy, making the going slow. Hector climbed as fast as he could, trying to make as little noise as possible, only using his torch for short flashes to make sure he was heading in the right direction. It was hard work; he was hot and out of breath by the time he reached the top. By his reckoning he was about a hundred yards from where he had seen the mysterious smoker. He hadn't told his dad about smelling the smoke, feeling it was unwise to admit he recognised the smell of weed, and thinking if he was lucky he might find the boy's stash. Not to smoke, but he knew plenty of kids who'd pay for it in cash or favours.

Crashing noises, like bears blundering across a wilderness, broke through the pounding of blood in his ears. That would be Fred and his mates making a mess of the search. Hunkering down, Hector settled himself to watch the show.

Fred came into view and crossed a patch of moonlight illuminating a clearing, sweeping at a thicket of brambles with a stick.

Clanging. Wonder of wonders the dumb fuck had found the door! Shouting to his mates, his father started pulling at the undergrowth, cursing as thorns tore his hands. Two of his militia sidekicks burst into the clearing to help him, and between them the door was uncovered in a matter of minutes. Fred grabbed the handle, turned it and pushed. Nothing happened. He tried pulling. Nothing.

'OK, plan B.' Fred took something off his belt. Hector knew this was a highly personalised multi-tool kit that contained – among pointy and stabby objects suitable for threatening and causing pain to uncooperative people – pliers and a screwdriver. Telling one of his companions to hold his torch so he could see, Fred began working on the door.

This could take a while. Hector eased himself to the ground and stifled a yawn, tired from all the running around he had been doing. The ground under him was covered in shallow roots, one of which was poking him in the bum. He sidled a bit to the right, found a patch cushioned in ivy and leaned back against the bole of a tree.

Five minutes later Fred had unscrewed one hinge of three. There was a distinct air of anticlimax, compounded by the fact clouds now obscured the moon and Hector could only see what progress was being made intermittently, by the light of the torch, when it wasn't blocked by his father's body. He was getting bored. Also, a little worried that, unlikely as it seemed, there would be nothing of interest behind the door and his dad would give him shit for wasting his time. He'd have to rush home to be sure of getting there before Fred did, and sneak into the house. Being here was feeling more and more like a bad idea, and maybe an example of the poor impulse control his mother was always banging on about.

A rustling in the undergrowth beside him. Hector pushed himself away on his hands and heels and then scrabbled around on the ground to find a weapon in case it turned out to be a rat. He was scared of rats.

The moon broke free of clouds and illuminated a pale hand protruding from the ground; like something from one of the old horror DVDs he watched on the laptop his grandfather had given him. Hector squeaked and waved the stick in front of him before the significance of what he was seeing broke through his fright. The hand was pushing up a hinging lid. Another hand joined it. Now a head and shoulders appeared.

He recognised the boy he had seen earlier that day, who was wide-eyed and panting hard, as if he was scared. Knowing that made Hector's own fear recede.

Hector withdrew into shadows and waited for the whole of the boy's body to emerge and then, aiming just below the knees now level with his face, drew his arms back and swiped at them with the stick as hard as he could. Even sitting down, he managed to put enough force into the blow to send the boy flying sideways, hitting the ground hard. There was a whoof as air left the stranger's lungs, and he lay winded and unmoving.

Hector bellowed, '*DAD!*'

★

Fred was brought up short by the sound of Junior shouting for him. What the hell was the little shit doing here, when he'd been given a direct order to go to bed?

'DAD, *HELP!*'

Hector's voice was coming from a dense net of shadows across the clearing. Fred grabbed the torch and ran, to see Junior crouched against the roots of a towering oak, holding a stick in front of him like he had been fending off an attack. Close by, a stranger was lying on his back on the ground, and beside him was a hatchway. An escape route! Clearly the foreigner – Fred didn't recognise him, he had to have come from outside the village at least – had become aware of their attempts to break into his hideaway and had been trying to run away. Now why would he do that if he wasn't up to no good?

The foreigner rolled over and started scrambling to his knees, obviously trying to escape. Fred hit him with the torch where he thought his head should be – the beam sweeping wildly across Hector's face, a crazed tangle of tree limbs and white, outstretched hands – and heard a satisfying craack as he connected with bone. The torch winked out as the glass and the bulb broke. Dug and Biff appeared.

'Whoa,' said Dug. 'We got someone?'

'Looks that way. And who's the we? Took you long enough.'

'What's Junior doing here?' Biff wanted to know.

So did Fred, but now was not the time to go into that.

'I was worried Dad,' Hector told them, eyes wide in the bullshit way he pulled when he was lying but thought he could get away with it. 'Who knows what these people are up to? I wanted to be sure you'd be OK.'

Biff had another question. 'How'd he get over 'ere?'

'Tunnel. Looks like we don't need to dick around with the door. My torch's bust, give me yours.'

'Ain't got one.'

'I've got one Dad.' Hector rummaged in his jacket pocket and pulled out an expensive torch Fred recognised as one he thought he'd lost months ago. He'd got an earful from Spight about carelessness and waste at the time, something else to discuss with his son later. For now, he just grabbed it and switched it on.

By its light they could see that the body collapsed at their feet was that of a boy of about sixteen, unknown to any of them and still out cold. He was dressed in the insurrectionist uniform Junior had described and had a hand-held radio in the side pocket of his trousers, but no weapons beyond a pocket knife. Fred removed the walkie-talkie and knife and put them in his own pocket.

What to do with him? If they took him back to the village it would be like saying they were waiting for Spight's return. Besides, where to put him? Fred came to a decision, and the outline of a plan. But before that, he wanted to see what was at the end of the tunnel.

'Biff, you stay here with Junior and the prisoner. I'm going down. Dug, you come with me in case there's more of 'em.'

'What do I do if he wakes up? Or they come out that door? You didn't say to come armed, I got nothin'.'

Fred brought out an ancient pair of handcuffs from another pocket, turned the stranger over to snap them closed on his wrists and left him lying face down. He knew those cuffs would come in handy some day; it was worth having carried them around for the last three years, and the price he'd paid.

'There, that should keep him in line if he wakes up. If any more come running, yell.' He grinned mirthlessly at Biff. 'But I reckon he's the only one here. Now you,' and he pointed the torch in Junior's direction, 'stay put or I'll beat you bloody when I find you.'

Hector Jr's Adam's apple bobbed as he swallowed and nodded.

A ladder led down into darkness. Stepping onto it with the torch held between his teeth, Fred saw it was old, and pitted with rust that flaked away under his hands. So, this tunnel had been here a while. How come he had never heard about it? He was born and bred in the village. It offended him that something existed within the parish boundary about which he knew nothing.

At the bottom, about ten feet down, he found a tunnel with a dirt floor leading away behind him. It was a tight fit to turn around, and as he was shuffling his feet Dug started his descent, sifting rust into his hair and almost kicking him in the face.

'Oy, wait!' he shouted. The feet paused. Fred stooped. He was six foot two and the tunnel barely five foot eight, so he had to walk with his neck severely cocked. 'Right, come on then,' he called back to Dug as he started down the tunnel. The torch held in front of him showed him the tunnel was about fifteen feet long and ended at an open door, dim light spilling out to pool on the rough ground. Excitement mounted as he neared it; there was a chance he'd be bursting in on a whole gang and there'd be more violence. He tightened his grip on the torch in his left hand, and brought out his multitool, extracting the sharpest knife from its nest and holding it in front of him in his right.

When he got to the door he waited for Dug to catch up, not moving until he felt the man's breath on his neck, then pulled the door open to its widest extent and leapt inside, knife hand extended.

He was in a room of about twenty feet by fifteen and seven feet high, full of clutter and a rank stench but otherwise empty. A sturdy wooden door with a lock was to his right, and another to his left. The door to the left was unlocked and led to another, shorter, tunnel, and a big steel door that looked like the inside of the door he'd been trying to unlock. The door to the right was locked.

A table in the centre of the room was covered in maps held down by half full mugs. The top one was of Plymouth and its harbour.

'This proves they hijacked the shipment!' Dug was a master at stating the bleeding obvious. 'Spight's gonna give us a medal for finding this lot.'

Fred doubted Spight would give him credit for finding anything if he could help it. He pulled the Plymouth map aside. Underneath were maps of Longmarsh, Bodingleigh and other villages in the parish, with mysterious red symbols on them. Something was seriously afoot.

'Dug, go check the prisoner for keys. We need to get in that locked room.'

A search of the prisoner's pockets produced no keys, but did rouse him to incoherent protests and a bout of vomiting. Dug reported this back. Reluctantly, Fred conceded it was time to do something about him. He rolled up the maps and tucked them under his arm before he and Dug returned to the surface, where Dug was instructed to stay and watch to see if anyone returned. If they did, he was to do nothing but wait for Fred to return. Junior was to accompany Fred and Biff back to the Land Rover with the prisoner, keeping his mouth shut.

Between them, Biff and Fred hoisted up the now semi-conscious prisoner and half-dragged, half-carried him through the woods to the driveway, where they had stashed the Land Rover. After throwing him into the back seat and telling Biff to get in and keep him from getting out, Fred climbed behind the wheel and started the engine. Junior pulled himself up onto the passenger seat and Fred threw the roll of maps into his lap.

Instead of turning around, Fred carried on up the drive towards the fat farm.

Biff was confused. 'Eh? Aren't we going back to the village?'

'Nope.'

There were no lights in any of the windows when they drew up outside the farm. Fred checked his watch and saw it was after midnight. Too bad. He cut the engine and climbed out, telling the others to stay put.

The front door was locked. The knocker, a large iron ring, made an almighty *boom* when he dropped it against the plate. He knocked again, and again, and again, until eventually the door was opened by Dorcas wrapped in a tartan dressing gown. Behind her, lights were appearing in the hallway as members of staff crept down the stairs with candles to see what was going on.

'What the hell … Fred? What are you doing back here? Do you know what time it is?'

'Do you know you have a secret hideout in the grounds, and it's the HQ for some secret army that's plotting to steal our shipments and God knows what else?'

'What? Are you mad? What are you talking about?'

He grabbed her by the arm and dragged her down the steps to the back door of the Land Rover. 'There, see him? He's one of them and we just arrested him in your back garden.' At a nod from Fred, Biff dragged the boy into a sitting position. He was now awake, but still groggy, staring at them with eyes wide with terror. Fred released Dorcas, who stepped back, rubbing her arm and looking shocked. Fred opened the back door and grabbed his prisoner instead, pulling him out.

'Dorcas, look after my son, there's things about to happen he's still too young to see. Biff, go get Dr Harrow.'

DARKNESS WAS COMPLETE

The first part of their journey downriver was made more or less in silence. Spight occasionally received a call or text on his satellite phone and replied tersely to it. Bob rowed, taking rests when his arms grew too tired. Eventually Spight took pity on him and allowed him to start the engine. Everything was taking too long. He wanted to be in Dartmouth well before dawn, when the skipper was threatening to leave, having found potential markets for his cargo in Dorset. Customers who could pay cash, which was in short supply in Devon.

Besides themselves, there was no other traffic on the river. Intermittent moonlight showed dark woods massed on either bank and silvered the tree tops before falling to the water to light their spreading wake. The river twisted its sinuous way through loops and wide turns, passing ancient estate houses now crumbling into decay. A small Gothic boathouse with turrets jutted into the water, half submerged but with a candle burning in a top window. An owl swept past them on silent wings. Spight appreciated nothing of this.

He was counting off landmarks. The rotting hulk of an old plague ship, used as a smallpox hospital ward, burned out and abandoned. A village that had lost half its houses to rising waters and another that climbed up the steep hills as the river narrowed. Both appeared deserted and he approved; it meant the residents were observing the curfew, and not wasting resources by burning candles. He'd instituted the curfew as an energy-saving measure, citing the need to snuff the candles illuminating streetlights to conserve scant resources, and the dangers that people, particularly teenagers and women, might face wandering the streets after dark. It kept people indoors and under control and to his mind that could only be a good thing.

At last the outskirts of Dartmouth began to spread across the hills to either side. Again, most houses were dark. As they reached the town centre, Bob cut the engine and steered for the harbour wall, the skiff drifting in to bump against a protective shield of old tyres next to the stone steps. The height of the tide meant they were almost level with the top of the quay and it was easy to climb back on to dry land.

The cargo ship was moored out in deeper water, Spight had been informed during one phone call. The skipper had come in on a tender and was stopping overnight at his usual hotel next to the harbour. With Bob at his elbow, Spight crossed the square and tried the hotel door, the ancient Tudor building bulging out above him. It was locked, so he banged on it until someone came to open up, then pushed his way inside.

The interior appeared opulent in lighting kept deliberately dim, to hide its deficiencies as well as make the patrons and whores more attractive. This late, most activity had retired upstairs, but the ground-floor bar was still lit by a few lamps. The sleepy-looking man who had let them in returned to his station behind it and asked if they wanted a drink. Spight ordered a coffee, and on an afterthought, another one for Bob. To hell with the extravagance, he needed them both to be sharp.

'Over here.' The voice came from a chair in the shadows beside the fire, which had burned down to a glowing heap of embers. Spight told Bob to bring the drinks, crossed the room and drew up another chair. Sitting, he extended his hands to the glow. The trip on the river had left him chilled to the bone even if it was summer.

The skipper leaned forward in his chair. He was big. Not just well-covered, but tall, large-featured. The hand he extended for Spight to shake was huge, crushing his in its grip, and shockingly warm against his own chilled flesh. This was not the first time they had done business, but that didn't mean he trusted the man an inch, and coming in to negotiations in such a weak position made Spight twitchy and irritable. He had had plenty of time to think about how to approach things and looking at the man now he decided the best way to proceed was to go on the attack. Dwight came from a society that despised weakness. Millions had died during the Trump years, both at home and as a result of his callous indifference to calamities abroad, and people much like Dwight had watched it happen, with dispassion and a belief that their own survival depended on not heeding the suffering of others.

Bob brought their drinks over and was dismissed back to the bar.

'What the hell were you doing, being made a fool of by bloody insurgents?' Spight took a leisurely sip of his coffee. It was too hot and burned his mouth. He didn't let it show as he said, 'All you had to do was run them over and anchor for the night, we'd have the cargo unloaded by now and you'd be on your way back to New Jersey.'

Dwight's lip curled. It was not a smile. He was drinking whisky, the bottle on a small table by his side. He topped up his glass but didn't offer any to Spight. The 'real' American took a sip before replying. 'What the hell were you doing letting them float about your harbour?' he growled, in a voice like boots on gravel. 'I'm not part of your war, I just bring the cargo. And I take it where I'll get the best return. I don't give a

fuck about your dumbass little internal disputes. And I don't
kill people for you unless you pay me. Clean up your own
mess.'

He had a point. Time to change tack. 'I can top any offer
you've had from Dorset. We can unload here, and you don't
have to spend any more time or fuel.'

'I'm listening.'

'I can up my offer of livestock from fifty units to seventy-
five, on top of our other cargo.' He had no idea how he would
do it, but he had to have his shipment.

'That's pretty sweet, but where am I going to put another
twenty-five? I haven't time to make the arrangements to keep
'em healthy.'

'Keep them on deck if you have to.'

'Now that's hardly humane. 'Sides, they needs to be in good
shape when we get there or they're no good to me.' Dwight
sat back in his chair and took a long swallow from his glass.
'But I see you're desperate.' As he put down the tumbler his
manner became businesslike. 'OK, I'll take 'em, but they got to
be fatties so they got some surplus to burn, and they gotta be
young. No more offloading oldies on me.'

Relieved, ignoring the slur, Spight reached out his hand for
another grappling match and tried not to wince. 'Done.'

★

There had been something of a delay, as it turned out Dr
Harrow didn't live in the fat farm building, as Fred had
assumed, but in the gatehouse with his family. While he
waited, Fred dragged the prisoner down to the basement, at
the insistence of Dorcas who didn't want her residents
disturbed more than they had been already. As part of Spight's

inner cadre, she knew all about the more brutal realities of life in modern Devon, but it was something that was kept at a remove from the general population, and she didn't want it intruding at the farm.

Once there, the boy was recuffed to the leg of a heavy steel table supporting the fat rendering equipment, so that he was forced to sit on the floor. By now he was fully conscious, silent and pale with fright. Good, the more scared he was, the easier it would be to extract information.

Dr Harrow came in yawning, looking like he had dressed in a hurry. He stopped short when he saw the boy cuffed to the table and put down the black bag he was carrying.

'Dug said there was a problem at the farm. What's going on? I thought it was one of my patients.'

Patients? Was the man mad? They were cattle, like Spight said in his more unguarded moments. Stupid, greedy cattle. Or rather pigs. Livestock.

'We found him down in the woods in a secret hideout. We need to know what he was doing, and who else he's working with. What are the maps about?' This last was barked at his prisoner.

'I don't know what you mean, what maps?' It was the first time the boy had spoken. His voice squeaked with fright, wobbling between two registers. If his balls had dropped yet, it sounded like they were trying to creep back up into his body.

Fred took the roll of maps from where he had put them on the workbench running along the wall of the basement. He smacked them against the leg of the table the prisoner was shackled to. The boy flinched but said nothing. 'Don't play dumb, kid, you were in the bunker, these maps were in that bunker. Don't pretend you don't know what they are.'

The boy trembled, but his face remained blank and still he

said nothing.

'OK Doc, over to you. There's no time to beat it out of him.'

'What do you want me to do?' Harrow's worried frown said he had a fair idea, but needed it spelled out.

'Do what you do. I'm sure there's a bit of fat on 'im, time to donate it to the cause. No need to waste anaesthetic.'

'I'm really not sure …'

'I don't give a *fuck*, Harrow, just get it done, and don't make me have to tell the Mayor you didn't want to cooperate.'

Harrow opened his mouth a few times like he was going to protest, then shrugged. He didn't look the prisoner in the eye as he said, 'I'll need a table, and a power supply.'

The collapsible gurney had been brought downstairs from its usual place in the treatment room, with a great deal of difficulty and swearing, by Biff and Fred. They set it up next to the portable generator, before moving the table to which their prisoner was handcuffed. This was accomplished with considerably more difficulty, as it was steel and heavy, and the vat even heavier. The boy sat, shuffling along with the table when kicked, and said nothing.

When the gurney was ready, Biff freed the prisoner, stripping him of his jacket and hauling him up onto the cold steel surface. Reattaching the cuff to one of the supports left the prisoner's arm twisted at an awkward angle.

Dr Harrow pulled up the boy's jumper and t-shirt, unbuckled his belt and unfastened his trousers, exposing a flat, quivering white stomach and bony ribs.

'I don't see much fat here.'

'Fuck's sake Harrow, does that really matter? This i'n't really about the fat, right?'

'Yes, right.' Harrow's hands were shaking as he swabbed a wad of cotton with iodine and swept it across pristine skin, leaving a brown stain. For someone who cut people all the time, the man was a pussy.

'Don't know why you're bothering with that.'

'I don't want him catching an infection.'

'Yeah, right, his life expectancy is gonna be that long.' Fred was bluffing, he knew it was more likely Spight would send the boy to New Jersey. Young as he was he would fetch a very good price; the Mayor would want him in reasonable shape, for at least as long as it took to get him to a cargo ship and payment. But the prisoner didn't know that, and the more scared he was the more likely it was he would break and talk. All Fred wanted was for him to talk. Torture didn't bother him, but it took time, and he wanted this information nailed before Spight came back and took over. He wanted his father-in-law's respect, sod it! Not to say: Well, I caught this terrorist but he ain't talking, over to you.

The doctor's equipment consisted of a needle connected to a cannula, in turn connected to a flexible hose, and powered by a generator. Harrow picked up the needle, and stood, hesitating. Fred switched on the generator. It belched smoke into the room and he wondered if they should be doing this somewhere with better ventilation. But it was too late now. He plugged the hose into a socket and switched it on.

Biff gave Harrow a gentle shove towards the gurney.

The doctor's face was pale but his voice steady as he said, 'You'll have to hold him down, he's going to struggle.'

Biff took hold of the prisoner's shoulders and Fred grabbed him around the knees.

'Last chance kid.' Fred kept his tone gentle. The boy's face was white, his eyes screwed shut. He didn't speak.

Harrow made a small puncture with the needle. The flesh he pierced spasmed but the boy only gasped as blood welled and tears leaked from his eyes. Harrow pressed a button and a sucking noise filled the room. It was almost loud enough to drown out the sound of screaming as Harrow began to work the needle into the fatty layer beneath the skin, the doctor's hands steadying as professional habits took over. Clots of yellow, threaded with red, moved up the tube.

Holding on to the bucking, thrashing body and bringing his full weight to bear to keep it on the trolley, Fred was too distracted to see his son standing in the doorway, his eyes wide.

★

It didn't take long for Mal to break. Yes, he wanted to see the light return to darkest Devon, but not at this price. He had been warned he might face torture if he fell into the hands of Spight's empire, but it had been something he hadn't really believed. His family were from Devon, these were their neighbours and friends. Surely the rumours of people dying or disappearing were false, exaggerated. If he'd known it was all true he might not have volunteered.

He told them everything he knew about the disruption of the shipment, the monitoring of the Mayor and his minions and the plan to get Spight out of the way. It took them a while to believe that finer details and their final objective had been kept from him, the one holding his legs swapping with the doctor to become creative with the needle, culminating in holding it above Mal's twitching eyeball. Here, the doctor intervened, switching off the generator and declaring to the red-faced man that that was enough, it was clear this was just some footsoldier, and if they wanted more answers they'd have to go further up the chain of command.

Mal collapsed back onto the gurney and wept. It was at this point he became aware of the boy, the one from the woods who had knocked him over, standing just inside the plastic curtain in the doorway, watching him. What sort of monsters were these people?

Generator fumes fouled the air, which reeked of blood and burned bacon. All of them were coughing. Mal retched weakly over the side of the gurney, crying out with pain as the spasms racking his stomach aggravated his wounds, blood pulsing and spattering the floor. The short, fierce-looking woman appeared behind the boy and shoved him towards the stairs.

'Get out of here Hector, before I smack you one. I might have known this was where you'd sneak off to,' she said sharply to the boy, then turned to the man who seemed permanently angry. 'And you, Fred, have completely freaked out my residents. They can hear the screaming way up to the roof. I'm not having any more of it, you hear me?'

'We've got what we wanted.'

'Good, now clean him up. He might be a terrorist, but there's no need to kill him when we can make something from him. And clean up this bloody mess – we need this room to finish rendering the next batch.'

'I need somewhere secure to put him.' Fred's tone was stubborn. Fred ... the Mayor's son-in-law. Stories about his violent temper were widespread in the Saltash training camp and turned out to have a basis in fact. And that greedy-eyed boy, who had ignored the woman's instruction and was still hovering at her elbow, must be the Hector Jr Mal had heard about. He gave a mental shrug. It wasn't as though the information was going to help him now.

The woman replied, 'He can go in the old pantry. It's got no windows and the lock's secure. I'll get him a blanket so he don't freeze. You, clean him up.' This last was said to the doctor as she whisked back out of the room.

The clean-up was almost as bad as the torture. The doctor suggested some poppy juice, but the angry man, Fred, refused; Mal's open wounds were swabbed with disinfectant, and his mouth muffled when he screamed. After that, bandages were wrapped around his torso and his clothing was restored, before Fred and the other man dragged him up the stairs and through the kitchen to a corridor and a dark room lined with shelves stocked with tins and jars. A blanket had been thrown on the floor, which was just about long enough for him to lie down fully.

'Night-night,' said Fred as he pushed him inside. Mal knew, from a brief glimpse out of the kitchen window, that dawn was breaking. Once the door was slammed closed and locked, there was no way to tell. Darkness was complete. Falling to his knees and feeling his way to the blanket, Mal wrapped himself up and lay down. The burning of his wounds was nothing to the tortuous thoughts that crowded his mind as he wondered what would come next.

⋆

The journey upriver to Littlemarsh took longer than the journey down. Spight was too impatient to wait for the tide to turn, so they were battling the current. It was illogical; waiting another hour would make their return journey quicker, but he didn't want to be sitting still when there was so much to organise. He had to find another twenty-five bodies – and young, well-fleshed and healthy ones at that – by the following evening, or the deal was off. Dorcas wouldn't want to give up any of her fatties except the one they'd already agreed, which reduced his options considerably.

He already had a few spares lined up, being held under guard in warehouses near the dock in Plymouth. For the most part, they were older than the skipper had specified, but Spight hoped if he salted the shipment with enough younger bodies the others might not be noticed until the boat was underway. What happened to them after Dwight gave them a closer inspection was not his concern. It might sour relations for the next load, but that was tomorrow's problem, and besides his special project might be up and running by then.

He sat in the prow of the dinghy as Bob steered the boat, and schemed. He couldn't call anyone, as the battery of his satellite phone had died while he was talking to Dwight; all he could do was lay plans and will the landscape to pass faster.

'We're going to have to do a raid in Plymouth,' he told Bob as they entered the last bend before Longmarsh. Dawn had well and truly broken, birds making a damned racket in the trees to either side. Tendrils of mist clung to the water and drifted across the boat. Spight batted at them irritably.

'A raid?' Bob looked doubtful. The man was a wuss.

They'd done street raids in the past and yes, it was risky; someone who looked friendless and vulnerable could turn out to be anything but, and a situation could turn ugly in a moment but, as he pointed out, 'Where else am I going to get twenty-five pieces of meat at short notice?'

'Twenty-five?'

'What are you, a damn parrot? Yes, twenty-five. And they have to be young. Young as you can. It'll have to be today – we have to get them to Dartmouth by tomorrow night.'

'Can't Dwight meet us back in Plymouth?'

'Of course he could, but he won't. This is going to cost us a lot in fuel. Come on, man, we have to get moving!'

The quay was in sight. Beyond it lay the town, the church steeple on the hill jutting from the mist and sparking light as the sun rose over distant hills. From here, in these conditions, it was possible to think the town was in good repair; even the wharfside developments – built so close to the river they flooded at every spring tide and had been abandoned to rats and stray dogs – looked habitable.

While Bob offloaded the remaining fuel, stowing it in the back of the Land Rover waiting for them on the quayside, Spight started the engine and plugged his phone into a USB adaptor to put it on charge. As soon as the phone blinked back into life a text came through. It was from Dorcas and characteristically terse.

Come to fat farm asap

What the hell was it now?

It turned out to be a prisoner in the pantry, mutilated by his son-in-law – now roaming the woods doing God only knew what – and a fuming Matron threatening bodily harm to his brat of a grandson if he, Spight, didn't take him home right now. The Mayor heard Dorcas's story in silence, inspected the unconscious prisoner from the pantry doorway and grabbed his grandson by the ear before dragged him out to the Land Rover and throwing him into the passenger seat.

Spight got into the driver's seat.

Junior wouldn't shut up, insistent on telling his story and the important part he had played in the capture of the terrorist.

'Where's your father now?' growled Spight.

'He went with Biff, back to the hideout to see if Dug seen anything. Can we go too? I can show you the way.'

'You should be home in bed.'

'But it's morning! Can't go to bed now! I got some sleep anyway, I'm not tired.' Big eyes looked at him pleadingly. The boy certainly had an appetite for action ... a proper chip off the old block. A surge of familial pride led him to ruffle the boy's hair. His grandson beamed with pleasure.

'OK, let's go look at this bunker, see what Fred has to say. And then, later, we'll have a chat about sneaking out in the night and refusing to do what you're told.'

The boy looked a good deal less pleased by that prospect but kept quiet.

Bob was hovering by the Land Rover's door, looking a little queasy. Dorcas had been graphic in her description of the violence that had been visited on the prisoner. Spight told him to stay at the fat farm and make sure his phone had plenty of charge. He would be needed later, but first he was allowed to get some sleep in one of the spare rooms.

By the time they found the clearing, Hector Jr was back to his bumptious self, telling his grandfather in detail about how he had captured the insurgent single-handed, and then watched as Fred forced him to tell them what he knew. The boy's high, slightly nasal voice was carrying through the woods. If there were any more conspirators in the neighbourhood they'd be long gone.

They found Fred and his friends standing in the middle of the clearing when they eventually found it. Fred didn't look happy to see his father-in-law, or son, but said nothing as he showed them the main entrance, now open after a close inspection of the bunker disclosed a key on a nail just inside the door. Spight pulled the ivy aside and ducked into the tunnel, followed by his family and the two militia men.

He was disturbed to discover something like this had been hidden from view on his own turf. He looked around him, taking in the evidence of long habitation; clothes strewn over the single cot, plates and food scraps piled up on the countertop, the smell of unwashed bodies thickening the air. A folder on the table caught his eye and he moved closer to have a look. Inside was a stack of photos. At the top was a picture of him, with his name written neatly below it. The candid shot had caught him in mid-speech, mouth open and brow furrowed, over a sea of heads. There were also labelled photos of Bob, Fred, several other militia officers and key personnel from Bodingleigh and across Devon, and his grandson. This last enraged him. How dare they threaten his family?

Fred hadn't had any luck in finding the key to the other locked door. Spight ordered him to break it in and Fred complied willingly, kicking at it until the wood splintered around the lock and the door swung open.

Spight strode in and looked around him at the massed radio and IT equipment. More than the other room, this tangible evidence of a concerted, organised and resourced effort to thwart his empire and his plans enraged him. He knew he had enemies, and the loss of his shipment proved they meant business, but this was something else; this felt like the whole outside world ganging up on him and his vision of a good life for his people. Yes, his vision might be at the expense of the freedom of choice of a few, but when had the system ever looked out for everyone? No one who cooperated had to starve in his Devon, and no one was without work or a useful niche to fill. That was a distinct improvement on how things had been when he first became Mayor.

In a fit of temper, he pulled at cables and smacked a radio

antenna off the worktop, threw batteries at the wall and ground circuits into the dirt floor.

'What we gonna do if they come back? They're gonna know we've been in here, if you trash the place,' Fred pointed out.

'By the time they do, we'll have them.' Spight swept a monitor onto the floor. The crash of glass was gratifying.

'OK, you got a point. But we could sell this stuff. Or use it ourselves.'

Spight pulled himself together. It was true, this was merchandise. Besides, he was feeling calmer now. 'OK, lock up, and Dug, you stay to watch. You see or hear anyone, you get word out to me and I'll send you backup with guns. Any luck, we'll round these renegades up and send them off with Dwight. Serve them right. Fred, Biff, come with me, I need you to go to Plymouth to lead a raid.'

Junior was hovering in the doorway. Spight hadn't forgotten his promise to him, and rounded him up as they left the room. He was proud of the boy, but there were some serious discipline issues he needed to address. First, he had other business to attend to.

There were no lights on in the fat farm's gatehouse. Spight left Junior in the Land Rover – despite his protestations the boy had fallen asleep in his seat almost as soon as the engine started – and strode to the front door, thumping on it loudly. Mrs Harrow answered it wrapped in an old dressing gown and scowling, which was quite an achievement considering all the facial surgery that had attempted to remove this ability. When she recognised the Mayor on her doorstep her eyes widened with terror but she let him in and offered him tea. He refused and demanded to see her husband.

'He's still asleep, he's had a very disturbed night.'

Spight barked a laugh. 'Haven't we all! Fetch him.'

Mouth twisted in disapproval at being ordered about in her own home, she led him to the kitchen and went to wake her husband. Spight crossed the room to the door at the far end and unlocked it with a key from the bunch in his pocket. When Dr Harrow came in a few minutes later, in dressing gown and pyjamas, face lined with exhaustion, he found the Mayor examining the paraphernalia of his laboratory. There was a faint smell of almonds in the air.

'How is our special project coming along?' Spight picked up a glass retort stoppered with a cork bung and stared at the colourless contents, shaking it to set them swirling.

'Don't touch that!' Harrow snatched the glass out of Spight's hand and set it gently on the worktop. 'It's volatile, and there isn't enough ventilation in here if some gets out.'

'It works then?'

The doctor pursed his lips as he considerd the question. 'We're close. Efficacy on subjects has been one hundred per cent. But as I say, it's volatile. The problem is keeping the gas from breaking down before it's done its job. Works fine in an enclosed space, but if you want to promote it as a chemical weapon, it needs to operate within acceptable parameters when dispersed in the outdoors.'

'How long?'

'Weeks, maybe months.'

'You've been saying that for the last eighteen months.'

'We're doing something new. If you want this done properly, without silly accidents, you have to give me the time I need.'

'I need something saleable ready by the time the next cargo exchange takes place. It's getting too risky to keep going as we have been. We need something new to offer, and this is going to be it. This is going to put Devon on the map and make us a global player.'

'I need more laurel to work with.'

'I'll have some cut and the leaves brought to you.'

'Make sure they're not shredded this time. As soon as the leaves are damaged we start losing the cyanates. I need more subjects too. Not cats this time.' The light of scientific fervour was in Harrow's eyes as he said, 'We'll need to test on a ... er ... human subject. Preferably someone young and fairly fit, so we can be sure of the result.'

'That shouldn't be a problem. I believe you've just met and ministered to him. We'll just have to heal him from that, first.' Spight headed towards the door. 'Of course, it doesn't need to be said that this project remains top secret. No one is to know about this until we are ready to launch our product. Not your wife, not Bob, and definitely not Fred. Understood?'

'Of course, Sir. You can count on my discretion.'

★

The narrow bed in a tiny attic room was lumpy but that wasn't why Bob couldn't sleep. The events of the last day kept playing through his mind. Ever since he had woken Spight to tell him about the sabotaged shipment, things had felt like they were spiralling out of control. More to the point, Spight was out of control. His casual insistence that they snatch twenty-five people from the streets of Plymouth in broad daylight was proof of it. So was his acceptance of Fred torturing someone who had, at most, helped thwart him. Not harmed him, not harmed anyone, just got in the way of his plans. What happened when Bob, or someone he cared about, got in the way? They'd end up on a boat to New Jersey for a life of hell, at the very least. It was the threat they had all lived with for years; it was beginning to feel like an inevitability.

Bob knew what faced the people who were freighted to the Real USA. In the beginning, he told himself they were offering at least some of them opportunities they would never have in Devon, but casual jokes and asides from Dwight and his crew had killed that illusion. Most of them ended up in baby farms, brothels or as slave labour. A handful might be married off, but the net result was the same.

Despite what his family or the rest of the village might think, Bob was not proud to be working for the Mayor, but what other choice did he have? He relied on Spight for imported drugs to manage the progression of a degenerative disease that could kill him in a matter of a few years if it remained untreated. He flattered himself he had softened some of Spight's worst excesses, but it was becoming clear that any influence he might once have had was waning just as it was most needed.

Now it seemed like the insurgency he had always taken for a bit of a joke, something that only fretted at their borders, was actually an organisation that, with a little help, might at least get this one boy out of harm's way. And Bob had a pretty shrewd idea who could put him in touch with them.

How much should he tell her? Could he tell her everything? He wasn't sure he could bear the shame.

Before he left he checked on the prisoner and found him blearily awake and flinching away from the intrusion of light into his cell. Bob said nothing, just closed the door gently and relocked it. He was tempted to set the boy free, but it was too risky, and for the moment he was probably safe enough, now Fred was off the premises. If all went well, the prisoner's colleagues would be along to rescue him before too long. He would benefit more from time to heal.

Dorcas offered him breakfast as he passed the kitchen, where she was sweating over a huge pan of crisping bacon from a neighbouring farm's pigs. He thanked her but said he needed to be on his way and asked if he could borrow one of the farm's bicycles.

'Yeah. They're all bone-shakers, but you're welcome, so long as someone gets it back here. Round by the garage.'

There were three bikes leaning against the garage wall, with torn seats and rusted suspension. He took the one with pumped tyres and set off down the drive, weaving from side to side to avoid the potholes. The sun was blazing overhead, beating into his scalp, and it was a relief to disappear under the dense woodland canopy shrouding the lane. By the time he emerged above the village, clouds had rolled in, the wind had changed direction and the temperature had dropped. Seagulls screamed overhead, presaging the approach of a storm. Sweat cooled against his skin and he batted at horseflies clustered above his head.

The last bit of his journey had to be circumspect. It was important no one should see him approach the house. A couple of Door Knockers were out by the church noticeboard, taking down posters advertising last night's meeting, chatting about what they were anticipating in the delayed cargo. He parked the bike behind the churchyard wall and slipped down an alley before they saw him.

As he went through the gate and up the path, he noticed the curtains in the windows of the cottage were drawn. He knocked on the door. Then checked his watch. Of course, she would be at the schoolhouse, teaching.

But the door opened and Mrs Prendaghast stood there,

looking tired and strained. She blinked at him in surprise.

'Good morning, Aunty Iris, can I come in?'

Fat drops of rain began to fall and a rumble of thunder could be heard in the distance.

*

The unexpected knock at the front door had brought a clutch of fear to Primrose's heart and sent her running upstairs to Mrs Prendaghast's room, where she stood behind the door and wondered what to do if someone came in, looking for her. Of course, it could just be someone concerned that the teacher had put a note on the schoolroom gate that morning, saying school was closed for the day because she was sick; someone wanting to know if they could do anything for her. Primrose strained to hear what was being said downstairs, but rain began beating against the windows and she couldn't make out anything except a man's voice, unfamiliar.

The tone was urgent and fanned the flames of her fear. She crouched down, ignoring the pain of her wounds, wrapping her arms around her knees and trying to make herself as small as possible.

After a few minutes, the door creaked open and Mrs Prendaghast's face appeared around it, seeking her out. She looked excited but weary. To Primrose's young eyes she looked not just old but suddenly ancient.

'It's alright, you can come back downstairs.'

'Has he gone?'

'Yes, and I didn't tell him about you, though I don't think it would have mattered. It appears my nephew has had a long overdue change of heart.'

This didn't mean much to Primrose, but she was pleased to

be able to return downstairs, where she perched on the edge of the chair by the stove, which retained a bit of warmth. Her heart still had a rabbity beat.

'What did he want?'

'He wanted me to get a message to someone. Funnily enough, I was planning to do that anyway, about you, but it's become even more urgent. I'm going to have to go out for a while, and I need you to promise me you will stay in the house, and not set a foot outside it, or let anyone see you. If anyone else comes to the door, go back upstairs and keep quiet. I'll lock it behind me.'

'I promise.'

'Good girl. I'll be back as quick as I can. Help yourself to food, and there are some books in the bedroom if you get bored.'

The teacher bustled about fetching a raincoat. After checking there was no one in the lane outside, she went out into the downpour and Primrose heard the *snick* of the door being locked.

What a luxury, to be awake, and alone in a house. She couldn't remember that ever happening to her before. There had always been siblings, parents, other fat farm residents. She stretched out and examined the room, dim behind drawn curtains; after a few minutes, she wasn't sure what to do with herself. She could sleep, but the cuts under her bandages must be starting to heal, because they itched like crazy. She scratched at an arm, but remembered Dorcas telling her she'd be scarred if she did that, so she stopped.

Reading, that would keep her occupied.

Most of the books in the bookcase under the window in the bedroom were dull-looking theory textbooks on teaching, philosophy and other dry stuff. But there were also thrillers, many of them translations of Scandinavian and African authors, according to the descriptions on the covers, and Primrose looked at these with excitement. Foreign books were never seen in the classroom. How curious that her teacher should have a library of them at home. She picked up a stack and took them to the bed. To have a bit more light, she opened the curtains a crack – no one would be able to see in up here. The house opposite showed her a blank wall with no windows. She was safe.

Sitting against the headboard, she felt the weight of the books in her hand, stroked the well-worn covers. Looking inside, she saw that none had been published after 2030, which was still more than ten years before she was born, and a few years after Devon's Devolution. She didn't know much about the details, it was something no one she knew talked about, except to say it was a good thing, without explaining why. Her dad had, sometimes, when he'd had a few drinks and come back from the pub, said it meant they'd sent all the Pakis packing. He'd laugh at that, but she didn't get it and he never bothered to explain. What were Pakis?

One of the author photos on the back of a book showed a woman with dark skin, almost black. Primrose had never seen such a thing before. Everyone she knew was pale, or grey after a long winter. She stroked the photo, and wondered what it would be like, and if it would feel any different.

She opened the book at a random page and started reading. The story drew her into a world so different from hers it might as well have been science fiction. The world it evoked was hot, dry, full of the names of foods she had never heard of, wildlife she had never seen, families exchanging remarks made in anger that couldn't hide the warmth at their core.

It was too much; the contrast to her own life was so stark it made her sad. She put the book aside and lay back against the pillows feeling scared and frustrated. There really was a whole world outside the borders of the place she had always called home, but she'd never learned about it, or seen it. Unless Mrs Prendaghast managed to find someone who could smuggle her out, she never would. And if she did leave, then what? She'd know no one, have nothing, be fit for nothing and the thought was terrifying. Maybe she would be better off back at the farm. She was useful there and she knew the rules.

Lightning flared through the gap in the curtains and a moment later a *BOOOMMM* of thunder overhead made the cottage shake and Primrose jump. Mood dark and mind whirling, she slumped down into the bed. Something was digging into her. She reached back and rummaged under the pillows and a hardback book emerged in her hand. The front two-thirds of the lined pages were filled with handwriting she recognised from Mrs Prendaghast scribbling on the board in school. This must be a diary, Mrs Prendaghast's diary. Guiltily, but with no idea of replacing it, she turned to the beginning and read the title at the head of the first page.

A record of events in the County of Devon,
from the time of Devolution to the present day
by Mrs Iris Prendaghast

This wasn't a diary, it was a secret history. Surely it was meant to be read, and Mrs Prendaghast wouldn't mind if she had a look. After all, she had told Primrose to read what she wanted from the bedroom.

I do not pretend this will be anything other than a partial record. As it will probably remain unread, that doesn't seem to matter. But sometimes I find myself so at odds with what I see happening around me, I feel the need to write as faithful a record as I can just to try and understand it, and to convince myself the world is out of joint, not I; perhaps if I commit my thoughts and observations to paper the world will make more sense.

So. Where to start?

The fat farm. In the parlance of my teenage years, what the fuck?

It was proposed to us initially as a way to run essential services. Volunteers were invited to donate a kilo or two of excess fat, rather like we used to do with blood before we ran out of ways to store it, and this was rendered into biodiesel and stored for emergency use. Once we were all acclimatised to the idea it was suggested some citizens might like to become permanent donors in exchange for a guaranteed home and as much food as they could eat. Things had already started to get tough, but I was still surprised how many put their hands up. Mostly older people who were struggling with the return to a largely manual labour force and had no family to support them through old age. (It would have been called retirement once, but fat chance of that now. Pun intended.)

Once this pattern had been established, and around the time the newly elected Mayor Spight decided it was essential he have fuel for his fleet of cars and boats (I suspect he had been raiding the civic store for some time already), it was decided at a Council meeting that families should be given the opportunity to 'safeguard the future' of one of their offspring. No reward was offered, but it has often struck me how the fortunes of families have improved rapidly soon after they have offered up their child. Usually girls, as they are more efficient at storing fat cells. The birth rate has rocketed in recent years, with most families (and young, single people) having limited or no access to birth control, so I understand some parents might think they are doing the child a kindness, but I have heard stories of some having a child with the deliberate intention of giving them to the farm as soon *as they are old enough. The youngest child I have lost from my class was poor, dear Primrose at eleven years old, but I hear stories sometimes of much younger children, some as young as eight or nine, from other settlements. I have no way of corroborating this.*

Primrose put down the notebook. The thought of a child as young as eight enduring the harvesting process and its aftermath was repugnant. She was also touched by Mrs Prendaghast's obvious affection, and dismay at what had happened to her, which she had suspected but not known for sure. Swallowing the lump in her throat, she resumed reading.

Each community now has at least one, managed by a Matron and a skeleton (pun also intended) staff. Their food comes from the local farms and community gardens, but is also heavily reliant on expensive, poor-quality but high-calorie imports; I have often thought it a ridiculously unbalanced energy input to output ratio. Rather like running an internal combustion engine in order to deliver transport. In one, possibly quite unexpected way, it was a stroke of genius for Spight to set them up. Everyone in the county is now complicit in their existence; we are tied by our collective guilt.

Where Spight gets the money to pay for all the crap he brings in is something no one has managed yet to ascertain. There is no real economy to speak of. Devon has limited exports: perishable foods such as meat and dairy, and some vegetables and fruit. The 'Real' USA states we trade with are in dire need of our comparatively clean foodstuffs – having destroyed much of their agricultural land, poisoned their air and water, and precipitated an ecological collapse even before their own disunity and our Devolution – but as we import their chemical insecticides and fertilisers in exchange, I am not sure how much longer that will pertain. Thankfully we do not have the resources to buy them in bulk; it is largely those farms owned by

Spight's family that use them.

So, an unexpected bonus of the straits in which we find ourselves, is the return of flora and fauna that were in serious trouble in my youth, in some unmanaged areas at least. In particular, solitary bees seem to be making a comeback, as well as butterflies and moths, and this has had a concomitant effect on bat and some bird populations. However larger birds are in decline as they are trapped for food.

Primrose stopped reading and started flicking at random through the pages. She wasn't so interested in bees, or birds. There had to be juicier stuff than this.

A few pages on she found it.

Gloria knows her husband is having an affair with the Matron, but she doesn't care. She is happy that he is happy elsewhere; literally as his trysts with Dorcas take them away from the farm. I warned her before she married him that material security was never going to be enough to outweigh the loss of freedom and stultifying tedium of being married to Spight and having to conform to his narrow definition of a woman's place and a wife's duties.

I think Gloria might be looking to have her own fun elsewhere too. There is a sparkle in her eye these days that goes beyond having a bit of time off from her husband, but she won't tell me anything. I wish good luck to her, if so. I just hope she can remain discreet. I don't think Spight would be as forgiving as she. At the moment, no doubt to assuage his guilt at betraying his marriage vows, he is nice as pie to Gloria, but I believe him to have an evil temper. There are stories that followed him from his time as Captain of the Militia, though none ever led to an inquiry or prosecution – not surprising as he either presides over or is cronies with all those who would be tasked with looking into such matters.

The joys of a small community and its intrigues. It feels like being back at my old secondary school, with all the secrets and illicit passions, requited and otherwise. I am grateful my own urges are abating as I age. Not that I don't still have my moments from time to time. There was one time ...

Primrose shut the book hurriedly. She did not want to know the details of Mrs Prendaghast's sex life.

LAMPS HAD BEEN LIT
AGAINST THE DARK

It had been a long day and night of meetings and briefings. Will had had barely two hours of sleep since he woke up in the bunker, nearly seventy-two hours before. His eyes stung from tiredness and his stomach was rumbling. They were due to return to Bodingleigh within the hour; he hoped someone had factored in a meal before then, as he hadn't eaten since a bit of bread and cheese on their arrival.

He was sitting in the wood-panelled hallway of the rather grand safe house they had gone to after the blockade, the Major having decided it was too dangerous to risk journeying all the way back to the bunker in broad daylight. He had also wanted to finalise their plans for Stage Three face to face, a long process as teams across Devon and Cornwall were alerted and mobilised. Sunlight slanted in through the open door, the storm that had overtaken them as they drove away from Plymouth having moved east. The beams picked out specks of dust. Will let his gaze follow them. His eyelids drifted closed.

Somewhere deeper inside the house a telephone rang. It was a rare sound in Devon and brought him back to full awareness. He heard a voice answering it, there was a brief lull and then footsteps pounded down the corridor from the library in which they held their meetings.

It was one of the older Cornish agents, Merryn, who barked at him, 'Where's the Major?'

'Outside on the terrace I think.'

'Fetch him now, please.'

Will leaped up and ran out into baking sunshine. The Major
was sitting on a low wall on the edge of a stone-flagged terrace,
in close conversation with Mrs Mason. Behind them, a long
swathe of meadow ended in sun-drenched woodland.
Butterflies were dancing above the meadow. Steam rose from
the rapidly drying stone. 'Major!'

'What is it?'

'There's a phone call, sounds urgent.'

Mrs Mason and the Major exchanged a look before getting
up to follow Will to the library.

The room was long and lined with bookcases stuffed with
leather-bound books. There was no sign of a phone. Merryn
beckoned them to the conference table in the centre of the
room and told them to sit down. 'You too,' he said to Will as
the boy headed for the door. Several others from the resistance
were already there. From the looks on the faces of those
already seated, the news was significant.

'We've had a call from Bodingleigh.'

'From who?' Will blurted. 'Mal?'

'No. Somehow the bunker has been compromised. Mal has
been taken to the fat farm and tortured. It's probable our plans
are now known by Spight. Enough, at least, to compromise
them irraparably.'

'Tortured?' The Major's face was ashen. 'He's only a boy!'

Will felt sick. Tortured ... That could so easily have been
him. Poor Mal.

'So far as they are concerned he is an agent of a foreign
power,' Merryn pointed out.

'Foreign?' The Major laughed bitterly, 'Mal's from Exeter!'

'It doesn't matter, Spight will spin it to make Mal seem like the advance guard of barbarian hordes, you know his style of rhetoric.'

Merryn paused to let his words sink in, then continued in a grim tone: 'So, everything we've planned is in jeopardy. What do we do now?'

★

The itching was becoming unbearable. It was no good, she would have to do something about the bandages. Primrose put the journal back under the pillow where she had found it and climbed off the bed.

Mrs Prendaghast had given her some old tights to wear under the dress, to keep her warm in the chilly cottage, and once they were off Primrose thought her legs looked a lot less swollen than they had the day before, and certainly a lot less fat than they had been in some time. Hopefully it would be safe to take the dressings off and have a look at the punctures.

Taking them off her legs was reasonably straightforward. Her skin was lined and puckered from the tight wrappings, but otherwise looked smooth and unpuffy despite wounds that were different from how she'd expected; the skin had been pulled tight before it had been stitched up neatly.

In some places, the bandages stuck to her skin and she had to pull, which hurt, but she gritted her teeth and persevered. Once they were off, she removed the jumper and dress and managed to release one arm, but unwrapping the bandages from the other, or her torso, proved to be more than she could manage, as the ends were pinned out of reach. When she heard the front door close downstairs she froze, caught half-naked and wrapped in grubby linen strips, but then she heard Mrs Prendaghast calling her name softly and let out a pent-up breath. A moment later the teacher appeared in the doorway.

Primrose gestured at herself and said, 'I kind of need a hand.'

Things proceeded much more easily with two of them. Before long she was standing in the middle of the bedroom naked and shivering in the cold, a pool of blood-stained linens around her feet. A few of the cuts had opened up during her initial struggles, but most of her smaller wounds had scabbed over and were healing nicely. She stopped twisting around and examining herself to catch Mrs Prendaghast looking at her oddly. They caught each other's eye and Primrose blushed. She was so used to being treated like a piece of meat at the fat farm, she had lost all modesty years ago, but it must be odd for the teacher to have her former pupil standing there starkers. Something that was borne out by her next remark.

'Well, Primrose, you've changed a little.'

'It has been five years.'

'There's a mirror in the bathroom. Go and have a look.'

Mystified, Primrose went into the small bathroom adjoining the bedroom. The mirror in the cabinet showed her straggly hair and a grubby face, and a neck also in need of a good wash, but not much else as it cut her off at the shoulders. Alternately standing and kneeling on the edge of the old bath, she contorted and stretched until she could see the whole of her body.

She didn't recognise herself. When she had had 'treatment' before, she had been left looking very lumpy, with flaps of skin, pockets of fat and silvery stretch marks where she had shrunk. This time, it was as though she had been sculpted into one of those plastic dolls, the ones the younger girls at school used to fight over. Barbies. She looked like a Barbie doll. Some of her boobs were gone, but they were still full. Her waist was tiny and her bum shapely. Some time in the last couple of years she had grown taller, and it seemed to be all leg.

What to make of it? It made her feel strange. Slightly tingly and excited, but also confused and alien in her own body.

There was a towelling dressing gown hanging on the back of the door. Primrose put it on and returned to the bedroom, where Mrs Prendaghast was sitting on the bed. She patted the mattress beside her and Primrose sat.

'It was my nephew who came here before. He had a message for me to pass on.' Mrs Prendaghast took one of Primrose's hands and held it loosely. 'He wanted me to contact the resistance.'

'The rebels?' Primrose was shocked. 'You can do that?' A terrifying thought occurred to her. 'Are you one of them?' The rebels were violent brigands, determined to make everyone in Devon conform to some extreme agenda. She wasn't sure what that agenda was, but everyone she knew had been saying bad things about it since as long as she could remember. She felt like pulling her hand away, but this was Mrs Prendaghast, who had given her sanctuary. She forced herself to stay still.

'No, not exactly, at least not actively. I'm too old, and the Mayor keeps too close an eye on me because of my dubious past.'

The teacher had a past? That seemed so unlikely Primrose laughed out loud, then clapped her hands over her mouth in apology. 'Really Mrs P?'

'Yes, really.'

'But you're a respectable old widow! You're the schoolteacher!'

'Yes dear, but I'm also a lesbian, and these days that isn't socially acceptable. You know what that means I suppose?'

Primrose knew – it was a common insult at the fat farm

even among the girls who had sex with each other – and she blushed. 'But you were married!'

'Yes, to my wife. Gay marriage was allowed at the time.'

She had been standing there naked a matter of minutes ago, her hand was still warm from where the teacher had held it. Primrose blushed again and felt very uncomfortable. Mrs Prendaghast seemed to follow her thinking and laughed shortly.

'Don't worry, my dear. I said I was a lesbian, not a paedophile, you're quite safe. But we're getting off-topic. I am not an active member of the resistance, but I know some who are, and I know how to get a message through if need be. Last night my nephew wanted me to get a message out about a young man up at the farm who needs their help. It seems young Fred has been getting out of hand. I thought you should know it's possible I'll need to go out again.'

*

'We have to rescue him.'

It was three hours later and they were no further along. The only good thing that had happened was that someone had thought to bring in a plate of sandwiches. Sickened by thoughts of what Mal must be going through, Will had at first been unable to eat, but after the plate had been in front of him for a while, and feeling he had nothing to contribute to the discussion besides making it clear he supported the Major's plan for a rescue, he had nibbled listlessly at a cheese and pickle and found himself to be ravenous.

'We've been through this already.' Merryn, the dark and stocky Cornishman who had ordered him to fetch the Major, was growing tired and irritable and it showed in his voice. 'We all agree we want to do something to help Mal, but blundering in to save him is not going to achieve our goals, and we're so close! We've been planning this for years damn it!'

'Yes, and why?' the Major asked.

'What?'

'Why have we been planning it? Because we all agree Spight is like a toxic cloud, poisoning everything he touches, and we aren't prepared to let events take their course. We've decided we're better than he is, we've set ourselves on an elevated moral plane, and now we're going to abandon one of our own? How does that make us superior to Spight?'

'That's a specious argument and you know it. Thousands … tens of thousands of people's lives are going to be improved if we …'

'So it's a numbers game?' the Major asked.

'That's not what I said.'

'No, because I interrupted once I could see where you were going. Thousands of lives weighed up against one … blah blah blah.'

'What we are losing sight of,' said Mrs Mason, breaking in to what had become a tedious restating of positions already entrenched two hours before, 'is that our plans have already been changed for us. We cannot proceed as we intended. We should be grateful we found out now, not after we returned to the bunker, or we could all be in Mal's position. The point being, is there a way we can continue with Stage Two? Do we abandon everything we've worked and sacrificed for? Or is there a way to incorporate a rescue?'

This brought a fresh round of argument. Maps and flipcharts were brought out. Will laid his head down on his forearms on the table, just for a moment, and slept.

★

Primrose had to be replaced in the shipment, and Dorcas had Alise in mind. The girl was older, and less beautiful, but she had a more tractable temperament, demonstrated by the fact she was still present in her room, munching away on crackers and cheese as a snack to tide her over until lunch. More worrying was that the treatment had to be undertaken today and Alise would not be fully recovered before she had to leave for Dartmouth. Dorcas was a pragmatic and self-serving woman, not a deliberately cruel one, and she wouldn't want one of her charges to suffer unnecessarily, but neither did she want to get on the rough side of Spight or his son-in-law. Alise would have to go, and she just hoped Spight wouldn't spot the substitution.

Summoned from the gatehouse, Dr Harrow looked haggard, etched by all seventy-seven of his years. His activities of the previous night seemed to weigh heavy on him. Dorcas sympathised, but she couldn't afford to show it, so she offered him an instant coffee and told him he was going to have a busy day, with a stern admonition to: 'Mind you don't make her too skinny. She's going to need some reserves to get her through the journey, Spight says.'

Dr Harrow now looked old, haggard and unhappy, but also resigned. 'I'll need the girl's charts. Has she been put on nil by mouth?'

'Er, no, I'll get Agnes on that right away.'

'We might have to pump her stomach, don't want to risk her choking.' He looked up from checking through his bag to see what additional equipment he would need. 'What happened to Primrose? I thought she was slated for this shipment? That was some of my best work.'

It was true the doctor took pride in his surgery. Conventional demand for his cosmetic services had died with the departure of people who could afford them and left him with no money to relocate; after several years making do as a GP he had jumped at the chance to work at the farm, with a comfortable home thrown in. Now he was too old to do anything else, she almost felt sorry for him.

She could hardly tell the doctor the girl was sick. With no credible alternative presenting itself, Dorcas plumped reluctantly for the truth.

'We've mislaid her, temporarily. I've got people out looking for her. The girl's family will bring her back if she turns up there, and she hasn't had any visitors in all the time she's been here so she can't have any friends who would take her in. We'll find her. But in case it isn't before the shipment leaves, we need a back-up.'

'Well well, little girl's found her backbone under all that blubber eh?' The doctor's pinched features looked momentarily amused.

Irritated, Dorcas snapped, 'Perhaps you'd like to check in on your other patient, see if he survived the night?' She knew the prisoner in the larder was still alive, she had checked on him several times already, but pity for the doctor often switched abruptly to revulsion. She needed him, and he was good at what he did, but his professional, doctorly callousness grated on what survived of her conscience.

Dr Harrow flinched and she knew she had hit some remaining nerve still connecting him to his Hippocratic Oath. Smiling icily, she swept out of the cramped office to which he had been summoned, shouting for Agnes to go and remove the plate of crackers and cheese from Alise's grip.

★

When Will awoke, stormy-looking clouds were dimming the day outside the mullioned windows and lamps had been lit against the dark, casting warm pools of light across the room. The Major was shaking him by the shoulder.

'Sorry, shouldn't have gone to sleep.' Will wiped at the corner of his mouth, where it felt like he had drooled a little. His neck was stiff.

'Most sensible thing you could have done, in the circumstances.'

'What's happening?'

'Nothing for now, at least not for you and me. We need more intel. I think the best thing we can do is go and check on your friend. I hear he's been giving a little trouble.'

'Friend?' Head muzzy with sleep, he didn't know what the Major meant.

'The old man. He should be sobering up by now.'

'God, I forgot all about him. Has anyone taken him anything to eat? Or drink?' Will's conscience was stricken. They had delivered the old man to the owner of the house when they arrived and Will had pretty much forgotten about him since.

The Major laughed. 'Oh, he's been well taken care of. But don't expect any thanks.'

Will was led out into the rain and around to the back of the house, to a ramshackle outbuilding that looked like it was used to store tools.

'We couldn't let him in the house, too many sensitive conversations taking place,' the Major explained. As they drew closer they could hear loud shouting. An angry stream of swearing.

'Is he locked in?' Will was horrified.

'Yes. Partly for his own safety. He's taken a long time to sober up, and we didn't want him getting into any more trouble.' The Major produced a key and unlocked the sagging wooden door.

The smell as they walked in was powerful. Similar to that of the bunker, but with an additional fug of damp, stale alcohol fumes and old urine. The shouting stopped as soon as the door opened.

The old man was sitting on the edge of the sort of sun lounger no one bothered to own anymore, having neither the leisure nor the reliable weather to make use of one. A blanket was thrown over his knees. On a side table were an empty plate and several mugs half full of cold tea. A stoppered bottle of water lay untouched on the dirt floor. Rain drummed loudly on the corrugated iron roof and plinked to the table from a hole.

There was no sign of any tools. Will supposed it might be unwise to leave sharp objects in reach of someone so clearly enraged; a scowl distorted the old man's features. At least he appeared to be sober, if angry. His hand shook as he pointed at them.

'You bastards remembered me at last?'

'It's been a disturbing day, I apologise if you feel neglected. I can see someone has been taking care of you.' The Major leaned against the doorjamb. Will hovered at his shoulder.

'Locked me up is what you've done. Held me against my will. Who are you, thinking you can lock me up? Thought I was back with that monster Spight. Might be safer with him, for all I know.'

Will started at the sound of the Mayor's name. If the Major was surprised he showed no sign, but his voice was curious as he said, 'You've had dealings with our illustrious Mayor?'

'Illustrious? Spight? Don't make me puke. I know what the fucker's done. Should do, I helped him enough times.'

'Helped him how?'

Will's heart sank. He thought he'd done the right thing, pulling the old man out of the flames, but now it sounded like he was just another bad guy. Then he caught himself, remembering how the Major had reacted when he'd called Primrose the enemy. And realised he would never have been able to live with himself if he had left the old man to burn, however many bad things he might have done.

The old man looked ashamed. 'Can't tell you ... don't like to remember. S'why I drink.' A crafty look stole across his grimy features as he said, 'Don't suppose you've got anything on you? A flask or some such? I'm awful thirsty.'

'There's water there, on the floor.'

'Water,' the old man spat, as if the Major had suggested he drink acid. 'Can't stomach water. If you give me something with a bit of welly, I'll tell you what I done. What Spight and I done.' His voice was wheedling. 'I've a terrible headache ... can't think with this headache.' He clutched at his forehead, eyes screwed closed in apparent pain, but Will could see a glint of light reflecting from one that had opened slightly and was regarding them slyly.

'No! I'm not giving alcohol to an alcoholic!'

Their host, Rowena, was a stern-looking woman of about seventy with very erect posture and silver hair tied up in an elaborate knot. Wisps of hair flew free as she shook her head to emphasise her refusal.

'I quite understand how you feel, and in normal circumstances I wouldn't dream of suggesting it, but these aren't normal circumstances.'

Will agreed privately with Rowena, but he was torn. He really wanted to know what the old man knew, in case it helped Mal.

'Ah, the special circumstances defence, I know it well. I'll have no truck with it, and this is my home.' Rowena's tone was unyielding.

The Major nodded his head and Will supposed that was that. He was astonished when the Major said, 'Then the only thing we can do, I suppose, is take him with us.'

Rowena looked as surprised as Will felt. Surely nothing had changed enough that they were ready to leave, something she echoed when she said, 'You know we aren't anywhere near that yet.'

'But I am. I'm going to go get Mal out of whatever hell-hole they've put him, and if it means giving an old man what he wants in the meantime, to find out what he knows, then I'll find a way to do that. Tell Merryn he can get hold of me at the barn. We'll head there when we've got the boy.'

Lips pursed in disapproval, Rowena nodded. 'I'll tell him. But if you screw this up for us, Major, you'll have to live with that.' She turned on her heel and left the kitchen where they had found her. A couple of young cadets washing up plates in the large sinks across the room looked at each other with raised eyebrows but said nothing. Their looks of disapproval switched to Will and he avoided them by following the Major out. The Major was stomping back across the lawn and Will had to run to catch up. His head was full of questions, but the look on the man's face put him off voicing them for the moment.

When they got back to the shed the Major unlocked the door and flung it open.

'Right, you can stay locked up here like a prisoner, with that bottle of water for company, or you can come with us and I'll see what I can do about getting you a proper drink.'

The old man jumped up from his lounger, staggered a little, still clutching the blanket. 'I'm coming with you!'

'I'll expect you to tell me everything you know about Spight.'

'I'll do that, but it'll take a drink or two. It's a long tale, and not a pretty one.'

Mrs Mason didn't come with them, and she also forbade Tom, Dick and Harriet from leaving.

'They can come back with me when we know what we're doing, and that might just be a few hours, when we've heard from everyone. Please, Paul, take your time and think this through.' She put her hand on the Major's arm. Will was shocked to hear the Major had a given name.

The Major shook her off, but gently. He pulled her into a quick hug before stepping back. 'I'm not going to do anything stupid. You know me better than that, I hope.'

She gave him a rueful smile. 'I know you well enough to be sure you'll try.'

That had been half an hour ago. Now, they were bouncing around in an electric vehicle the Major had 'borrowed' from their host, lifting the key fob from a rack by the front door as they left. Apart from the sound of its tyres hissing and throwing back mud on the road it was silent. Travelling on little-used lanes, the Major professed confidence they could make it back to Bodingleigh unnoticed.

A direct route would take them through villages. Even with the heavy rain keeping people indoors, their passage might be remarked upon, or stopped. The additional distance meant it could be at least another hour before they got back and, as less-used roads received no upkeep, the car's suspension was already struggling. The old man in the back seat was complaining the bouncing around was making him feel sick. The few hours of sleep Will had managed at the conference table were not enough to have left him feeling rested, and the constant jouncing was making his head pound too. So was the old man's complaining. It was a relief when the Major drove through an open gateway into a fallow field and switched off the car's battery. Without the windscreen wipers sweeping away rain the windows were obscured. They wouldn't see anyone who might creep up on them. Will hoped this wouldn't take long.

The Major turned around in his seat to regard their passenger, who blinked back at him.

'Right then, time we had our little talk.'

'You promised me a drink.'

The Major reached into his jacket pocket and brought out a hip flask. He unscrewed the lid and sniffed at it. The fumes of whisky were strong enough to reach Will and, apparently the old man, who leaned forward and reached out with shaking hands. The Major held the flask out of reach.

'You promised!' The old man looked to be on the verge of tears.

Will felt sick, revolted by what they were doing to him. He wanted to cry at the old man's weakness.

Some of his feelings seemed to be shared by the Major; his voice was gentle as he said, 'I'm not happy to be doing this. I'm not happy to be exploiting a sickness like this. So, please give us some information on account. Before I hand this over, you go back to ruin, and we can't make any more sense out of you.'

The old man looked at them both, blinking. His eyes were watering. He nodded slowly.

People were being sold off as slaves. It was happening in the place Will had lived, and all over the county of Devon. He, Jeremiah, had been responsible for making collections, as he described them. Picking people up, keeping them locked up, fed and watered, and delivering them to the docks. He said he tried to treat them as well as he could, but he couldn't always control what went on when he was sleeping, or away on a collection, and sometimes he had returned to find his subordinates mistreating the stock – that was how he described his prisoners – and taking advantage of the younger and prettier ones. He started drinking, and when that didn't numb him sufficiently and he couldn't handle it anymore, he'd quit.

He had known if he told Spight he no longer wanted to work for him, the Mayor might use his family to make him change his mind, so he just walked away one day; walked to the outskirts of Plymouth where he knew he could disappear and find work labouring. He was no longer married, his wife having died in the 'flu pandemic of '27, but he still had two children.

'Kids'll be long grown, might have little uns of they own. S'best I keep away from 'em,' he mumbled through tears.

Some time in the last year or so things had become too dangerous in the suburbs, with fires breaking out in the new towns built at the turn of the century, and he started to drift around the city, begging and working for scraps of food or, more often, drink.

He didn't drink much whisky; Will reckoned his liver was so soaked it had only taken a few mouthfuls to fill it brimful. When he stopped speaking and slumped back against the headrest, the Major removed the flask from his hand, gently, screwed the top back on and slipped the flask back into his pocket.

The scale of what they were up against had just multiplied beyond Will's capacity to calculate. He felt ill.

'How come we don't know about this? How come everyone doesn't know?' he blurted out.

Jeremiah's eyes opened blearily as he mumbled, 'There's some does, and they just turn a blind eye. Folk go missing, who you gonna tell? Spight? One of the others he controls? If they've come from the fat farm, and most does, they've been written off already. Family don't want to know 'em anymore. Too 'shamed of themselves I reckon, and too glad of the extra food and stuff.'

Primrose. Will was chilled by the thought that perhaps export for slavery was in store for her. If only he had helped her when he could.

'And if it's kids …' Here Jeremiah's breath hitched and he had trouble swallowing. 'Well, not everyone can feed all the kids they has, or love 'em enough to want to hang on to 'em. Or they lets 'em out to play and they don't come back. People just disappear sometimes, 'specially somewhere like Plymouth.' Jeremiah leaned forward and Will recoiled from the stench of his breath. 'He doesn't take 'em from everywhere, he's too smart for that. Places people might ask too many questions, like Bodingleigh, or Longmarsh, he plays it careful. Too smart to shit on his own doorstep, is Spight. If folk there knew what were going on, that might give him personal trouble.'

'But what about the resistance?' Will asked. 'How come we … they don't know?' They had not spelled out to Jeremiah who they were. Perhaps he had worked it out for himself, but it was safer for everyone that it not be confirmed.

'Ha! Don't make me laugh. Clueless bunch of do-gooders, the lot of 'em.'

A hot defence rose in Will's throat, but the Major coughed and shot him a look that told him to keep his mouth shut, before turning the car on again and backing out of the field.

Once they were underway, Will asked, 'Where did you get the flask?'

The Major looked a little ashamed. 'I pinched it out of Mrs Mason's pocket. She always carries whisky, for emergencies, but I knew she wouldn't hand it over once she knew why I wanted it, and I didn't want to lie.'

So that was why he had hugged her. Will had been sure there was something more to it than that but supposed he was wrong. He leaned back in his seat, numb to the resumed bouncing around, and wondered where she got her whisky from. Mrs Mason must be connected to have a regular supply of imported alcohol.

His mind switched to the more urgent matter of mulling over what they had been told. In the back seat, Jeremiah, sang softly to himself. The song sounded sweet, and sad.

'What are we going to do now?' asked Will.

'You heard the man. It's time the people of Bodingleigh knew what was happening under their noses.'

'And Mal?'

'And it's time he was rescued.'

GLINTING IN THE
SHADOWS

Organising the logistics of transport and storage had taken some time, but they were ready to start. Fred's fingers drummed on the rim of the open van window as Dug drove them through the outskirts of Plymouth. It meant the three militia men he'd picked up in Ivybridge, who now sat on the floor in the back, were getting wet, but he liked the way it made him feel; like someone from one of the old action movies in his DVD collection. Badass.

The streets were twilit but not yet deserted. It was coming up to nine. They had two hours until curfew; they needed to get a move on to be sure of snatching their share of the twenty-five bodies needed.

The few pedestrians out in the wet streets watched the van pass but without making it obvious. The panel van marked them apart as Spight's men, and that made people wary. The Mayor had made it very clear no one was to know what they were up to, on pain of becoming part of the shipment, which meant they needed to park up somewhere and proceed on foot.

He and the other gang leaders had divided the city into five sectors, five people to be taken from each. Fred had chosen to take Stonehouse and Millbay. These had once been known as rough neighbourhoods, before everywhere got rough, but the residents here were more dispirited and less organised than some of the others. Fred's crew might have to fight to get what they'd come for, but there would be no coordinated response. Perfect. Fred liked to play to his strengths.

They parked the van at Devil's Point, in the shadows of the once-exclusive Royal William Yard, converted from Napoleonic barracks at the end of the twentieth century and now a crumbling area of dark alleyways – down which the wind howled in off the Atlantic – and cavernous fortified squats that no one visited after sunset unless they had a death wish or their own nefarious business in mind. Fred left Dug behind the wheel, prepared to come and collect, or to move the van if it started getting the wrong kind of attention, and proceeded with his muscle back towards the westerly end of Union Street. They walked through the rubble of old streets that had burned down or fallen to scouring storms. Dressed in scruffy civilian clothing rather than militia uniform, they looked like any other small feral pack, of which they saw several. Fred ignored them as they ignored him. So long as they didn't step deliberately on anyone's toes, they might get away without attracting too much attention. He knew the Mayor would prefer it that way, but part of him, the part that had been roused by the violence he had visited on the insurgent spy, was itching to lash out.

They found their first target in the shadows of a semi-derelict block on the edge of a housing estate. Much of the building remained intact, although all the entryway doors had been kicked in and hung drunkenly off their hinges if they hadn't been taken away for firewood. A young man was hurrying towards the westernmost stairwell, alone and hunched up against the rain; otherwise the street was deserted. Silently, Fred signalled to one of his men to head their prey off before he reached the comparative shelter of the estate, while he and the other two blocked his escape. When he became aware of them, the young man began to run, but couldn't twist out of the way of the hands reaching for his shoulders and pulling him off his feet. Fred smacked him over the back of his head with the coin-weighted sock and he went down without a fight, to be slung over a shoulder, while Fred radioed for Dug to come and collect.

Their next was a twofer. Two young women, no doubt considering themselves safer together, in one of the smaller side streets. One of them produced a knife, handling it in a practised manner. Her friend, instead of staying close, backed away in panic and tried to run for it, only to have her feet swept away from under her by a scything size eleven boot. Distracted, her protector lost the knife to a swift kick from Fred. Shrieking and clutching her broken wrist, she put up little more resistance besides screaming obscenities at them, until Fred punched her, and she went down hard.

Two to go.

*

When no one showed up at the bunker within twenty-four hours, Spight assumed that somehow the rebels now knew he had invaded their HQ and taken their man. Swallowing his rage, he told Dorcas there was a chance someone would come to rescue the prisoner, but she was to tell her staff nothing, and, while the door to the larder should remain locked, the door should not be guarded. Similarly, he kept the perimeter around the bunker loose.

Let the idiots think he was too caught up in arrangements for his shipment to have proper security in place. Not that it wasn't close to the truth. Keeping on top of updates from his

subordinates in Plymouth was time-consuming, and he'd lost
key personnel to the captaining of the raids. Bob wasn't much
use to him, having turned up late, looking tired and pale.
Spight hoped the man wasn't coming down with something,
or forgetting to take his medication; he needed him at his side,
focused. In the meantime, he'd sent him to the kitchen to fetch
some supper, while Spight sat with his satellite phone and a
walkie-talkie at the ready, in Dorcas's poorly lit and cramped
study, hastily scrawled notes spread out on the desk before him
as he kept tabs on his different teams. The last of the day
drained away into an early dusk brought on by the storm
lashing the trees. Rain battered against the window.

It sounded like he'd have all he needed from Plymouth
within another hour or two, stored securely near the river in
Longmarsh and ready for transport to Dartmouth on the
morning tide. His existing stock would be transported by road
in the morning. He had called in all his most trusted people.
Some of them were bringing additional boats but a goodly
number were tied up in securing the perimeter of the fat farm.
His resources were stretched too thin and that irked him.

Bob came in carrying two plates piled high with food. As
Spight took one, the walkie-talkie crackled into life, vibrating
against the desk.

'Number Five to Number One, Number Five to Number
One, over.'

Spight pushed the plate to one side and snatched up the
radio. Number Five was deep in the woods, between him and
the bunker. A tingle of excitement ran up his spine.

'Number One to Number Five, receiving. Over.'

'We've two insurgents come past us, headed for you. Both
male. Over.'

Spight pulled a map towards him and found the spot

Number Five should be radioing from. He traced an imaginary line from there to the house and worked out the distance. They should be here any moment now.

'Roger that, Five. Stay there and await my command. Out.'

The walkie-talkie buzzed again. 'Number Three to Number One, Number Three to Number One, over.'

Number Three should be down by the entrance to the drive. 'Number One to Number Three, receiving. Over.'

'Six insurgents moved past us, proceeding up the side of the drive, staying under cover. What you want us to do? Over.'

'Stay there, await my command. Out.'

That made at least eight insurgents on their way to the house. It was quite possible more had slipped through unseen. He'd have them any minute now. He made sure the door to the corridor was open so he could hear what was happening in the hallway. The larder was two doors down and he defied anyone to get in and out unheard.

'What do we do now?' asked Bob.

'First, put out the light.'

Bob blew out the candles on the desk, so the room was in darkness.

'Now, we wait.'

★

Far above, the last of the day's storm-dimmed light was losing a battle to penetrate the woodland canopy, which swayed and bent before violent gusts of wind. A branch snapped off and sent a litter of leaves swirling as it crashed to the ground nearby. The pressure of powerful gusts was painful against Will's ears as he staggered through the wood in the dark, hands out to cushion himself in case he tripped over an

invisible root or fallen branch. Deafened by the wind's roar, he
could barely hear the Major, who was shouting in Will's ear
that they needed to head further east in order to find the path
that bordered the drive.

Will was questioning the wisdom of the Major's plan.
Which didn't seem to be so much a plan as a headlong rush
into potential disaster. There were eight of them involved in
the rescue attempt, all that the Major had managed to pull
together in the two hours since their return. They had met in
the old, disused barn to the north of the fat farm, where the
Major told them he and Will would be taking care of releasing
Mal; the others were to remain outside the house and act as
lookouts, or backup if needed.

Looking at their pale faces, illuminated by flashlight, Will
had not rated their potential as reinforcements very highly.
Irma and Greg were extremely young, Simon middle-aged and
overweight, and all three of them were sweating with nerves.
Two other men, who arrived late and didn't get an
introduction, appeared more capable, but even they seemed
unnerved to be venturing to the heart of Spight's empire. And
then there was Jeremiah, who was still with them. He had
refused to be left in the barn, or to go with the team of
anonymous strangers when their paths diverged. Will could
hear the old man behind him, blundering into bushes and
cursing.

The Major had forbidden them to use torches, so all they
had to see by was the last of the twilight filtering through the
dense canopy that swayed overhead. Soon that would be gone.
The driveway to their right gave them a rough guide to the
direction in which they needed to go, but their progress was
painfully slow as they made their way towards the house,
pausing in the comparative shelter of an overgrown hedge

once they got there.

Here they left the old man, as well as Irma, Greg and Simon. Jeremiah cursed them, but the Major was adamant he could not go with them into the house. Eventually, promised more whisky after they came back with Mal, he sat down on the sodden ground and promptly went to sleep sitting up. Will took off his scarf and wrapped it around Jeremiah's scrawny neck. He was hot from the climb and sweating so much from nerves he didn't need it, and Jeremiah might. The Major patted him on the back approvingly.

'Right then, lad, let's go get Mal away from these bastards, shall we?'

What had happened to 'These people are not our enemy?' Will wondered. Maybe that ceased to be the case when those people resorted to torture.

The Major led him around the east wing of the house, keeping within the tree line until they were forced out into the open to reach the kitchen at the rear. Several windows on the first floor were lit, but only two on the ground floor, and both of those were over in the west wing and nowhere near the kitchen. Will's heart was hammering in his ears, knowing he had to follow. He felt sick as the Major stepped out into the open, crossed the yard and opened the kitchen door. The Major acted as if he had every right to be there, and Will tried to emulate him, standing up straight and holding his shoulders back, when all he wanted to do was cringe and hide his face from the crescent moon, briefly visible between speeding clouds.

The kitchen was dark and deserted and the din of the storm dropped away as they stepped inside. Switching on a torch and shading it with his hand to keep the beam from betraying their presence to anyone who might be passing the uncurtained window, the Major strode across to a door on the far side, and through it into a corridor. He seemed to know exactly where he was going as he turned right, Will trotting along behind him, aware he was leaving soggy footprints. They walked along a threadbare carpet runner over scuffed and squeaky floorboards and stopped at the first door on the left. The Major tried the handle. It was locked. He passed the torch to Will and indicated with a nod of his head that he wanted the beam shone onto the lock. Will did his best to keep it steady.

The Major rummaged in an inside pocket of his jacket and brought out a pair of long, thin tools. Kneeling so the lock was at eye level, he inserted them and fiddled about. Will was impressed. Clearly his own training was incomplete. After a few moments, there was a click that seemed loud in the silence of the building, and it struck Will that the house was eerily quiet for a place that housed at least a couple of dozen people.

The door opened onto a small, dark and windowless room about two metres square. Torchlight showed shelves lining three walls. It smelled of vinegar and the contents of a bucket with a lid in one corner, that had been used as a toilet. A long shape shrouded in a blanket lay across the floor. It didn't move as they entered and Will wondered if they were too late. His mouth was dry as the Major knelt down and reached out with one hand to touch the blanket. The body beneath flinched. The Major grabbed a handful of the wool and tugged, and Mal's battered face was revealed. He curled into a foetal position, wrapping his arms over his head, not looking at them.

'Mal, hey, it's us,' the Major whispered, patting the boy's arm. 'We've come to get you out of here.'

Mal's eyes flickered open. He stared at them blankly for a moment, then his face crumpled and he started to sob. The Major pulled him up into a rough hug, then started pulling at the blanket to free Mal's legs so he could stand.

'Come on, we have to get out of here before someone comes to check on you. Can you walk?'

Mal sniffed hard and nodded. His eyes met Will's and he tried to smile. Will smiled back around the lump in this throat. Between them, he and the Major managed to get Mal on his feet and his arms around their shoulders so they could take his weight. Will put his head out of the door to check the corridor was still deserted. Once they were out of the larder he pulled the door closed quietly, and they hobbled as fast as they could for the kitchen.

The full force of the storm lashed them as they went back out by the back door. Will switched off the torch and they headed for the shadows of the trees, where they retrieved Jeremiah and the others and had a short and silent argument over whether Jeremiah should be allowed a pull on the flask, which the old man lost. From there they headed deeper into the woods, and once properly out of sight of the house the Major pulled out his radio and quietly called their backup team to meet them at the barn. He also allowed Will to switch the torch back on; it was too difficult to make good time through slippery mud and overgrowth in the dark, with two of them still supporting Mal. Now their objective had been achieved they were more concerned with getting Mal to safety than in stealth, and the sound and violence of the storm was enough to cover the noise of their progress and, hopefully, keep people indoors.

The other team was already back in the comparative shelter of the barn when they got there, and they set Simon as the first sentry before hastening inside. Greg and Irma lit a few lanterns and a Primus stove, after covering the windows with old sacking to keep them blacked out. There was an air of

jubilation as everyone greeted Mal, slapping him on the arm
and ruffling his hair until he pushed them away with a weak
laugh and fell into a chair. Will collapsed into another beside
him and breathed deeply, feeling the tension still thrumming
through his body.

Once Jeremiah had been handed Mrs Mason's flask, now
almost empty, the Major brought out his satellite phone and
rang the safe house to let them know Mal had been retrieved;
Will detected a note of smugness in his voice as he promised
the three, sorry, four of them would be back there by dawn,
with some brand-new intel courtesy of the old man.

Will half listened, letting his thoughts wander, and before
long he began to doze. The door slamming open woke him,
and he stared at a group of militia framed in the doorway,
most of them holding weapons, ranging from cricket bats to
axes to guns. At their front was Simon, who was pushed
forward and fell to the floor. Behind him, Mayor Spight,
holding a furled umbrella and a pistol, stepped into the room.
One of his minions took the umbrella.

'Well, well, well, thank you for making this so easy.'

Behind Will, Jeremiah squeaked with dismay and dropped
the flask. The Mayor looked him over dismissively, then did a
double take.

'Well *indeed*! I do believe I see old Jeremiah lurking behind
all that dirt and stink. What are you doing, throwing your lot
in with these losers? Oh, yeah, you're an even bigger loser.
Well, guess what? You're all winners now – you've won tickets
to the Real USA.' He looked at Irma and Greg, then Will, and
nodded approvingly. 'Nice … some young blood. I'm sure
you'll be made very welcome.'

When he spotted the Major on the other side of the room,
he began to laugh. Will thought he sounded a bit unhinged,

and he saw a couple of Spight's men look at each other behind their leader's back as though they agreed.

'You! Well, who would have thought I'd have the pleasure. I wondered if it was you trying to make life difficult for me. What's the matter? Run out of agitators and having to do your own dirty work? I see you still need a gang of kids around you for a bit of hero worship.'

He turned to Will and the others. 'Do you think he's a hero? Do you think he's a proper military man, chest full of ribbons?'

They didn't do medals in the resistance, but Will nodded defiantly anyway, wanting to wipe the smug smirk of the Mayor's face.

Spight sneered at him, 'He's a joke – a joke in very bad taste. He's no Major. He's a puffed-up trombonist, in a band called The Militia. Calls himself the Major, but he ducked his duty as a sergeant in the *real* militia, ran away like a coward and was courtmartialled in his absence for desertion. *That's* your *Major!*' Spight was red in the face from the fury of his denunciation; spittle hung from his lower lip.

Will looked to the Major for a denial, but his idol merely shrugged and looked regretful, avoiding looking him in the eye.

Spight resumed his tirade, turning his back on the shocked faces of Will and the others and addressing their leader. 'Or did you come back for her? It won't do you any good you know, she's long-since forgotten about you, but I'll be sure to send your regards if you like. In the meantime ...' He made a sudden lunge for Irma, who was closest to him, grabbing and twisting her arm so it was pulled into a painful angle behind her back. Irma's face screwed up with pain but she made no sound. Spight nodded at one of his subordinates, who came forward and took up the grip, pulling her away from her comrades.

'Now, I want you all to behave yourselves, or I promise you things will get very unpleasant for this young woman. Your friend there can confirm I follow through on my promises. So, you will come with me, you will climb into the vehicle we have waiting, and you will *not* try to escape.'

How could they have been so stupid? Poor Mal, returned to the clutches of his tormentors. How could he, Will, have idolised the Major – *Paul* – so completely? The man was just a ... a *musician*. Will could not stop berating himself as they were led along a deer track through the storm-lashed woods to a gate onto the lane. In just a few minutes they had emerged, and there was the vehicle Spight had spoken of, parked so that it was heading in the direction of Longmarsh; an ancient Land Rover with its engine running, belching out foul-smelling smoke, rain slanting through the beams of its headlights. He recognised the man behind the wheel as the Mayor's chief flunkey, Bob. He looked as agitated as Will felt.

Bob jumped out and moved towards the back of the Land Rover, where they were all huddled together. As he passed Will, who was standing at the edge of the group, he hissed out of the side of his mouth, 'Go to the teacher.'

What? Before the word had time to leave his mouth, Bob had tripped and crashed into the man holding Irma by the arm, who had to let go to stop himself falling over. In the confusion Will found himself unguarded. Seizing the chance, before giving himself time to fear that he might be shot, he turned on his heel and fled down the road towards the village. Shouts and a roar of rage from Spight followed him around the bend. Shots were fired and a tree splintered just to his right.

As soon as he was out of sight of the Land Rover he sprinted as fast as he could down the lane to a dip, and an old stone drain that emptied out into a culvert beside the road. Squeezing himself inside, he lay half-submerged in the freezing stream, heart hammering. Feet passed him and pounded on to the next bend, where the road straightened out. There they faltered and stopped. He could hear them conferring, shouting over the wind, then two sets of footsteps making their way back up the hill.

'We lost him,' one of them shouted as they turned the corner. 'He just disappeared.'

'Fuckwits! How could he just disappear? Flat-footed cocksuckers!' Spight was screeching with rage. A pause, and he continued in a calmer voice that Will could barely hear, saying, 'At least we still have the rest, even if a couple of them are past it. Bob, get on to the Door Knockers to spread the word to watch out for the boy. You lot, get in the fucking truck or I'll beat you senseless. And if you fall over yourself again Bob, you won't get a cruise to the US because I'll fucking kill you.'

There were scuffling sounds and a low cry of pain that sounded like it came from Mal. Will was torn. Should he try to free the others, or should he do what Bob had told him and go find the teacher? He must mean Mrs Prendaghast, who used to live in the cottage next to the school. What on earth use could an old woman like her be to him?

The sound of the engine grew louder as it was put in gear and started driving away. Well that made his decision easier, but he cursed himself for not taking them all on single-handed, even though he knew the Major would bawl him out if he got himself captured again. The Major ... What a joke! He couldn't begin to ponder that betrayal of trust.

He would go to the village. The old woman might not be

much help, but it was somewhere to go; presumably Bob had
meant she would take him in and give him shelter. Lying in the
frigid water, with every friend he had being taken off to
imprisonment and slavery, that seemed good enough to Will.
He pulled himself out of the culvert and crouched, dripping, by
the side of the road for a moment until he was sure no one had
been left behind to look for him. The storm was easing but a
cold wind knifed through his soaked clothing. He needed to
get somewhere dry.

It had been years since he had been into Bodingleigh but not
much had changed. Some of the out-lying buildings looked
more dilapidated; roofs fallen in and windows broken, their
hard edges softened by growths of moss that appeared black in
the fitful moonlight appearing between scudding clouds.

Checking his watch, he saw there was still a quarter of an
hour to go until curfew, but the streets were already deserted,
and most of the windows of the houses he passed were dark,
until he neared the pub. Someone was playing a piano, which
needed tuning but still provided a melody for raised voices to
follow. They were singing a standard from the last century,
something about a Wonderwall, with much wailing at the end
of the chorus. The pub was close by the school and he was
forced to cross the open square in front of it, lit by one
streetlight, the corners yawning with shadows.

Remembering how the Major – Paul – had made himself
look as if he belonged where he didn't, Will forced himself to
stand erect and walk without hurrying, as if he had every right
to be there. And didn't he? He and his ancestors had been born
here after all, and that was what counted in Devon. Striding
out of the shadows and into the square, he was half-way across
when the door of the pub opened, and two men dressed in

uniform spilled out of the door, staggering down the steps.

They were still singing, serenading each other and roaring with laughter. Will recognised them from the mug shots in the bunker. Low-level Spight flunkies, cronies of Fred's. He forced himself to continue at the same casual pace. The men staggered to the railings at the edge of the square next to the church and opened up their trousers to pee into the churchyard. The sound of two urine streams hitting a gravestone was loud in the quiet that descended as the song ended.

''S good, room for more cider now,' one of them slurred.

His companion guffawed, staggered, cursed as urine splashed back on to his shoes, and said in a slightly less slurry voice, 'You gon' bring down the wrath of Spight, you too bladdered to take stock down Dartmouth at sparrer's fart.'

'He'll be madder at you for talkin' 'bout it 'ere in public. He don' wan' folk to know what we been up to.'

'What public – you mean that bey over there? Hey, bey!'

Will was almost across the square. He froze and half turned, keeping his head down and face in shadow.

'Yeah?'

'You 'ear what we been on 'bout?'

'What? No.'

'See, ain't no one listenin'. Now you bugger off before curfew bey.'

Will nodded and hurried away before they changed their minds. Behind him, the noise from the pub increased as the door opened and they staggered back in.

★

A knock on the door so late at night had to be trouble. It was her third unexpected caller in as many days. It could not be good news. Mrs Prendaghast told Primrose to go upstairs and be quiet, before creeping to the front door, guarding a candle flame against the many draughts. Its light threw wavering shadows across the walls.

She put her mouth up against the door and called softly, 'Who is it?'

'Mrs Prendaghast?' The voice was young, male and unfamiliar. He wasn't shouting, so he didn't want to be heard by any neighbours still up. She had a bad feeling this was going to add to her troubles.

'Yes, this is my home.' A note of asperity crept into her tone. 'Who are you? What do you want?'

'I was sent here by Bob, I need your help.' His voice was pitched so low she had to strain to hear it.

Praying this was not an elaborate trap designed by Spight to catch her out, she put the chain on the door and opened it a crack. A tall young man stood on the step, dressed in soaking black clothes stained with mud, his blond hair sticking up in all directions. He was shivering and looking at her with a hopeful expression.

She looked back at him blankly. 'Do I know you?'

'No. Well, you used to. I was in your class but my parents took me away. Five years ago. I'm Will.'

'Will?' Looking closer, she could almost see the gawky thirteen-year-old he'd been, with scabby knees and cheeky grin.

'Look, can we talk inside? I'm kind of on the run.'

She hesitated a moment longer before taking the chain off

the door and opening it wide enough for him to come in. Once he had done so they stood on either side of the table in the small room. He was so tall his head practically touched the ceiling. She checked the windows were still curtained.

'What sort of help do you think I can give you?' She was wary. 'And what are you doing back in Bodingleigh? I thought you and your family went to Cornwall?'

'We did.'

He looked to be in the grip of an internal struggle. She remembered him as an idealistic boy, prone to saving injured wild animals and devastated if they died. His parents had been founders of SCREW and vocal opponents to the more extreme ideas of the Council and Spight, ending up as social pariahs, everyone too afraid to be seen associating with them. Then they disappeared; the first she had known about it was when Will failed to turn up for school. She had hoped they got away, wished them well and had pretty much forgotten about them.

A decision must have been reached because Will went on, 'We moved to Saltash and I signed up with the resistance as soon as I could. I've been back, up at the fat farm, in a bunker with a bunch of other agents, working to get the Mayor out. So people can live the way they want to.'

She laughed. 'You know you sound just like him – the Mayor. That's the reason he gives for getting rid of the resistance. Only he calls you insurgents.'

The boy's face flushed. 'I can't help it if he's a liar. We never locked anyone up. Or tortured them. Or fed them up so we could suck the fat out of them. Or sold them.'

'*Sold* them?'

'Yes, we just found out about it, the Major and me … I mean, Paul and me … from the old man.'

He wasn't making sense. But before she unravelled his

meaning, she wanted to know what he was doing in her house, inviting trouble to her door.

'Why are you here, Will?'

'I really don't know. We were caught by Spight when we rescued Mal, and we were all ordered into a truck, then Bob fell over so I got free. He told me to come to you. I've nowhere else to go, Mrs P. And something bad is about to happen to a whole bunch of people and I don't know what to do ...'

Gibberish. But ... Mrs P. He used to call her that when he was very young, unable to pronounce her name.

Behind her, she felt a draught as the door to the stairs opened. 'You have to help him, Mrs Prendaghast.' Primrose came into the room and clutched her arm, then turned to the boy and smiled awkwardly. 'Hi, Will.'

The two youngsters were sharing the one armchair, Primrose in the chair and Will perched on one of the arms, wrapped in the crocheted throw. He kept stealing glances at the girl, still dressed in Mrs Prendaghast's bathrobe, as if he couldn't believe what he was seeing. Mrs Prendaghast snorted quietly to herself. Ah, hormones.

He had given her a second, more detailed account of the last few days and she was badly worried. A lot of people were about to be shipped out and there was little time to do anything about it. She had no way of contacting Bob, without putting both of them in danger. Besides, she was furious with him for only giving her part of the story. She could only assume he had been too ashamed to tell her all of it.

She would have to go direct to the resistance again. It was risky, but Primrose was right. They had to help.

Mrs Prendaghast poured out the camomile tea she had

been making while Will told his story, and passed them a mug each, then held her cup up to her nose so she could breathe in the steam and steady her nerves. She regarded them both over the rim.

'We're going to go make a phone call. You'd best come with me, Will, so you can fill in the details I'll forget. You too Primrose. I've wanted to shield you, but I'm your teacher, and I'm not doing you any favours by standing between you and what's really happening. This is the world you live in, and if you don't like it, it's up to you to do something about it.'

★

Primrose was excited. Instead of skulking inside – when she had done pretty much nothing else but that for the last five years – she was going to get to do something brave and useful, and to help people. The fact that, until yesterday, she had thought the resistance was a dangerous gang of delinquents out to destroy society, no longer seemed to matter. If Will was one of them they must be OK. She had liked Will at school, had thought him handsome and had a bit of a crush on him before she was sent to the farm. He had been one of the friends she missed most in the first few confusing and miserable months away from home.

Sitting close to him now was another thing giving her little quivers of nervous energy and making it hard for her to sit still. Every time he looked down at her, and he seemed to do that quite often, sparks ignited in her chest, and her belly felt a bit fluttery.

Mrs Prendaghast took her upstairs to get dressed, and to find some of her dad's old trousers and a jumper for Will, who was shivering in his wet clothes.

As she helped Mrs Prendaghast rummage through old boxes stacked in a corner of the bedroom, Primrose wondered aloud at the information Will had brought them, saying how terrible it must be for the poor souls being sent away. Mrs Prendaghast told her to sit down for a moment. She did so and looked up at the teacher expectantly.

'You do know that could have been you, don't you?' Mrs Prendaghast said, sitting beside her. 'If you hadn't run away, you'd be part of that shipment of people leaving tomorrow.'

Primrose was confused.

The teacher went on, 'Why else do you think the last harvesting was so extreme? To make you look like you do now, so that when you arrived in New Jersey you'd fetch a higher price.'

It took a while for that to sink in. 'But what good am I if I'm not fat?' she asked.

Mrs Prendaghast's eyes filled with tears. 'You're plenty good just as you are, or as you were, Primrose. But, you see, New Jersey has plenty of fat people. They don't farm them because they still have oil fields, and coal, and they don't care about climate collapse, but they have terrible food so most of them are very fat. The poor people anyway. What they want, what they pay for, is young, beautiful girls. Like you. Boys too.'

'I'm beautiful?'

'Of course you are, dear.'

This was such a novel concept it quite distracted Primrose from the seriousness of what Mrs Prendaghast was telling her, or what she could see the teacher thought was serious. To Primrose, who had been a thing to be used for so long, it didn't seem so outlandish that people should be sold off, like cows or sheep, no matter how much it shocked Will and Mrs

Prendaghast. She knew it was wrong, but was not surprised.

The teacher was still talking but Primrose got up from the bed and went to the bathroom, where she stared at herself in the mirror, trying to see beauty there.

Mrs Prendaghast came to the door and watched her with an amused but somewhat exasperated expression, which Primrose noticed after some moments spent studying her own small nose and full mouth, set in a heart-shaped face atop what were now her slender neck and shoulders.

'I'm sorry, it's just no one ever said I was beautiful before.'

'I think you may be missing the point here, dear. It wouldn't have done you any favours, you'd still be just a breeder to them ...' She saw Primrose's expression and stopped.

'Breeder?' Now Primrose really was shocked. So that was what all the fuss was about. That was why the two of them were so upset. And now she was too. Breed? Despite plenty of offers at the fat farm, she hadn't even kissed anyone yet, let alone ... She felt like an idiot for being so naive. Of course, that was how they made new cows and sheep.

'You see, conception rates have dropped like a stone over there. They need young people like you, with healthy bodies.'

In the parlance of Mrs Prendaghast's youth: what the fuck?

Somewhat subdued, Primrose continued rummaging through boxes and eventually found some things that fitted her better than the clothes she had taken from the farm, and dark enough not to show up at night. Will was given a jumper, jacket and trousers that smelled of thirty years of storage, but didn't complain, stripping and pulling on the dry clothes while Primrose averted her eyes from his skinny body and Mrs Prendaghast hung his wet things over the bath to dry.

By the time they were ready it was well past curfew. To make it less likely they'd meet one of the enforcers, Mrs Prendaghast took them out through the door that connected her kitchen to the school, and from there to an entrance into the empty building next door, so that if they were seen emerging, it wouldn't be from her home.

'This was the girls' school, back when sexes were segregated in village schools, and there were enough children to need two buildings,' Mrs Prendaghast explained as they walked through the empty rooms, which still carried the faint smell of chalk dust. 'Then it was sold off to become someone's second home, but they left after Devolution, and no one had any money to buy it, or any need for somewhere so hard to heat. Spight was going to use it as a store room but he decided it wasn't secure. It's been empty ever since.'

A back entrance let them out into a quiet alley with blank stone walls. No windows overlooked it. From there they slipped down another alley that led them steeply to the bottom of the village. They walked in silence, Mrs Prendaghast leading, followed by Primrose with Will at the rear. Once, they heard someone coming towards them and ducked into a front yard to hide behind a hedge, but it turned out to be a hedgehog, snuffling and pushing its way through the undergrowth to the side of the path. Primrose stifled a laugh. This was so different from her flights from the fat farm and their solitary terrors. She was no longer alone.

The storm had swollen the stream at the bottom of the hill and it had overspilled its banks. The nearest bridge was in the village, next to a house with lit windows, so they were forced to walk beside it for several hundred metres over uneven ground pocked with waterlogged holes, before they could find somewhere to cross without getting more than their feet wet.

The shock of the cold water sobered Primrose a little; that and the rubbing of wet leather against her feet, which made her hobble.

Mrs Prendaghast turned right at the next crossroads, and then left into a driveway marked as private by a battered sign. An ornate but abandoned gatehouse stood back a little from the road, and she took them around to the side, where a door hung off its hinges. With a good deal of effort, she squeezed through the gap in the wood and beckoned them to follow. Primrose got through with little trouble but she could hear Will struggling to fold his frame small enough, cursing as bits of him caught on splinters. On the other side of the broken door was a heavy black drape, being held back by Mrs Prendaghast so they could slip past. Once all three of them were safely through, she dropped the fabric and switched on a torch.

They were standing in a small, square room. The large, carved-stone window frames she had seen from outside were hidden by another set of blackout curtains. The room was dusty, empty, with a padlocked door in the far wall. Mrs Prendaghast crossed to this door and drew a slender chain from within her clothing, at the end of which hung a key. She used this to open the padlock, before unbolting the door and opening it into another blacked-out room with a desk and chair atop a dusty rug. Pulling the chair aside, shoving the desk a few inches, Mrs Prendaghast stooped and flipped back the rug to reveal a sturdy trapdoor, with an iron ring set into it. She pushed herself up to standing and gestured to the ring.

'One of you open that, please, I'm pooped.' She sat herself down heavily on the chair while Will grabbed the ring and heaved. A yawning black hole appeared, leading down to a basement. Primrose could see the top of a ladder.

'Can one of you go down and fetch a phone please.'

Will switched on a torch and headed down into the dark without even looking to see if Primrose wanted to oblige. Somewhat piqued, she climbed down after him. The basement was bare and windowless; she could just about stand comfortably, but Will was having to bend his neck and couldn't stand upright. He was looking around with wonder.

'How come I never heard of this place?' he called up to Mrs Prendaghast.

Primrose's eye was caught by something glinting in the shadows. She took Will's torch from him, jumping slightly as their hands touched. He was so warm. Directing the beam revealed a metal box with a hasp but no padlock. Inside were old papers, which she ignored, and a bundle of shiny plastic phones, which she recognised from old movies, with another device attached to one of them. She snatched them up eagerly and flourished them at Will. They were bulky and made it difficult to climb back up the ladder, but she managed and passed them to Mrs Prendaghast with a triumphant air.

Will climbed back out and repeated his question. He sounded offended, as though secrets had been kept from him, an insurgent. A member of the resistance, she amended.

Mrs Prendaghast's amusement showed as she replied, 'Very few people know about this place. Or rather, they know there is an abandoned gatehouse here, but they don't know it's a secret lair.' Will was glowering, and she went on, 'Don't worry, lad, I doubt your Major knows about it either. It's a bolthole for one of your lot, who happens to be a good friend of mine. She told me about it, in strictest confidence, so I could communicate with the resistance if she wasn't around and the need arose. I never used it until yesterday, and I hope, after tonight, I won't have to again.'

'She? Do you mean Mrs M? Mrs Mason?' A thought seemed to strike Will then and he exclaimed, 'Was it *you* who rang the safe house to tell us about Mal?' He looked at the old woman with a noticeable increase in respect.

'Mrs Mason, is that what she's calling herself?' Mrs Prendaghast chuckled. 'That's a bit close to the bone. And yes, that was me. Right, let's get on with making this call then shall we?' She powered up one of the phones.

'I didn't think mobile phones worked anymore,' said Primrose.

'They don't, dear, since the masts all went down, but this is a satellite phone, and so long as they don't fall down, it should be working fine.' Primrose wasn't sure what a mast was. She imagined a line of old sailing ships toppling. Satellites were more familiar to her. The moon was one, so maybe that's what Mrs P – she copied Will unconsciously – meant. The moon certainly wasn't going to fall down any time soon.

From being excited she was feeling despondent again. There really was so much she didn't know. Or maybe it was hunger dragging her mood down. She was so used to eating whenever she was awake, and she and Mrs P had been on their way to bed when Will came to the door. It had now been hours since their spartan supper of soup with a bit of cheese. Her stomach rumbled and she flashed an embarrassed smile, but no one seemed to have noticed.

'Right, where's the call history? Ah, here we go.' There was a long pause before a tinny ringing sounded.

A voice came on the line. Mrs P put the phone to her ear and asked for Mrs Mason. There was a wait of a couple of minutes, while they all stared aimlessly around the featureless room, and then, faintly, they could hear the voice of a woman with a no-nonsense voice say, 'Hello? Iris? Why are you calling again? Everything alright?'

'I'm fine. I have someone here who needs to talk to you.' Mrs Prendaghast handed the phone to Will. He looked nervous as he took it and held it away from his face so they could all hear both sides of the conversation.

'Mrs M? I mean, Mrs Mason, it's me, Will.'

'Will? What's happened? I thought you and the Major were on your way back with news for us. We're waiting on you before we pull out.'

'Well, here's the thing ...' Will gave a brief sketch of events since the Major had last rung the safe house, told her what he had overheard in the village square, and what they had been told about people-selling by Jeremiah. When he finished there was a long pause. When she spoke again, Mrs Mason sounded odd, her voice tight.

'Will, thank you, and well done for getting this information to us – it explains a lot. I need to share everything, so we can decide what to do. Please stay where you are and wait for instructions.' He opened his mouth to reply but the line was buzzing. The call was over. Will passed the phone to Mrs P, who handed it straight back.

'No, you hang on to it. It's you she wants to talk to. In the meantime,' she looked around the room, 'let's try and make ourselves comfortable, shall we?'

They made a nest with a pile of blackout material found in a corner of the first room they had entered. Mrs Prendaghast preferred to stay in the chair, wrapped in a swathe of dusty black cloth, saying she wouldn't be able to get up again if she lay on the floor, but she insisted the other two lie down and try to get some sleep. Lying next to Will in the dark, Primrose's heartbeat speeded up and sleep felt impossible. The teacher seemed to have dropped off despite being seated; the girl could hear faint snores coming from that corner of the room.

Her mind was filled with new information and ideas, thoughts about what might have happened to her if she hadn't escaped. She couldn't get comfortable and kept turning over, trying to be quiet so she wouldn't wake Will. When he spoke, she jumped in shock.

'Can't you sleep?'

'No, there's too much to think about.'

He laughed and said, 'Ain't that the truth!'

She liked his laugh. It had deepened in the last few years. The thought of that change, and other changes that had happened to both of them, made her feel hot and she pushed the blackout curtain away, her hand coming in contact with his again. She snatched it back.

'Sorry,' she mumbled, feeling foolish.

'Don't be.' His hand found hers and held it. Their fingers entwined, and his thumb stroked her palm.

All of her seemed to throb.

There was no way she would be able to sleep now.

THE LIGHTLESS PIT OF
DESPAIR THAT YAWNED

The prisoners had been taken to a damp and leaky boatshed on the quayside of the river in Longmarsh. The journey had been conducted in silence, with only a sobbed apology from Irma, barely heard over the sound of the Land Rover's engine. The Major, next to her, patted her hand and told her it wasn't her fault. She had swiftly broken contact, and he cursed Spight for destroying her trust in him. So what if he wasn't really a former army officer? He had years of experience in the field; if they went in for rank in the resistance, he'd probably be a General by now. But it was true he had deserted the militia. Cowing the local populace under the guise of keeping them secure had not suited his temperament in the way it had others, such as Fred and the then Captain Spight.

Two of the men who had abducted them sat on the bench seat in front, next to Bob, who drove. The seven prisoners sat on uncushioned metal seats flanking both sides of the vehicle, with two more of Spight's men to one side and one squatting between their knees in the middle, all of them bouncing up and down painfully as they were driven at speed over uneven ground. Spight was being driven directly behind them in his old Audi, which had maintained a tight tail. Even if he could have managed to get past their guards and jump from the back, the Major thought, Spight would just have had his driver run over him. There was no love lost between the two men.

Besides, he was responsible for his team, he couldn't abandon them.

Once at the quay, they were taken out singly from the Land Rover, at gunpoint, and pushed into the shed, where they milled about in the dark, tripping over what turned out to be old fishing nets. They were all frisked on the way in. The Major lost his satellite phone and torch, and the knife he kept on his belt. Now he sat against a wall and tried to keep from falling into the lightless pit of despair that yawned before him.

Three guards had been left outside. He could hear them talking in low voices, smell cigarette smoke that wafted in through gaps in the aged wooden walls and awoke his tobacco cravings. It had resumed raining an hour or so after their arrival, and it was then they discovered the shed leaked. All of them had found somewhere reasonably dry to sit by now and waited there in silence for whatever came next. No one had a plan.

Mal was close by; his laboured breathing was audible. When the Major asked him how he was, the boy swore at him.

The only one who seemed unconcerned was Jeremiah, who was sleeping off the booze. He had managed to grab the flask and drain its contents in one swallow, before it was taken away. Currently, his head lolled on the Major's shoulder, whisky-stinking snores vibrating through the wood they leaned against.

The Major was pleased Will had got free, he just hoped he had managed to find somewhere safe to hole up and didn't have any crazy ideas about coming to rescue them all. Once they were missed at the safe house, which he reckoned would be when they were at least a couple of hours late for their dawn rendezvous – so, say, about seven a.m. – Mrs Mason and the others would know something was wrong. What they could do about it was another matter. They would have no way of knowing what had happened, or where he and the others were. He could only hope they would proceed with Stage Two. If he'd messed that up with his insistence on returning to Bodingleigh he would never forgive himself. He didn't think Mrs Mason would forgive him either, particularly when she found out about Devon's slave trade.

He estimated the time to be about midnight. He should get some sleep while he could, or he wouldn't be fit to take advantage of any other lapses by their guards, like Bob falling over himself. How incredibly fortuitous that had been. Pushing Jeremiah upright – the old man didn't wake but the pitch of his snoring moved up an octave – he took off his scarf and folded it into a pillow, before lying down with his coat wrapped around himself tightly to keep out the cold, and willing himself to sleep.

Waking some unknown time later he lay still for a moment. He could hear men's voices and laughter outside, and the sound of vehicle doors slamming. He drew himself up to a sitting position and wondered if it was time for them to be moved on to Dartmouth. Surely it wasn't dawn yet. It was too dark to see if anyone else was awake, but he could feel an edge of tension in the air.

The door they had been pushed through was unlocked, unbolted and opened, creating a paler square in the blackness. A torch beam was shone inside the shed, its brightness painful to eyes accustomed to the dark.

'Right, you lot, in you go. No rushing now.' Mocking laughter greeted this witticism. He knew that voice. Fred. Had Spight told him he, the Major, was here? That could get ugly fast.

People started filing in, hunched over as if terrified or in pain. The Major counted twenty but there could have been more; it was difficult to see.

'Make yourselves comfortable, we'll be back to collect you for the commencement of your cruise in approximately four hours, so I'd make the most of it, I was you. And thank fuck I ain't!' More laughter. That Fred, such a card. He seemed to be feeling pleased with himself. But he didn't seem to be aware of the Major's presence yet, and some of the tension left his body as he settled in to wait.

★

Fred was, indeed, feeling pleased with himself. He had filled his quota before the call came through from Spight that he had an additional seven bodies available for shipping, though some of them might not be suitable for market. They would run inventory in the morning, weeding out the less desirable.

'What will we do with those?' he had asked.

'I'm sure we can find a use for them. Everyone has their aptitude. I should think they'll find themselves so grateful not to be going as part of the shipment, they'll be willing enough to comply. We might have trouble with one or two, but I foresee no lasting difficulties.' Spight had rung off then, leaving Fred to coordinate the transport of all those taken from Plymouth. That, and the journey itself, had taken some time, so it was very late, or very early, when they arrived at the quayside. It was hardly worth going home to catch a few hours of sleep, so he bedded down in the back of his Transit van, sending the rest of his crew off to fend for themselves.

Adrenaline was still pumping around his system and he found it difficult to go to sleep. Instead he lay and calculated how long he might have to wait before it could legitimately be said Spight was too old to be holding all the reins. Surely only another year or two. The man was still fit, but everyone was vulnerable to accidents, and no one was immune from illness. The Mayor had better recourse to treatment than most, but he was still human. Fred should start building alliances now. Discreetly of course. A couple of hours were spent scheming before exhaustion pushed ambition aside and claimed him for a restless sleep full of dreams of chasing, but never quite reaching, a quarry he could not see.

Spight had decreed that his men should be ready for action at dawn. Fred had delegated Dug to make sure everyone was up, and to put in an order for flasks of tea and bacon sandwiches from the Knockers. As dawn broke, Dug bellowed at them all to shake a leg. The door to Fred's van slid open, screeching loudly, and he sat up, yawning. Dug handed him a mug of tepid tea and he gulped it down. The temperature and humidity had risen with the sun. Even with a breeze whipping up the surface of the river and rustling the limp leaves of trees on both banks, it was going to be an unpleasantly hot voyage to Dartmouth. The smell of the bacon sandwich Dug was offering was making Fred feel a bit sick as he contemplated the hours ahead.

When he emerged from the van he could see Spight supervising the flotilla they would be using for transport of the cargo, moored further downriver overnight and now making its way to the quayside on the last of the incoming tide. They would load up as it turned slack, then float down as it ebbed, using engines to supplement their speed, but only if it looked like they weren't going to get to their destination in time for the agreed rendezvous. The last few days had almost sucked the last of their fuel reserves dry; thankfully, some fossil-based oil was part of the new deal Spight had negotiated with

Dwight, or they might not get all their supplies back from the coast. If that happened, Spight would probably make them all get out and carry it back on their heads like some goddamn safari.

He could hear more vehicles approaching, and saw a small convoy coming over the bridge. That would be Dorcas, with offerings from the county's fat farms. Now therewas someone he needed to keep sweet if he was ever going to take his rightful place ...

'Why have you brought me here?' Stood on the side of the quay wrapped in a blanket, with bare, scabbed legs, her feet pushed into well-worn slippers, the girl sounded sleepy, confused and pissed off, but not scared. She was neither as young nor as pretty as he'd been led to believe by Dorcas's description of her. But she'd do.

'Primrose, you are about to embark on a great adventure.' Fred threw his arms wide in the direction of the river, as if offering her the world.

'Why you calling me Primrose? I'm Alise.'

Fred turned to Dorcas, who wouldn't meet his eye.

'I thought you said you were sending some young maid called Primrose?'

'I couldn't, she's not very ...'

'She done a bunk,' finished Alise, oblivious to the spasm of rage that flickered across the older woman's face. Or was it fear? This could do him some good.

'Really, and how come we don't know anything about this?' Putting stress on the *we*, making a point of his closeness to Spight. 'Of course, seeing as you and me work so close, I wouldn't want to see you in the shit with my father-in-law. I know any lapse in security won't happen again. I could cover for you, this one time.'

Dorcas looked at him suspiciously but forced a smile and nodded. 'I would be grateful.'

'Of course, we'll need your cooperation too, young lady,' Fred said to Alise, with an attempt at a charming smile. 'There's no harm in forgetting your real name for one day, is there? Soon as you're safely on the boat, it won't matter if it turns out you're ... Alice? That's a pretty name.'

She pouted. 'Alise,' she said and turned to Dorcas. 'I can smell bacon sarnies. I'm starved.'

The Matron scowled, but Fred said immediately, 'Of course, let me get you one of those. And tea?'

'I want ketchup, and three sugars.'

'Coming right up.'

He fetched the sandwich and the tea, dipping into his own prized stash of ketchup and sugar sachets from the glove compartment of the van. Alise took the sandwich and stuffed it into her mouth, ketchup oozing down her chin. Her eyes screwed up with pleasure. She seemed oblivious to the hostile stares being sent her way by the other fat farm inmates standing close by in ill-fitting clothes

Fred nodded to them and said to Dorcas, 'It'd be a good idea to get this lot fed and watered too, or we'll never get them on the boats.'

She nodded understanding and called to Agnes, busy talking to one of the skivvies from a Torquay farm. 'Here, you two, get this lot fed.'

Still eating as they went, Alise and the others were loaded onto the first two boats to be brought to the quayside, ten in each, with two members of crew to 'help' in case any of them decided they didn't fancy a cruise and a new life abroad. So far there had been no trouble; they were used to doing what they were told in the expectation their needs would be met in exchange. The Knockers sent them off with boxes of biscuits and flapjacks, that were already being consumed. Heaven help them if their new bodies got too out of shape before they docked in New Jersey.

Additional cargo was being moved from storage in Plymouth, Kingsbridge and Salcombe, to rendezvous with them in Dartmouth. Now loaded, the first two boats cast off and floated a little way downstream, anchoring before the bend in the river to await the rest of the flotilla. Spight was taking no chances that their primary cargo might be spooked by the loading of prisoners and rebels onto the remaining four boats. Fred was practically rubbing his hands with delight when these prisoners were eventually led out of the shed, blinking as they emerged into bright daylight.

There didn't seem any need for the heavily armed presence that greeted them as they came out to stand in a dejected group on the quayside. One of them was so old and doddery Fred was surprised he had been considered fit for sale, and as he thought this Spight had the man removed from the pack and shoved to one side, where he stood swaying on his feet, only the militia man gripping his arm keeping him upright.

'I've given this some thought, Jeremiah, and there's no market for the likes of you – even your organs are worthless,' the Mayor said, to sniggering from a couple of his men. Fred looked again at the old man, and now he remembered him. The crust of dirt and accumulation of years had made their old colleague almost unrecognisable. Well, well, what was he doing with this bunch of renegades?

'I could let you go,' Spight continued, 'but that would hardly send out the message people need to hear. People need to know there are penalties for treason.'

Jeremiah laughed. 'Treason?' he snorted, 'You think you're royalty or summat? You're just a puffed-up, evil old git.' Much louder laughter greeted this remark.

Spight looked furious, his usually pale face flushing all the way over the dome of his balding head. Fred caught himself just in time, keeping his own face straight.

Jeremiah smirked, hawked and spat at the Mayor, the gob of phlegm hitting the midpoint of Spight's immaculate suit. The hawking set him off coughing and he doubled over, his face turning purple behind the dirt. When the coughing trailed off he was hauled upright again, his chin shining with spit and streaks of blood.

Spight drew a handkerchief from his pocket and dabbed at the shiny mucus, his voice tight with suppressed rage as he grated out, 'You appear to be unwell Jeremiah. I think I should put you out of your misery, you traitorous shit. Give me your weapon.' Fred barely saw the gun being snatched from one of his men before the Mayor had fired it and Jeremiah sagged against the man holding him. Blood from the crater in the back of his head, blown out by the point-blank shot, spattered in a wide arc, smears of fluid and brain matter blotching the wooden boards of the shed. The bloodied guard looked at the body sagging against him and almost thrust it away. Jeremiah fell to the cracked concrete and lay still, his head twisted to the side, eyes wide and staring. The hole in his forehead leaked a little.

Echoes of the gunshot rolled downstream. Birds flew from the trees and fled squawking. Fred could see heads craning on the boats moored in the river. Even he was shocked by his father-in-law's actions. He had never seen the man lose control before.

As if he could tell what Fred was thinking, Spight drew himself to his fullest height and smoothed his expression into a neutral mask as he handed the gun back.

'That,' he said, 'was a lesson in what happens to those who betray me.' Did it mean anything that his eyes swept across Fred's face before moving on to the rest of his men?

Fred didn't have time to think about it, as the Mayor started shouting orders to get the boats boarded, they were running out of tide.

Defeat was written in the slumped shoulders and downcast eyes of those that remained. Fred could see the boy he had tortured in their midst, looking pale and sick. He felt a twinge of something and squashed it ruthlessly. There was no room for softness in his world. If he weren't hard and ungiving, he'd never survive to fill Spight's shoes and make the decades of self-sacrifice worthwhile.

His father-in-law had also noticed the boy. He issued an instruction and the youth was dragged from the crowd to stand before the Mayor. Fred saw him try to draw himself erect, but pain kept him stooped. His face was white and dark blood stained the front of his clothes.

Spight grabbed the boy's chin and twisted his face up to look into his own. 'You're no good to me either. There's no way you'll be accepted as cargo. Your friends didn't exactly do you any favours by rescuing you, did they?' He turned to the men who had led the prisoners out. 'Take him back to Bodingleigh. I have another use in mind for him if he heals, and if he doesn't, we'll hang him as a terrorist once we're done in Dartmouth.'

There were a few half-hearted cheers, and cries of dismay from the boy's friends as he was dragged away from them. A middle-aged man lunged forward before being beaten back. He looked familiar. As if he could feel Fred's eyes on him, the man's head turned until their eyes met. The prisoner's face paled, but he didn't look away.

A shock of recognition and a flare of rage shot through Fred as he realised he was looking at an old and unloved acquaintance. The further realisation that Spight must have known the man was there, and hadn't told him, stoked his fury. The heat that spread from his head down his spine made him feel he might combust where he stood.

'Why didn't you tell me you had the Major locked up in that shed? I would have liked to have some time alone with him.' Fred was keeping his voice low, but he knew it must be clear to anyone watching that he was furious with his father-in-law, if only from the way he had stalked up to Spight and was hissing in his ear. He could see Dug and some of the others straining to hear what was being said; he tried to relax and unclench his fists.

Spight looked at him coldly. 'That's precisely why I didn't tell you – I didn't want you damaging the livestock or upsetting the rest of it while you indulged yourself in some stupid vendetta.'

As if shooting the old man hadn't upset them! While they argued he could see consternation spreading all across the flotilla as speculation mounted about what had happened. With Fred still struggling to articulate his outrage, Spight continued, 'I don't know why you're still obsessed. After all, you could say you won, in the end. You got Flora and your place in my household.'

The old man knew why Fred had married his daughter. So what? If anyone approved of a practical over a romantic motivation for marriage, it should be him. It wasn't as if Fred hadn't loved Flora, even after she had betrayed him, and it wasn't as if there had been others lining up to marry a woman pregnant with another man's child. Particularly a woman with a tongue as sharp as Flora's. Spight had played a significant part in returning society to a state in which single women, particularly unwed mothers, were fair game for any man who wanted to take advantage; he should be grateful that Fred had ignored the sly comments of the villagers and got her down the aisle before the bump that would turn into Hector Jr was too visible.

And then he'd raised the boy, enduring people's whispers about Hector Jr's true paternity. It had not been an easy row he'd been hoeing all these years.

Remembering that, and knowing he still had some way to go before he could enjoy the harvest, Fred nodded in seeming acquiescence and forced an ingratiating grin.

'And I'm happy to be part of it still, Sir.'

*

Seeing his father and grandfather in close proximity to each other made Junior nervous. It always had. There was an air of incipient violence whenever the two men were close together for longer than a few minutes. Which could be why they all lived in such a big house with plenty of rooms.

At least if they were looking daggers at each other they wouldn't have eyes for him. He had spotted them from the road before turning his bike onto the quay and they were far enough away for him to be able to slip into shadows before they saw him. Dismounting from the bike, he stashed it in a hedge and crept closer to find a place from which he could observe what was going on without being noticed and sent home.

People were being put on a boat, and it wasn't being done gently. Men were standing by cleats, ready to slip the mooring. If he was going to make a move he had only a few minutes left in which to do it.

At last all of the passengers were on board. The crew were onshore having a last cigarette, waiting for the boats ahead of them to move out into the river and the order to move off. While their backs were turned, Hector crept forward and ran for the stern. There was no ladder, he had to climb down using his toes – jamming them into gaps between the stones of the wall – and then drop, landing as quietly as he could. He picked up one corner of an old tarpaulin lying on the deck and crawled under it, cursing as cold rainwater trickled from its creases and down his neck.

A couple of minutes later he heard other feet landing on the deck and coachroof, men's voices shouting to cast off. The engine rumbled into life below him, sending vibrations throughout the boat.

'Right, let's get this lot downriver then.' His father's voice, sounding bullish, like it always did when he knew he wasn't in charge but was hoping no one else had noticed. Too late to get off the boat now. Hector Jr had better keep his head down if he didn't want a beating.

★

Primrose and Will abandoned the electric car in a derelict farmyard soon after dawn and proceeded on foot. Here, so far from Bodingleigh and anyone who might know them – or wonder why they didn't – they could walk openly on the road, which made progress easier, even on a surface pocked with craters. They were on the outskirts of Dartmouth, still a large town by post-Devolution standards, with a lively if illegal market in goods from traders sailing over from the Brittany coast; strangers were more common and less remarked upon here than elsewhere in Devon.

Other people were heading in the same direction, carrying wares or empty sacks, hoping to do business with the traders, or the small fishing fleet that brought in a daily if somewhat meagre catch. Will heard someone they overtook talking to their companion about the freighter standing offshore, and the deals it was offering. It must be the one Spight was on his way to meet. He checked his watch for the seventh time since they had left the car, and saw they needed to be at their rendezvous within forty minutes or they would be late. They still had two and a half miles to go. It was going to be tight.

Beside him, Primrose was clearly struggling but trying not to show it. Despite the huge weight loss, which must make walking less arduous in the sweltering heat, she could hardly be used to this much exertion after five years of doing little but eat. They had already been walking fast for an hour. Her face was shiny with sweat and she winced frequently as her feet rubbed in the ill-fitting shoes. Pennywort was growing on the shaded side of the road and he picked some for her, showing her how to extract water from the fleshy little pockets. She flashed him a tired smile of gratitude.

She also seemed awed by her new surroundings and overwhelmed by the numbers of people around them. It must all be a big change from life at the fat farm. Will sympathised, but he was frustrated by their slow rate of progress and terrified they would be late. It was hard not to let that show in his voice when he encouraged her to go just a little faster. He should have insisted she go back to Mrs P's house, but she wouldn't hear of it and he hadn't had the heart to leave her behind.

When she'd called back, Mrs Mason had told him to rendezvous with the resistance in Dartmouth at eleven a.m., when they estimated all the 'cargo' would be assembled, but before it reached the freighter. Will checked his watch again and saw it was nearly ten-thirty. At least, from here, the route was downhill all the way. Trees grew to either side of the road and there was some shelter from the sun burning overhead, but it was still hard going.

He stole another look at Primrose as she struggled along beside him, biting her lip, tears glistening in her eyes as each step caused her pain. He could barely recognise the child he had played with at school, or the immense girl he had seen staggering in the dark just a few days before, trying to escape from the fat farm. He was impressed she'd had the courage to make another attempt, on her own; he had never heard of it happening before. If he had helped her the first time, she wouldn't have had to undergo the extreme procedure that had turned her from morbidly obese to disturbingly rounded. And if he was honest with himself, would he still feel the same way about her bravery then? It was all very confusing.

As were the memories of the night before, of him holding and stroking her hand and hearing her breathe in the dark beside him. He had developed a painful erection, which had made sleep impossible. Just thinking about it now was enough to send the blood surging south from his brain.

He was aware of the admiring glances and open leers Primrose was receiving from men they passed. If she noticed the attention, she didn't seem pleased about it. Her head was bent and she avoided eye contact as the crowds thickened. Will was annoyed on her behalf, as well as feeling a hot sort of possessiveness at the thought she might be tempted to smile back, or that one of them might like to take it further than looking. He would punch anyone who tried.

He pushed these thoughts and urges to violence aside. He had a mission to perform, he couldn't afford to let himself become distracted by complicated feelings about girls.

*

A cool breeze blew across the surface of the river but still the heat under the cracked Plexiglass canopy of the old ferry was brutal. The prisoners lay in enervated heaps, too hot and depressed to move.

When he could see the austere, colonial grandeur of the old Royal Naval College up on the hill to his right, and the Major knew Dartmouth was only a short distance away, he stopped fighting it and finally allowed despondency to take a proper hold. All the way downriver he had been waiting for SCREW activists to appear and save the day. He was sure they would take the boats where the river was narrowest, hemmed in by thick woodland to either side. A rope stretched across and suddenly snapping taut as a prow hit it would be all it took to throw the lead boat into confusion and cause a pile-up.

He counted down in his head constantly, trying to work out how long it would have taken for Mrs Mason and the others to miss him and Will, and from there to come up with a plan.

But why should they come and rescue him, when he had gone against strict orders not to put Stage Two in jeopardy by mounting a rescue bid for Mal, and getting his own stupid self captured in turn?

Mal ... Spight had been right; taking him from the fat farm

so soon had put the boy's life in further jeopardy. Now, he would be hanged, and there was not one thing the Major could do to stop it.

As the time passed and nothing happened except the day growing lighter and hotter, he had to admit he was beaten. By the time Dartmouth itself came into view despondency had succumbed to despair.

At least Fred wasn't on this boat but the one keeping close behind, clearly not happy about it, but doing his duty as a good son-in-law. The Major wondered how long it would take for Fred to stick a knife in the old man's back, or in his own.

The Major expected the flotilla to continue on past the town and out into the deep water by the castle, to meet the freighter for a transfer of goods. But instead the small fleet headed for the old harbour and moored up, strung along the ancient pontoon or against the high wall, which loomed over them.

This was the time to throw despair down on the deck and give it a good kicking. This could be his moment.

But heat beat him down and he watched the bustle of the crew through eyes that remained glazed with apathy.

*

Spight had intended to proceed directly to the freighter. He couldn't relax until his cargo was aboard, his payment received and stowed on the boats, and he and it were safely on their way back to Longmarsh. But Dwight had called, insisting on coming on board to inspect the goods before he would sign off on payment. Reluctantly, Spight issued orders for all the boats to tie up.

Once on the quayside, he sent Fred off to find the skipper at the hotel and tell him the cargo awaited his pleasure. He just hoped the ex-fatties wouldn't get spooked. Perhaps shooting Jeremiah had been a bit of an over-reaction, but if there was one thing he could not tolerate it was betrayal. Jeremiah being in league with terrorists had been betrayal of the rankest kind, threatening his authority over his men as nothing else had in all his years in office. But at least he now had a suitable subject for Harrow's experiments, if the boy recovered from his infection. And if he didn't, he had someone for the populace to vent their frustrations on, and to use as a warning to any others seeking to undermine him. A hanging would suffice to serve both ends.

While Spight waited, he put Bob in charge of inspecting the perimeter he had ordered put in place around the ancient dock, to keep unwanted eyes from seeing what was tantamount to a slave auction. No one was to be allowed to come within one hundred yards of the boats, unless they were bringing the last consignment: children. The few businesses located nearby had already been told to take a holiday, and the fish market had been relocated to a dilapidated marina at Kingswear, across the river. Those traders that complained had been given the offer of turning the holiday into permanent retirement, and Spight was pleased to see no shutters had been raised. The hotel was exempt; he was confident its owner would not give them any trouble.

Bob returned and reported the perimeter was in place and being enforced. Shoppers coming in from the outlying villages were being diverted to an impromptu ferry service run by some enterprising youths with access to a pair of leaky rowing boats. Message delivered, Bob fell to biting his nails and staring across the river.

It was looking to Spight very much as if Bob would soon

benefit from permanent retirement himself, and then Spight would be stuck with Fred for his second-in-command. He supposed Fred had earned it. It couldn't be easy being married to Flora, she had a mouth on her that could strip paint. But the man was an oaf with no talent for the subtleties that had kept Spight in power all these years. It wasn't enough to threaten people; you had to know when to offer the carrot as well as to apply the stick, and to be able to read people in order to know which was going to be more effective. Fred just set about himself freely with the stick. He had no finesse.

Perhaps Spight would have to wait for his grandson to become old enough to take over. The boy showed aptitude, but that would mean another decade or so of hard work for Spight. He would be well on his way to eighty years old by then. The thought made him feel tired.

The sound of boots scuffing cobbles reached his ears and he turned to find Dwight almost upon him, huge hand extended to offer another bone-crushing grip. Spight steeled himself and put his hand in the vice-like grasp. Behind him, he could see Fred, and Dwight's Fred-equivalent, eyeing each other up.

''Bout time you showed, was thinkin we'd have to haul anchor to make it up the coast in time.'

Bluster, always bluster.

'I think when you see what we've brought, you'll be happy you stayed.'

The inspection took almost an hour, Dwight insisting on first visiting the warehouse where non-human goods were being stored. Meats, cheeses, vegetables and casks of cider filled the store, stacked high. He could have taken care of this bit of business earlier, Spight thought to himself, suppressing a snarl of impatience as he watched Dwight pawing through potatoes

like he was the King of Spuds and would know blight if it bit
his nose off, before proceeding to inspect every one of the six
boats carrying live cargo.

At least he wasn't stupid enough to say anything untoward
to any of the livestock, taking the hand of the simpering
maiden called Primrose and telling her he couldn't wait to
wine and dine her at the Captain's table, at which she giggled
and blushed prettily. Dorcas's eyes must be failing her if she
thought this girl was the best the West Country had to offer,
but Dwight seemed satisfied he would find a buyer for her.

When it came to the newly captured prisoners, the Captain
passed a cursory eye over them, prodded one or two to see if
they were as scrawny as he feared, and grudgingly
pronounced, 'They'll do.' Most of them looked at him with
blank incomprehension, too traumatised to summon the
energy to fight off his meaty hands, although Spight thought
he saw the Major – slumped on the deck, looking sweaty and
ill – tensing as if he was considering giving it a go. Go on, he
thought, give Fred an excuse to batter you. He could feel Fred
at his shoulder, willing the prisoner on. But the Major said and
did nothing.

'Cargo's not up to the usual standard, I have to say, Spight.
You're gonna have to up your game, you wanna keep doin'
business with us,' Dwight said as they left the last of the boats,
climbing up the ramp that led from the pontoon to the dock.

Spight bridled at this insult to his livestock but perhaps the
man had a point. The insurgents and other prisoners were a
motley bunch.

'I'm working on a new line of product,' he told the skipper
as he rubbed rust from the handrail off his palms.

'Good to know. What kind of product we talkin' about?'

'A new kind of chemical weapon. Air-borne and deadly. I

think your clients will be very happy with it.'

Dwight looked mildly interested as he said, 'I'll be sure and tell 'em. Where's the little 'uns?'

'Nearby, awaiting my word. We thought it better to bring them out last, when you're ready to leave. Which will be …' He made a show of checking his watch.

'Any moment now, don't you worry. I'm as keen to shuck the dust of this hick town off my shoes, as you are to show me the door.'

'And my cargo?' Spight had sent Bob to inspect their goods as soon as they arrived but turned to make a point of checking with his right-hand-man that he had indeed found everything to be as stipulated – though he knew this to be the case as they had discussed it already – and found that, some time during the tour, the man had slipped away.

'Safe,' replied Dwight. 'I'll give you the keys to the warehouse as soon as those babes arrive.'

Spight extended his hand for a final mangling, and they shook on the deal. That done, he keyed in the number programmed into his phone. When it was answered he said, 'Bring the first batch.'

★

The Major watched the two men shake hands and thought, this is it then. A few days at sea, and then what? He doubted he'd make it into a harem. Nope, for him it would be down the mines or into the tar sands for a short stint of soul- and body-destroying labour, speedily followed by an unpleasant death. Not the way he had envisaged rounding out an eventful life. His eyes lingered on Fred, standing next to Spight, just visible at the top of the ramp. If he could just shake off this lethargy and try to take him out, now, even if the attempt killed him …

The thought was interrupted.

From somewhere ashore, there was a bellow of 'NOW!' and a deafening cacophony of bells, whistles and shouting broke out. The Major could not be sure who was behind it, or what it meant, but he did know that right now, while everyone was distracted and looking around in confusion, was his chance. Pushing himself to his feet, he threw himself at a guard, who was staring up at the dock with his mouth open and didn't see the fist heading for his temple. Pole-axed by the blow, the militia man fell to the deck and the Major leapt over him to tackle another guard, alerted by the sound of the first guard falling and approaching fast.

Taken off balance by the motion of the boat, swinging wildly, the guard toppled into the Major's fist and fell hard and sideways. As the guard got to his feet, Irma threw her coat over his head and started beating at him through the heavy wool. Confused, he backed away until the gunwale of the boat was behind his knees, and he fell overboard. Despite the summer heat the water was icy cold; the Major could hear the man gasping for breath when he surfaced. He left him floundering and turned away, looking for the next foe. The remaining three guards were all under attack from their prisoners and the boat would soon be theirs.

The Major hurled himself across the deck, grasped the rusting ladder fixed to the harbour wall and scrambled up until he was standing on the quay.

The prisoners had been put in four boats to stop them conspiring with each other, but that meant there were now four groups of passengers fighting Spight's militia and fewer of them to come to the aid of Spight up on the dock. The Major recognised the gaudily dressed SCREW activists who were closing in on Spight, Fred, the Captain and his crewman. The Captain was grinning, a knife held in each of his enormous hands, and his mate was holding a gun produced from inside his jacket.

All four of them were facing away from the Major and towards the approaching, noisy crowd. Now that he was standing level with them, he could hear some of what was being shouted.

'Come and get it! Come and get some nice young flesh! See our specials! Today only!'

'Don't miss the dish of the day! Get it while it's hot!'

'BARGAINS! WE GOT SOME LOVELY BARGAINS!' This last was amplified and distorted through a megaphone. He recognised Mrs Mason wielding it, and felt a sudden and overwhelming rush of love for her. She hadn't seen him yet. She was too busy shouting at her father and her husband.

They seemed stunned.

★

Will and Primrose didn't hear the bellowed 'NOW!' but they did hear the din that followed. Thanks to the gradient of the hill they were stumbling down, they could see the dock from several streets away, and an acoustic trick of the river, and the hillside on its other side, meant that the brightly dressed people running out of buildings shouting for everyone to come and look at the bargains to be had that day, could be heard clearly in the streets above.

Will put out his hand out to clasp Primrose's arm, bringing her to a staggering stop so they could work out what was happening. He could see Mrs Mason with a loudhailer, berating the Mayor and Fred and two enormous men he didn't recognise, on the water's edge. The Major was behind the four men, and neither they nor Mrs M seemed to notice him as he ran at one of the huge strangers, until he took the man out at the knees with a rugby tackle.

A gun went off and people screamed. A tide of bodies overtook Spight and the others and they were borne to the ground by sheer weight of numbers. Crowds of curious people were emerging from side streets, come to see what was going on and if, indeed, there were bargains to be had. It all looked as if the rebellion was succeeding. The Major and everyone else would soon be rescued.

That was it then. The people destined for slavery were being saved from their unspeakable fate. At last they could pause and catch their breath. The two of them slumped against the wall of a nearby house and waited for their legs to stop trembling from the last sprint down the hill, ignoring the glances of curious and suspicious people emerging into the street to see what all the ruckus was about.

Primrose was clutching her ribs and slid down the wall until she was sitting with her back resting against it. Will joined her. Even here in the shade the heat was punishing.

So that was it. Mission accomplished. It felt like an anticlimax.

Sitting, they could see nothing, though the shouting of the crowds below was still at a high pitch.

Despite his aching legs Will couldn't sit still. After a couple of minutes, he stood and said, 'Prim, I've got to go on. They might still need me.'

Primrose whimpered and made a move to stand.

'No, you stay here, come down when you can.'

'Are you sure?' She looked torn between exhaustion, relief and disappointment.

'Yes.' He took one of the satellite phones Mrs P had given them out of his rucksack, fiddled with it and crouched to scribble something in a page torn from his notebook before handing them to her. 'I'll come back up, or call me when you're ready and I'll tell you where to meet me. The number is on this bit of paper. It's really simple, I've switched it on so just hit the numbers and press Send.'

She took the phone and the bit of paper, looked at the phone with a mixture of fascination and anxiety, and put them both in the pocket of her trousers.

'Well, go on then,' she said and smiled bravely.

He hesitated a moment, patted her clumsily on the arm and stood as he said, 'See you soon.'

★

As the inspection tour moved from the warehouse back to the boats, Bob had slipped away to return a phone call. His phone had been vibrating in his pocket, and Gloria Spight's name was on the screen. Why would she be ringing? Not wanting to draw the attention of her husband, he had waited and ducked down a narrow alley while Spight was distracted by Dwight's questions, before calling her back.

'What do you want?'

'Charming,' she laughed. 'You've been hanging around my husband too long.'

'I'm sorry, darling. Things are tense here.'

'You don't know the half of it. There's someone here who needs to talk to you.'

'Who?'

'Your aunt. Wait a sec.'

There was a moment's pause and then his Aunty Iris started

speaking. 'Sorry, Bob, didn't have your number and couldn't think how else to get hold of you, but Gloria's alright, you can trust her. More than I can trust you – I can't believe you didn't tell me about the live cargo! I'm very disappointed in you.' Bob felt sick with shame. She continued, more kindly, 'You need to know that Will got a message through to the resistance, and there's going to be an interruption to Spight's plans. You can either stay out of the way or help them. The choice is yours. I really hope you do the right thing, this time.'

'When?'

'Right about now, I imagine. Before the boats leave for the freighter. I don't know any more, I think the situation is what you call fluid. I just thought you should know.'

Any moment then. 'Thank you. And I'm sorry Aunty, I know I should have told you. I've got to go.'

'Go well, Bob.' In the background, as he pressed End, he could Gloria speaking to someone, sounding surprised and annoyed.

The call had only taken a matter of minutes, but Spight and the others had disappeared from view by the time Bob left the alley. Which gave him a few moments to decide what to do. It was hard to know what that should be with so little information. This was what he had wanted, the hope that had taken him to his aunt's door, but he risked messing things up if he got directly involved. It was probably better to stay out of the way. Busy with his thoughts, he didn't notice Hector and Gloria's daughter Flora, until he was standing almost on top of her. Dressed in garish red jacket and bright purple trousers, she was peering around the corner of the hotel, holding a stopwatch and a loudhailer in her hands.

'Flora! What are you doing here?'

'Doing a spot of shopping … What the hell do you think

I'm doing? I'm getting in Daddy's way. Don't interfere if you value your skin.'

It wasn't so difficult to make the decision after all, and as soon as it was made he felt much better about himself. This was more important than one person. 'Me, too. Getting in the way, I mean.'

'Really – you? Sorry but you always seemed so much the lickspittle. Though Mummy speaks highly of you.'

Bob coughed. Best not tell her why just now, too distracting. 'Anything I can do?'

'Only if you can get that minion out of the way.' She gestured towards the corner and Bob put his head round cautiously. One of the militia men forming the perimeter of Spight's negotiations was standing in the next street, smoking a cigarette and looking bored. Beyond him, Bob could see Spight, Fred and the others standing by the water's edge.

'When?'

Flora checked her stopwatch. 'Now would be good.'

Bob approached the militia man and told him he needed to move his post two streets out. The man shrugged and moved off in the direction Bob was indicating. Once he had passed her hiding place, Flora emerged, running into the square.

'NOW!' she shouted. Doors opened, and dozens of people boiled out of the buildings facing onto the open space. Bob stood and watched. The minion he had sent away was standing looking confused but, seeing Bob, seemed content to stay where he was for now.

★

Before Primrose had a chance to wish him luck Will had gone, running down the street towards the town square. She was

devastated to be left behind but he was right, she was in too
much pain to move just now, and Will had been training for
this for years, from what he had been telling her as they made
their journey. She couldn't ask him not to go, however
terrified she was to be left alone.

She leaned her head back against the wall and closed her
eyes. Colours flared before her eyes in time with her racing
pulse, the display slowing as her heartbeat and breathing
calmed.

Voices nearby brought her back to her surroundings.
People were still standing in the street looking down the hill
and muttering to each other, but it wasn't them she had heard.

A dozen yards from where she was sitting, a side street led
up from the dockside to the warren of alleys and terraces that
covered the hillside this side of the river. Hurrying up it,
moving away from the water, were a middle-aged woman and
a man with a beard, both pushing strollers holding babies of
about six months old. There were slightly older children
strapped to their chests and backs. Behind them was another
woman with a toddler propped on each hip.

The adults all looked strained. The man was speaking
angrily but Primrose couldn't hear what he was saying. None
of the children looked as though they were related to each
other, showing a variety of skin tones, hair colours and facial
features. Another moment and they had crossed the road and
disappeared. Primrose followed them with her gaze, Will's
words of the previous night reverberating around her head:
'They don't just sell grown ups. It's babies too.'

With difficulty, she pushed herself up to standing on shaky
legs.

What should she do? With no one to tell her, she was
almost paralysed with indecision. What would Will do? Or Mrs

P? That steadied her and enabled her to think. First, she needed to follow them and see where they went.

She hurried to the corner and turned right, then slowed down so she could keep them in sight but wouldn't catch up. The odd family group carried on up the road before going through the front door of a mid-terrace house. Should she call Will? Or should she find out more first? Primrose took the phone and Will's scrap of paper out of her pocket. She keyed in the number, then slipped the phone back in her pocket without pressing Send. She needed more information before she called for help.

Not giving herself time to think or talk herself out of it, Primrose went straight to the house, and knocked on the door. There was a moment of delay before it was opened by the woman who had been carrying the toddlers. With a shock, Primrose realised she knew her from her first year at the fat farm.

'What do you want?' the woman asked suspiciously, looking past her and up and down the street.

'Esther? It's me, Primrose, from the farm.'

'Primrose? What you doing here?'

'Oh, er, Spight sent me to lend a hand.'

'Spight? He looked like he had his own hands full.'

'That was just a trap to get the insurgents out in the open. He'll mop them up and then he'll send for the babies. He'll contact me when he's ready. See, he's given me a phone.' Primrose waved it at the woman before returning it to her back pocket.

'Well, you'd best come in then.' Esther turned and led the way into the house. Primrose took a deep breath and followed her inside.

EMERGING FROM THE SHADOWS

It was risky, working in daylight, but they were against the clock now. Merryn just had to hope no one would be passing who could see over the overgrown hedge and observe them clearing the overgrowth from the few solar panels that had been left by raiders, and bringing in more from the vans parked inside the field. Stage Three had to be complete by the time the call came in from Mrs Mason, or all their years of scheming would have been wasted. It was unlikely they would get another chance. Merryn was fully aware of the weight of responsibility resting on him but tried to concentrate on every separate electrical connector. If one failed it could ruin their plan.

It was stiflingly hot under the panels of black glass, but the appearance of the sun had been greeted with delight when it rose, bloated and red, from the horizon. The recent weeks of cloud and rain had been a worry, and had slowed down the work of local operatives, leaving him with more to do. He was falling behind.

It didn't help that Mrs Mason had taken a large proportion of their agents with her to Dartmouth and he was working with only the handful that could be spared. Everything had sped up after the mad and reckless actions of the Major. He couldn't fault the man for caring about his recruit, but could curse him as he set to the task of feverishly checking yet another set of connectors. They were rusted through. That was another twenty minutes or so gone while he replaced them. Meanwhile someone was cleaning the panel above him, and cold, dirty water was seeping through his shirt and soaking his skin.

★

Once she was inside the house Primrose had to admit to herself she had no idea what she was doing. Her plan had consisted of getting through the front door. Now here she was, being led along a dim and dingy corridor, past a small front room to a kitchen at the back of the house, lit by a small window and a glazed back door, but still gloomy. There was no sign of the two younger babies but the toddlers and the others, whom she guessed to be about a year old, were all in the kitchen.

The one year olds were sitting on the floor under a table, around which the toddlers were running, screaming with delight. Esther gestured towards a chair by the table. She looked exhausted, aged beyond her thirty something years, with grey streaks in dull brown hair that hadn't been washed in a while.

'Where are the others?' Primrose asked as she sat down. The toddlers started using her as something to attack each other from behind. She tried to ignore them.

'Upstairs, changing nappies.' Esther replied. 'How come you got out the farm?'

'Dorcas never got me to sign. I decided I'd had enough so I asked for something else to do. Spight calls me in when he needs to.' This was like lying to Agnes all over again. It was almost worrying how good she was at it. Maybe all those years of reading silly stories were paying off in this ability to spin a tale from a slender thread.

'Funny … he just called and didn't say nothing about traps. Or you.' Esther seemed more confused than suspicious.

'Well, like you saw, he's got his hands full. Guess it slipped his mind. I'm just here to help wipe bums and pass on instructions when there's a new rendezvous arranged.'

'You think he's going to get that rabble under control?'

'Sure. Like I said, it was all planned like that.' She shot out a hand and stopped one of the children from hitting the other on the head with a sauce bottle grabbed from the table. Taking the bottle off him, she put it gently down in the centre of the table, out of reach.

'Not what it looked like to me.'

'Well, who else knows you're here, eh?' Primrose put some tetchiness into her tone. It always worked for Dorcas. 'It's good to see you, Esther.'

The girl seemed underwhelmed at their reunion. 'Maybe you can help me get this pair washed up a bit. Don't want them starting new lives with mucky faces.'

★

When Will arrived at the dock it was to find that the day had not yet been decisively won. Emerging from the shadows of a lane running down the side of an old half-timbered building, he could see that Spight, Fred and the two big men were in custody, sitting on the ground with their arms tied behind their backs, being guarded by Mrs M, who was holding a gun. A larger group of underlings were tethered together nearby. As he drew closer he could see the Major and several members of the resistance down on the pontoons, trying to board boats containing caches of young people, who looked confused but were not getting involved in efforts to defend or board the boats. Knots of townspeople were standing around the quay and the square, watching what was going on, looking interested but not as though they had much stake in the outcome.

On one of the boats, a young woman pushed her way out of the cabin and stood on deck. 'What's going on?' she demanded.

The Major ducked under a heavy swipe from an oar, looking close to falling before spreading his legs wide to retrieve his balance.

'We're trying to rescue you,' he shouted to her.

'From what?' she asked.

'Being sold off to the highest bidder.'

She laughed shortly. 'I been property all my life love, what's the drama?'

Spight's men were looking uneasy, but the oar-wielding guard was edging closer again.

The Major shouted to her, 'What, exactly, do you think is going on here? Where do you think you're off to?' He signalled to his men and women to stop their attempts to board, and wait.

'I'm going to America to start a new life.'

'Doing what?' he asked.

'I dunno. Get myself a job I guess. Or find a rich man to marry.'

'Is that what they told you?'

'Didn't really tell me anything, just told me I had to go 'cos Primrose run off and they needed someone else to take her place.'

'They were going to send Primrose off to breed babies,'

Will shouted from the top of the wall. The Major looked up, astonishment and joy flitting across his face before he turned back to the girl on boat. He motioned for Will to continue.

'That's what she told me. She was going to be on a baby farm, but first they took all her fat off, so she'd be all like ...' He gestured with his hands in an hourglass shape and blushed. 'So that men would like her I guess.'

'Like this, you mean?' The girl was wearing a very worn and diaphanous nightgown, which she lifted up to her shoulders. Underneath, she was wearing nothing but an off-white pair of knickers; her pale skin glowed in the sunshine, where it wasn't marred by angry-looking wounds. She was more rounded than Primrose, or at least as much of Primrose as Will had seen in his furtive glances at her. He blushed harder and nodded. Most of the other men on the boat had stopped dead and jaws had dropped.

The girl shrugged and dropped the nightgown back in place, before stooping to pick up a boathook and one of the fenders lying at her feet, waving them in the direction of a man who was sidling closer, shouting at him, 'I'd like to get off this boat *right* now, *with* my friends, and if one of you twats gets too close, I'll kill you!'

★

Both toddlers were screaming at the indignity of having their faces and hands scrubbed. The younger children under the table were watching them solemnly, sucking on their fingers. The man and woman she had seen with the babies had not yet come downstairs. Primrose could hear the crying of more than one baby through the ceiling above her head. The house was small; she expected there to be only two bedrooms upstairs, maybe a bathroom. How many children were crammed in here?

Should she ring Will and ask to be rescued? It must have been at least fifteen minutes since she had entered the house, and he'd been gone nearly half an hour. What was happening down at the square?

Esther was offering her a drink from a collection in the cupboard above the counter. The vivid colours reminded her of fizzy sweetness and her tastebuds craved the sugar.

She was almost dribbling as she said, 'Yes, please.'

The sugar made her dizzy, swiftly followed by an acrid burning on her tongue. After a couple of huge glugs, she forced herself to put the glass down and asked for some water instead.

'Suit yourself.' Esther took her glass, drained it in one swallow and handed it back to her so Primrose could fill it from a jug on the counter top. Esther guzzled the rest of her own glass and refilled it. Her lips and teeth were stained orange as she smiled in satisfaction.

'So, new lives. Do you know where they're going?' Primrose asked.

'I dunno. Somewhere over there.' Esther gestured in the direction of the Atlantic. 'The Land of the Free they call it. One of these days Spight'll let me go with a batch, get myself a job as a nanny. Might even go see if I can find my own babies. They'd be mostly grown now.'

'You had more than one?' Esther had been one of the skivvies when Primrose first arrived at the fat farm. She had left suddenly, amid rumours that she was pregnant by one of the few male inmates. It was assumed she had been shipped off to relatives to hide her shame and give birth in secret. Her lover had also disappeared. It had been a huge scandal.

'Two girls. Twins. Lovely little things they were. I loved them to bits, but Mayor Spight explained how they would have much better lives over there. People to love 'em – not just me, but a proper family. Not people looking down their noses because I got myself pregnant without a hubby. Proper jobs when they grows up, not just labourin' in a factory or on a farm like here.'

'Got yourself pregnant?' Primrose didn't know a great deal about sex, but she knew making a child took two. 'How? I mean, I remember when you left, I heard it was one of us, one of the boys, that was the dad.'

'It's just a sayin'. You bit thick or something? Dorcas wouldn't break his contract and let him leave, but she chucked me out. The Mayor found me a place, with some other single mums, and let me stay there when my babies was gone. I been lookin' after babies ever since. I like bein' round them, and lookin' after 'em. Feels like they're mine then, for a while.' Esther looked sad as she cradled the glass of orange liquid to her cheek. At her feet, the two toddlers had stopped crying and were examining bits of fluff from under the dresser and smearing them on their faces.

A baby farm. That's what this sounded like. Primrose felt sick.

Heavy feet descended the stairs. The man she had seen earlier pushed into the room and glared at her.

'Thought I heard voices. Who the fuck are you?'

★

Outnumbered by their prisoners five to one, it didn't take long for the demoralised guards to surrender. With Spight captured, the fight was lost anyway.

As the Major took charge of organising erstwhile prisoners into jailers, Alise and the others disembarked and stood in chattering groups, trying to make sense of what they had been told. Will sat on the harbour wall and waited for the Major. After the last of the militia was herded onto the biggest boat and it had left the pontoon to moor up in the deepest part of the river, the Major climbed the ladder to the shore and sat down beside him.

'I'm guessing I have you to thank for getting word out to the resistance,' he said, and gave Will's shoulder a grateful squeeze.

'It's Bob we should thank. If he hadn't pretended to fall over and told me to go to Mrs P, I'd never have got away or known where to go.'

'Bob? And Mrs P? We've got plenty to talk about. But there's a lot to do first.'

'What do you want me to do? Only, I left someone up the hill, I should go find her and bring her down here.'

'A girl eh? That Primrose you were talking about?'

Will nodded and blushed.

'She escaped from the farm then? She sounds resourceful. By all means, go and get her. We'll be loading up and heading back to Longmarsh once we've had a chance to regroup.'

★

Esther repeated Primrose's story to the angry-looking man, calling him Trevor. He wasn't buying it. Nor was the woman who came in as Trevor was asking for the second time who was she really? Why was she there? The children were picking up on the tension in the room and starting to whine. Primrose reached out to the toddler nearest her and tried to soothe him, but he was snatched up into the arms of the nameless woman, who hissed at her and squeezed the child so hard he began to cry in earnest. Echoing cries answered him from upstairs. Primrose counted at least three different wails, then another two joined in.

'Look, I'm just here to help.' Which was true after a fashion. She was becoming too unnerved to lie now and had to put her hands under her legs, so no one could see they were starting to shake. What on earth had she been thinking, coming into the house?

Looming over her where she sat at the table, Trevor was big and real and his anger and suspicion was terrifying as he snarled, 'We don't need help.'

All the children in the kitchen were crying now. Esther looked confused and was looking from Primrose to Trevor and back again.

'I'll go then. Don't worry, I won't get you in trouble with Spight. I'll just tell him everything is, you know, fine. He can send someone else when he's ready for you.' Primrose stood up. The woman with the child was between her and the door. She edged in that direction and the woman moved out of the way, but Trevor moved into the space she vacated, and Primrose was trapped.

'Yeah, and how we gonna find out this new rendezvous Esther said you was here to arrange?'

'You just made that not my problem.' She tried to project some bravado into the words but her voice was wobbling.

'I think you'd best stay and wait 'til we hear from Spight. Sit. Or,' and he leered at her, 'maybe we should get to know each other upstairs. I get first dibs on all the breeders. Just ask Esther.' He moved closer and his hand cupped one of her breasts and squeezed, painfully.

Primrose cried out, too shocked to say anything and too scared to move. His other hand grabbed her arm and he started pulling her towards the door.

'You don't want to do this,' she said, resisting with all her strength but unable to stop herself being dragged across the room.

'Oh, but I do, girly.' The hand squeezing her breast let go and grabbed his groin. He grinned at her. His teeth looked mossy.

Her dad used to call her 'girly'. She hated it.

One of the chairs was within reach. She grabbed it with her free hand and managed to skid it across the linoleum until it slammed into the side of his knee. He yelped and let go of her arm. Primrose backed away, straight into Esther.

'Grab her!' screamed Trevor.

Esther grabbed Primrose by both arms, but her heart wasn't in it and she was a lot smaller than Trevor. Primrose wriggled free and ducked around the table until all three adults were on the other side of it. The kitchen door was behind her and she tried the handle without taking her eyes off Trevor. It was locked. Stalemate. She couldn't get out, they couldn't get to her.

Time to call Will. She reached for her back pocket.

Which was when she realised the phone had fallen out of her pocket in the struggle and was lying at Trevor's feet. His eyes tracked from her horrified gaze, to her breasts, and down to the phone. With a triumphant cry he picked it up and peered at the screen.

'Who's on this number then eh?' he sneered. 'The Mayor?' His thumb pressed the Send button.

⋆

The sun was still climbing a cloudless sky. The afternoon was stiflingly hot and Will was sweating as he trotted back up the hill. He was almost at the place he had left Primrose when the phone in his pocket rang and he stopped to answer it.

'Primrose?'

'Who's this?' It was a man's voice; an angry man. Was it someone from the rebellion? But he was sure the number on the screen was the one for the phone he had left with Primrose.

'This is Will. Who are you?'

'Never the fuck you mind.' The line went dead.

With a rising sense of dread, Will resumed his journey, increasing his pace into a full run. Nearly there.

She wasn't where he had left her. The people who had come out to investigate the commotion earlier had gone back into their houses. The streets were deserted.

⋆

Esther was looking shocked at the sight of the knives Trevor had found in a drawer and was holding in both hands; a carving knife in one and a bread knife in the other. The children were still crying. The other woman still hadn't spoken but hugged the child she was holding tightly.

Primrose knew she didn't have much time left. Trevor would back her into a corner and she had nowhere to go. She risked a quick look at the counter top to her right, searching for something she could use as a weapon. The best it could offer was a heavy frying pan and she grabbed it, holding it up in front of herself. Oil dripped onto her hands.

'So, who was that?' Trevor asked. 'Wasn't the fuckin' Mayor.'

'Probably one of his men.'

'Didn't sound like a man, sounded like a boy. I can show you the difference, you want to put that pan down and come with me.'

'I'm not going anywhere with you.'

Trevor snatched up a child from under the kitchen table and put the edge of the bread knife against its neck. The little girl's face, already red from crying, crumpled as she gave out an even louder wail.

'You don't do what I say, and this girl is goin' to suffer. That I can promise you.'

Horrified, Primrose stuttered, 'You can't!'

'Oh, but I can. I can do whatever I like.' He smiled at her with chilling confidence.

Esther's voice was distraught as she shouted, 'Trevor, put her down!'

'Don't be stupid, Esther!' Trevor's voice was contemptuous, ignoring Esther as he moved towards the kitchen table, the little girl held under one arm, the knife still at her throat. He didn't see Esther pick up a heavy saucepan from the stove to smack it across the back of his head with a loud *CLANNNGG*. He stood swaying for a moment before he toppled sideways, giving her time to pull the little girl away and hold her close, crooning soothing noises. Trevor hit the stained lino hard. The phone fell out of his shirt pocket, skittering across the floor and under the table. Primrose stooped and seized hold of it.

Will answered on the first ring, sounding frantic. 'Primrose?'

'Will! Come quick. There's babies here, they're going to

send them away.' The truth of what she was saying hit her hard and she was trying not to cry. Across the room, the two other women held the children and looked at her with empty eyes.

'Where are you?' he asked urgently.

★

The sound of several babies crying convinced Will he had found the right house. Half a dozen or so young voices raised in misery. When he banged on the front door no one came to answer it, but he could hear raised voices inside. He climbed onto the sill of the bay window beside the door and broke the glass with his elbow so he could release the catch. Dropping down onto the bare boards of an unfurnished room, he realised the voices had stopped. The crying continued.

In the kitchen at the back of the house he found two women looking at him fearfully over the heads of the children they were holding. Primrose was on the far side of the kitchen table, holding a heavy frying pan. A man lay on the floor, either dead or out cold.

'Will!' Primrose cried with evident relief, and put the pan down on the table with a bang. 'They won't believe me. I've been telling them what really happens to the babies and they won't believe me.'

'Don't worry about it Prim. I've called the Major and he's sending a team to help. They can argue the toss with them I want to get you out of here, now.' He turned to the two women, and said, 'The Mayor's been taken into custody on behalf of the free people of Devon. No one is coming for those children except us, and if you want to walk away from this with an amnesty, you'll give them up.'

There was a pounding on the front door, and he could hear the Major shouting his name. Will ran to let him in and found half a dozen SCREW activists including the Major and Mrs M waiting impatiently on the step. He led them back to the kitchen. One of the women was taking a key from a nail by the back door, thrusting the child she was carrying into Primrose's arms. She shot one terrified look over her shoulder as she opened the door and fled. Will made to follow her but the Major put a restraining hand on his arm.

'Let her go. It's going to be a whole new world for her out there, let her go to meet it. We came here for the kids.' He squatted down by the table and held out his hand to one of the toddlers sitting under it. It took one look at him and resumed crying in earnest.

Mrs M – the Major had filled him in on her true identity, but Will would never be able to think of her as anything else – examined the unconscious man and pronounced him likely to be concussed, and in need of medical observation.

'What will happen to them? The kids?' Primrose asked. They were sitting outside the back of the house, on a low wall, the hill looming above them. Six babies had been found upstairs and brought outside. They lay in the cardboard boxes they had been found in, kicking their legs and waving at sunbeams that shone through the leaves of a stunted cherry tree. The four older children were in the kitchen with Esther and the three activists, who were heating up jars of food they had found in one of the cupboards and trying to establish if the children could tell them their names.

'We'll try to identify their parents,' replied the Major. 'If we do, we'll have to establish whether the kids were snatched or sold. Which won't be easy. If they were sold, we'll have to find foster parents.'

Will asked, 'How come we only just found out this was happening? I mean, we've been watching Spight for years, and had no idea. And you ...?' He paused, not sure how to proceed.

Mrs M smiled ruefully. 'Me? His daughter? Well, funnily enough, he didn't talk business with me, at least not in detail. I knew something was going on besides the fat farms, and I wondered what happened to the people who just seemed to drop off the map, but I never thought ...' Her voice wavered and she cleared her throat. 'I'm guessing it started about a year after my son was born. Hardly any crops grew that summer, it was so wet and cold. Everyone got sick, so even when there was a crop there was no one to bring it in. Everything just rotted in the ground. The whole of Devon was close to starving, then suddenly there was imported food and medicines coming in. No one questioned it, we were just grateful. I reckon he kept it secret because he knew the reaction there'd be. Maybe Bob can tell us more.'

She looked sad. It couldn't be easy being the daughter of the bad guy, even, or maybe especially, if you were the good guy. Will remembered what the Major had told him about there being no bad guys, but he had trouble believing it.

The Major squeezed Mrs M's shoulder and changed the subject, saying, 'It's time to get going. If you two want a ride home, you'd better come with us. We aren't done yet.'

Primrose looked up. 'Aren't we?' she asked wearily.

Will sympathised, but a rising tide of excitement buoyed him up as he asked, 'Stage Three?'

'Stage Three. Don't worry, you can sleep on the boat.'

'How is Mal doing?' he asked, as he offered a hand to Primrose to help her up. He kept hold of it as they headed towards to the street.

'That's another reason to get a move on. He isn't here. Spight sent him back to the village, and if we don't get a move on he'll be executed or used as a hostage. And I'm sorry Will, but I've worse news about Jeremiah.'

The Major described what had happened on the Longmarsh quayside. Poor Jeremiah. Will felt sick at the thought of the helpless old man being shot down, his body left like so much rubbish.

They had to make sure something similar didn't happen to Mal. Will speeded up his pace as they headed down the hill and soon he was once more dragging Primrose along behind him.

The baby snatcher – head bandaged and walking but still groggy – was loaded onto the first boat, along with Spight and Fred. The other consignments coming from Plymouth, Salcombe and Kingsbridge had been headed off, the human cargo released and given shelter while Stage Three was completed. The militia were to be kept under restraint in the warehouse holding the New Jersey cargo, until the will of the people had been heard.

The skipper and his crew were allowed to leave, and warned they faced a hostile reception if they returned. The skipper shrugged, and said there were other British ports, ready and willing to trade for cash.

'Don't be so sure,' the Major told him. 'Word'll be getting out and you might find yourself less welcome than you think. We're sending people all over the country, telling everyone what's been going on here.'

Alise and the others were invited to join the flotilla for a ride back to Longmarsh but told they could do what they liked. They all elected to return. Alise seemed to sum up their feelings when she nodded towards Spight and said, 'I want to see that bastard get what's coming to him.' And she added, with a slight frown, "Sides, where else am I gonna go now?'

Bob was the only other of Spight's men to accompany the resistance, getting in the first boat but taking care to stay out of the way, particularly of Spight. The Mayor himself – whatever else he was, he was still the elected leader of the county – chose to sit on a hard bench at the front. Will thought it interesting that Fred did not join him, but went to the other end and sat above the engine. Fred's face was stony; his hands were bound in front of him but he was otherwise unshackled. He ignored his wife, who gave him a wide berth as she and the Major brought the children on board with the woman from the baby farm, who refused to be parted from them.

The toddlers were fascinated by the boat and the passage of water in its wake, and ran through and around the legs of the adults, shrieking. Primrose stayed close to them. So much for sleep, but she looked happy as she chased them and they squealed with pleasure. Will sat himself down out of the wind and closed his eyes. The movement of the boat lulled him and soon he was snoring peacefully.

★

Cold rage was a familiar state but could not describe his feelings now. Murderous fury was inadequate, but it came closer. Spight watched his enemies wandering around the boat – and the brats running – without a care, while his own mind was in turmoil and his feelings seethed. How had this happened? How could he have been betrayed so completely?

Refilled with diesel liberated from the skipper's cargo, the engines were run all the way upriver – such wastefulness, did they not know how hard he had worked to get that fuel? – and with that, and the rising tide running in their favour, it took just over an hour for the fleet to arrive in Longmarsh. While the boats were being tied up, Flora came and sat next to him. Spight thought he might actually have a stroke. He could not speak for the rage-fuelled bile choking his throat.

'Hello, Daddy,' she said.

He was wrong. He could speak, enough to say, 'You're no daughter of mine.'

'Sadly, I am. I checked with Mummy.' Her tone was light but her words bitter.

'Neither of us will ever be able to forgive you.'

'Oh, I think Mummy might – who do you think has been helping me all these years? Covering for me. Looking after Junior when I was away so much.'

Spight looked at his daughter in shock. This betrayal by those he held dear – even if he ignored them most of the time, hardly ever thought about them, and shouted at them when they came to him with inane concerns – had hit him hard. All that he did, he did for them, didn't they realise that?

His daughter seemed to sense his feelings. Her face softened as she said, 'We did this for you, Daddy.'

How dare she throw his own thoughts back at him as justification for stabbing him in the back? And not just her, but his wife too. There was only Fred and Junior left. And Bob. Where was Bob?

'It's his fault, isn't it?' He pointed at the Major, busy supervising the transfer of babies off the boat to God knew where. Some socialist love shack commune where they'd be raised like God-benighted hippies of the previous century.

Flora looked annoyed again. 'It's nothing to do with him.'

'I knew he'd be back to cause trouble sooner or later. After leaving you in the lurch.'

'There was no lurch Daddy, I made my own choices and I chose to stay. For my own reasons. So that this could happen.' She gestured up at the people milling on the quayside, clearly trying to hear what was being said.

Spight drew his spine erect and stood up, looming over her. 'Raising his spawn under my roof? I should have made you have an abortion. Or drowned him at birth!'

'Hector!' Flora looked aghast, staring beyond him.

'Grandad?' Spight turned to see his grandson standing behind him, looking between the two of them with a look of horror and confusion on his face.

★

Junior had fallen asleep on the journey downriver. When he awoke it was from a familiar nightmare, the sound of his own screaming loud in his ears: Dad! *Noooooo!* For a terrifying moment he thought he had actually yelled aloud, but all was quiet, no one coming to investigate. The sounds of the engine and water moving past the boat were gone, and he could hear voices nearby. They must have arrived. When he pushed back a corner of the tarpaulin and peeked out, the prisoners were standing on deck, guarded by men he recognised from the local troop of militia. He wiped away the tears that had leaked from his eyes.

There was no sign of his father, but he stayed undercover anyway, sure he would get in trouble if he was caught hiding. Hours must have passed; he was stiff, thirsty and hungry. All he had to eat was a couple of scavenged biscuits in the pocket of his coat, which made him thirstier but stopped the ache in his belly. It was while he was licking the crumbs from his fingers that the ruckus started, with a bellow of, '*NOW!*'

From where he was lying under the tarpaulin he couldn't tell what was going on or hear much beyond a general rabble of raised voices, but he could tell it was a big deal by the reaction of the people on the boat. His grandfather's men were twitchy, craning to see, gripping weapons harder. He could see the lines of tension in the prisoners' bodies. Loud footsteps sounded on metal. Someone was coming down a ramp from the quay. The prisoners were delighted, shouting greetings. Their jailers were spooked, backing away from the side of the boat and flourishing bats, knives, cudgels and guns he suspected would be unloaded.

A militia man rushed past him to the stern and started to untie the line attaching the boat to the wall. Another, backing away, was tripped by an ankle extended into his path. As he went down, prisoners swarmed him. A young woman emerged from the scrum with a cudgel and threw it, hard, at the man untying the line, and he went down, narrowly avoiding landing on Junior, who huddled, terrified, as terrorists jumped aboard and attacked his grandfather's men. Within moments the balance of power had shifted, and he was no longer hiding in expectation of a beating from his dad but in fear of his life.

What passed next was a chaotic whirl. The ongoing battles on the water culminated in a shouted conversation – between a barely clothed and then nearly naked girl on a boat, a middle-aged insurgent on a pontoon and a boy on the dock – that made no sense. His world, like the boat some time later, had become unmoored. When the unconscious body of the man lying next to him was removed, Junior remained as still as possible so they wouldn't discover him.

When next he dared to peek out, he saw his grandfather; unharmed, unshackled, but under guard, in the front of the boat. His mother – his *mother* – was walking around freely. What was *she* doing here? His father was sitting close by, head lowered, staring at the deck, not quite within reach if Junior were to stretch an arm out from under the tarp. Children had arrived from somewhere and were running around the boat, being chased by a girl who looked like a skinnier version of the fat girl he enjoyed baiting at the farm.

The noise of the engine was too loud for him to hear anything of what was being said, and it was a confusing hour or so that followed, in which he pondered what the near-naked girl had said, so disturbed he barely thought about her body at all.

She had been told everyone on the boat was being sold, along with a load of other people. Slavery was bad. His grandfather said so. It was why he worked so hard to do what he did, so his people would have choices, and wouldn't become slaves to repressive laws, like most of the rest of the world. In which case, what Junior had heard could not be true. The insurgent must have been lying. It was the only thing that made sense.

Silence. The engines had stopped and that brought immediate concern for his own safety, and that of his family. Maybe now he could do something to help his grandfather. He watched as his mother walked over to where the old man was sitting and they started talking. He couldn't hear the words, but his grandfather was obviously furious. His father was pulled to his feet and led ashore, then a bunch of babies were being handed over. This end of the boat was now empty, with no one nearby or looking in his direction; he could pretend he'd just climbed onboard. Hector Jr pushed the tarpaulin aside and stood up, stiff from all the hours of lying concealed, wobbling as the boat moved about on its mooring.

As he approached, his grandfather was saying something about it all being the fault of the man handing over the babies. Junior turned to look at him, curious. It was the insurgent who had been talking to the girl in the nightgown earlier. Mum was denying it. Nothing they were saying made sense. Until he heard his grandfather – the man he feared, respected and loved more than any other – say he should have drowned him, Junior, at birth, and his world came crashing down.

★

Once the flotilla arrived at the Longmarsh quay and the babies and children had been taken to a nearby safe house, where they could be looked after by volunteers, the Major contacted Merryn to ask how Stage Three was coming along, and to tell him about Mal. Flora was looking upset, which was understandable considering she had been talking with her father and there was no way that had gone well, but she took out her own phone to ask her mother to activate the Door Knockers, telling people from the village to come down the hill to a public meeting in Longmarsh that evening, and to organise transport.

While she was distracted, he had her father, husband and son taken off the boat. None of them were speaking to each other, the two men looking furious and Junior shocked. This was not the time to introduce himself as the boy's actual father. The very thought of that conversation made his hands sweat. It had been a long time since he had allowed himself to think that he had a son. The wound of losing Flora when she decided to stay with her father, then discovering she had given birth to his child, was still open. The times they had worked together since Hector Jr had been born had hardly been conducive to discussing their relationship, or any potential role he might have as a parent, only serving to tear the scab and remind him he still hadn't healed.

Several SCREW activists surrounded him as he took the three of them to the boatshed where he and the others had spent the night. Fred was pushed inside and the door locked, and the Major could not suppress a small stirring of satisfaction as he turned the key, removed from Fred's pocket, in the lock.

Jeremiah's body had already been taken away, but the stains of his blood and brain matter were barely dry on the concrete outside the shed. The Major paused a moment in sorrow, while Spight was put in a car, and three muscular agents detailed to keep him in it until he could be driven up to the Civic Square. Hector Junior regarded him with hostile eyes.

'What are you going to do with me?' he asked.

'Nothing. Your mother needs to talk to you. I know today must have been very confusing, but she can explain everything.' He wasn't in the habit of talking to children, only cadets. He was using his officer voice and it didn't seem to be going down well with Junior – a suspicion confirmed when the boy turned on his heel and fled away from the quayside. The Major shouted at him to stop but the boy kept running. Shit! What was he going to tell Flora?

When Flora arrived, clutching her phone, she was too worried to ask him where their son was.

'Mum didn't answer. I called Mrs Harrow – she said Mrs Prendaghast is being held at the school. Someone found her at the gatehouse, talking on a phone she shouldn't have had. Harrow's got a mob keeping her under guard. She's very pleased with herself. She's expecting Dad to have her hanged when he gets back, along with Mal. I asked about Mum and she got really cagey – I think they might be holding her, too, but Mrs Harrow doesn't want me to know.' Flora's voice was wobbling.

A further complication, and with Stage Three so close to completion. Mal already needed rescuing. Now Mrs Prendaghast and Flora's mother too. The three of them from two different locations. All the Major wanted was to lie down somewhere, preferably with this woman he loved, and sleep for a month or two.

'Does Mrs Harrow know about you? Does she know about any of this?' He gestured around them, at the ex-prisoners and fat farm residents gathered on the quayside.

'I don't think so, or she wouldn't have told me anything. I don't think even her grapevine is good enough to get word back that fast.'

'Well, that's something.'

'What do we do? It won't take long for news to spread, and then we don't know what will happen to them.' Her hands were clenching and twisting, wringing the phone. He took hold of them gently and removed it from her grasp.

'I'll go. I'll take Will and that young Primrose. You wait here for Merryn, he's on his way to take care of things at this end.' He squeezed her arm. 'And don't worry.'

'Very funny. And where's Hector got to?'

★

Junior had only run as far as would take him out of sight of the terrorist, then stopped and hid in a bush, waiting for the pounding of feet. Silence. No one was following him, he was safe.

What could he do? Something weird was going on, he

didn't understand what was happening to his family, or what his grandfather had meant when he'd said that hateful thing, but he had to do something. His grandfather was beyond his reach, there was nothing he could do under the eyes of the three guards, but maybe he could help his dad. Junior climbed out of the bush and started walking back towards the boatshed. The terrorist was standing some way off, talking to his mother. The way they stood, close together, made him grind his teeth until his jaw ached.

An armed guard was posted outside the door on the quayside, and besides he was no good with locks. Junior drew back before he was seen and moved towards the rear of the shed, examining the planks that made up the walls. Many of them looked old enough to be rotten. Maybe he could find a way in.

One of the corners at the back of the shed had a gap between the boards large enough for him to get a foot into. He pushed the toe of his shoe in and wiggled it around. Soft wood broke off and made the hole slightly bigger. He kneeled down and started pulling at the rotten wood with both hands; before long the hole was large enough for him to consider putting his head and shoulders through it and calling for Fred.

A hand shot out and wrapped itself around his ankle.

'Who is it?' It was Fred's voice, sounding angry but also shot through with fear. It must be dark in that shed.

'Dad, it's me, Hector.'

'Dad? I ain't your *dad*.' The hand pushed his foot away and disappeared. 'You want to talk to him, he's the fuckwad that put me in here.'

Hector staggered backwards, turned and fled. Behind him, he heard Fred shouting. He kept running.

AS IF THE LIGHTS WERE
MAGIC

It was the Major, Will, Primrose and Bob who left for Bodingleigh; when Bob overheard them saying Gloria was in trouble he insisted on going with them, producing keys to Spight's Land Rover. They drove as fast as they could all the way, not caring if they were seen as they bounced and shuddered up the hill. The Land Rover was left parked on the lane below the vacant gallows and they went the rest of the way on foot.

The streets at the top of the village were sweltering and deserted. The clamour of raised voices drew them further downhill to the square between the church and pub, where they encountered the rear end of an angry mob besieging the schoolhouse, shouting and crowding round the building. From the number of people they could see, most of the village must be there, their bodies so tightly packed there was no way the newcomers could get through even if it was safe to try.

'We'll have to go in the back,' said Will, and set off at a trot round to the rear and the door that opened into the empty half of the school. When the others followed, they found him gesturing impatiently for the Major to unpick the lock.

Once inside, they ran through the echoing rooms, heading for the door into the schoolhouse, and from there to Mrs P's kitchen. As they approached the door connecting the two buildings, the sounds of voices grew louder.

Will tried the door and found it unlocked. He opened it a crack and put his ear to it. It was the voices of the mob they had been able to hear, loud and angry through the window. The kitchen was empty, curtains closed. There were other voices upstairs, and Will ran up the narrow and winding staircase, Primrose close behind and Bob following. The Major stayed in the kitchen, with the gun Flora had given him, in case any of the mob decided to break down the door or come in through the windows.

Bursting into the bedroom, Will found the teacher and another woman seated beside each other on the bed. Standing in front of him, her back to the door, was a woman with a bobbed helmet of dyed blonde hair whom he assumed to be Mrs Harrow. She was saying that it wouldn't be long before Mr Spight came to sort them out, and then they would be sorry. She had spoken to Gloria's daughter but had spared her the devastation of hearing that her mother was implicated in an insurgent plot. She couldn't think why it was taking so long for someone to come and sort them out …

From the looks on the seated women's faces, this speech had been made more than once.

Mrs Harrow turned towards the door. At the sight of a stranger, a look of shock did its best to spread across her face. When Bob pushed past Will and she recognised him, relief replaced the panic.

'Bob! Is the Mayor coming?' she cried.

'No. He's a little tied up at the moment, but he expressly asked me to give you his commendations and thanks, and he wants me to bring these two to him,' Bob replied. He crossed the room to the bed and extended a hand to each of the women. They both took one and stood up.

Mrs Harrow looked disappointed. 'You're taking them

now?'

'Yes. There's another public meeting tonight, in Longmarsh, a big one. It's imperative you come, and that you spread the word as wide as you can. Make sure that lot know about it.' He pointed to the window and the unseen but still audible crowd beyond.

'But I don't understand ...'

'You will, Mrs Harrow, you soon will.'

★

The last time Hector Jr had allowed himself to love anything was a memory he found too painful to look at. He kept it locked up tight, though it leaked out into his dreams, causing him to wake up crying, his pillow wet with tears. When that happened, he would twist the skin on his forearm until it bruised, to give himself something 'real' to cry about, the bright new pain pushing away an old ache of grief and guilt.

The object of his affections had been a cat. A skinny little tabby thing that liked to creep into his bedroom. The first time he found it, it had been sat on his windowsill, watching the nuthatches and bluetits flitting about in the tree outside the open window. He tried to stroke it and it had leapt away, using the flagpole beneath his window as a springboard to the top of the garden wall beneath. The next time it came, he didn't approach, but sped to the kitchen to fetch a bowl of milk, which he put on the floor a few feet inside the room. He sat on his bed and watched the cat sniff the air and regard him suspiciously, holding his breath until hunger overcame its fear and it jumped down to lap at the milk with a dainty pink tongue.

Before long he was sneaking food into his room regularly,

feeding the cat and earning a reward in permitted caresses of its soft fur and occasional rasps from its rough tongue. Within a matter of weeks, the cat had become his best friend, sleeping on his bed at night and purring in his ear when he woke. It became fat, stretched out content on the bedspread, its tummy bulging.

He kept it a secret. People didn't have pets in Harbingford. There were some working dogs, and feral cats tolerated as long as they kept vermin away, but pets were seen as waste and indulgence, part of an old, soft way of life. In his own short lifetime there had been years when there was barely enough food for humans, and he'd heard whispers of people putting pets in the pot back in the day when times were hardest. His mum would probably be OK with him looking after a cat, but he knew his dad and granddad would disapprove. They had an image to uphold.

One day he went up to his room after school and there was no sign of the cat, although he had left the window open as usual. He threw himself on the bed and the old mattress squealed in protest. An answering chorus of high-pitched squeaks came from under it. Poking his head over the side he saw the cat nestled into one of his old jumpers, with three tiny kittens curled into the crook of her body, their little heads blind and weaving.

Astonished and awestruck, Hector Jr dropped beside the bed on his knees and stroked the mother cat's head. She awarded him one tongue rasp before turning to washing her babies. That night he could barely sleep for excitement.

But he did sleep, and when he woke his father was in his room, shaking him awake and saying, 'Happy Birthday Jr. Eight years old, eh? Get up. Your mum wants you downstairs for a special breakfast before school.'

Hector Jr mumbled and turned away, burying his head in the pillow. He had forgotten about the cats, until he heard his dad say, 'What's making that noise? We got rats in here?'

The kittens had resumed squeaking. There was nothing he could do – he told himself afterwards, before he forbade himself from ever thinking about it again – to stop Fred from kneeling beside the bed and peering underneath.

'What the ... they *are* fucking rats! What you doing keeping them in your room?'

'They're not rats, they're kittens!' Hector shouted as he struggled free of blankets and tried to push Fred away from the side of the bed.

'They're vermin is what they are!' Fred was pulling the old jumper out. The kittens were wriggling around. There was no sign of the cat.

Before Hector could stop him, Fred had picked up all three of the kittens and crossed the room.

'Dad! *Noooooo!*' Junior screamed in horror, as the tiny bodies were thrown out of the open first-floor window. He rushed across and leaned out. Far below, one of the kittens lay twitching on the concrete. The other two were still. He knew he should go and do something about the one still alive, but he was too horror-struck and sick. Fred gave him a smack around the head and told him to grow the fuck up and stop wailing like a girl.

After a furious row between his parents, and at Fred's insistence, Hector was sent to school. There had been no celebration breakfast. He sat in numb silence for the day, ignoring the questions of the teacher and the concern in her eyes. When he got home at lunchtime, steeling himself, he went into the back yard. The bodies were gone. He felt relief that he didn't have to do anything, and horribly guilty.

He went up to his room and found the cat sniffing under
the bed and crying. Terrified of what Fred would do if he came
home and found her there, he chased her away and threw soft
toys at her until she jumped up on the windowsill and hissed at
him before disappearing.

That night was the last time he had seen the cat, and the
last time he cried. Not even his mother could penetrate the
shell he put up around himself. He took refuge in small acts of
meanness that put friends at a distance and made sure he didn't
make new ones. Within a year, he had built a new persona and
rattled around inside it. He had been sure he would grow to fill
it one day.

Now, he could feel it cracking and disintegrating. Inside it,
he felt tiny, weak, blind and helpless. Just like those poor
kittens before Fred killed them.

*

He shouldn't have shouted at the boy. It had taken a good
twenty minutes after Junior had run off for Fred to finish the
work of making the gap in the wood large enough for his
considerable bulk. He was hampered by having to work
quietly for fear of alerting the guard he could hear walking up
and down outside the door, so he couldn't just kick it out.

No, he shouldn't have shouted at the boy, but it had felt
good to tell the truth. No point in pretending anymore.

No point in much of anything anymore. All Fred's dreams
of running Spight's empire were gone. All that was left to him
was the need for revenge. An overpowering wish to make the
world pay for what it had done to him, and then to get the hell
out of Devon with whatever he could take with him.

First things first. He would take out his rage on the boy

who had started the whole thing: that brat they'd found in the bunker. Everything had been going fine until he'd popped up. Fred would go after that boy before anyone else remembered him, and if the beating he administered didn't kill him first, he could use the terrorist agent as a hostage to get himself across the border into Dorset or Somerset.

Fred pushed his head out through the hole, looked around and, when he saw no one close by, forced his shoulders and then his belly through, ignoring the pain of splinters catching and needling through his shirt. Once free he stood hunched over, braced for a fight that didn't come. No one had noticed his escape.

He straightened up and lumbered away from the quayside, in the direction of a quiet stretch of river where it was safe to swim across; from there he would take the old paths towards Bodingleigh.

*

Once safely out of the schoolhouse and back on the outskirts of the village, the Major sent Gloria and Mrs Prendaghast back to Longmarsh in the Land Rover, with Bob and Primrose, while he and Will headed on foot for the fat farm. Primrose wanted to go with them, but the Major suggested she should be on hand to tell her story to the townspeople if needed. She looked petrified at the idea but agreed to go, clutching Mrs Prendaghast's hand. The old woman patted her on the arm and coaxed her into the back of the vehicle, while Gloria and Bob climbed into the front.

As he walked away backwards up the hill, the last Will saw of her was a pair of huge eyes staring at him out of the side window, her gaze following him until he turned the corner into the shadows of the lane and was lost to view. Once she was out of sight he shook himself and hurried after the Major.

They had no idea where Mal was, but the logical place to start was where he had been held before their last, botched attempt to rescue him – the larder at the fat farm – and that was where the Major decided they should go. Their last visit was preying on Will's mind as they hurried along the road. This was the first time he had had a chance to talk to the Major about Spight's revelations. He had so many questions, and no idea where to start.

They trotted along the road for a few minutes in silence. When the Major next spoke, as the neared the break in the hedge where they would enter the farm's woods, it was clear he had been thinking along the same lines.

'I owe you an explanation,' he said soberly.

Now the opportunity had presented itself, Will wasn't sure he wanted to know more, and shrugged his shoulders.

The Major climbed through the hedge and Will followed. There was a dense tangle of laurel to struggle through, and when they reached a clearing on the other side Will found the Major sitting on a fallen ash tree, waiting for him. He motioned for Will to sit next to him. Will sat. The Major picked up a dead branch and began stripping the bark as he spoke.

'First, I want you to know I never intended to lie to anyone. Major Pain was just a kind of joke nickname I had in the band we played in when we were kids. We all had one. The drummer was Sergeant, bassist was Private, lead singer was General Mayhem, backing singers were Corporals. Flora – Mrs M – was Corporal Punishment. We were all called up to the actual militia when we turned eighteen, training together. Flora and I were a couple but were posted apart. Fred was in her platoon and was obsessed with her. When I visited on leave he'd pick fights, but for the most part we ignored him and carried on seeing each other, even though it was frowned upon and her dad made it pretty clear he didn't approve. He was my commanding officer and didn't think I was good son-in-law material. Turned out he was right when I ran away.'

This was the bit Will was dreading. The militia were notorious for their brutality, but if the Major had deserted from cowardice he didn't think he could bear to hear about it. He didn't say anything though, staring at the ground while the man continued.

'I ran because I was good at fighting and strategy, and all I could see ahead of me was years of using brute force to terrorise people into falling in line. The last act I carried out as a militiaman was to help hang a sixteen-year-old boy for stealing a sheep to feed his family, who had been evicted from their home by the sheep's owner. Who was Spight, as it turned out. Because they hadn't paid the rent because the father had an accident working on Spight's farm. I was too scared to stand up for the boy, but I knew I couldn't do it again, so I ran. Friends helped me get to Cornwall, and I put my skills at the disposal of what was, at the time, a pretty random bunch of ex-Devonians who wanted their homes back. Our bassist was already there, he called me the Major, and that was that. We don't have ranks in our command chain, so I didn't think anything of it, but then the cadets started using it. It was a bit of a joke, but it wasn't meant to fool anyone or make them think it was a rank I had earned.'

The Major fell silent and dropped the now-shredded stick. Will didn't know what to say. He still had questions, but this was not the time to go into the details of the Major's relationship with Mrs M. His fears about the Major's honour had at least been allayed, and his trust proved not to be misplaced. The relief was overwhelming.

He said nothing but stood and gestured into the darkness of the woods, saying, 'Come on Major, we have a job to do,' before standing back and letting the other man lead the way.

*

Fever dreams had tormented him since he had been taken forcibly from his comrades on the quayside, and Mal had no idea how long he had been back in the chilly and unlit larder at the fat farm. It could have been hours, or days. Food had been brought when he first arrived but he'd had no appetite to eat, only managing to drink some water to slake a raging thirst. Blankets had been provided, but he had lost them somehow in the dark, and was now racked with chills as the cold of the stone floor sucked heat out of him, too weak to move.

When light flooded into the room he squinted painfully, holding up a hand to shield his eyes and wincing as his stinking wound flared. He coughed weakly, groaned as the pain stabbed harder.

'I can't have him dying in my larder, Doctor, so do something about it.' It was a woman's voice, the same woman who had overseen his previous imprisonment. It could have been her looming over him, but his vision was blurred from being in the dark so long. Rough wool was thrown over him and a pillow placed beneath his head.

He remembered the voice of the other speaker too, it was the doctor who had helped Fred torture him, and Mal cringed as he heard, 'He looks pretty far gone. I'm not sure what I can do for him.' Their voices were fading in and out and the light was growing dim.

'You're the bloody doctor! Figure something out or I'll be telling Spight you're past it.'

'I don't really see the point. If he recovers, Spight's plans for him ...'

'What plans?'

There was no reply.

'Fine, useless piece of shit, I'll go find a hedgewitch and see what she can do.'

'Steady on! No need to bring one of those heathens into it. I have some maggots that might clean out the infected flesh, then it's up to him. It'll help if you get him out of here and into a proper bed.'

Their words were making no sense, noise with no meaning, sounds pulsing in time with the blackness that was descending. Mal was back in the dark before the door had even closed.

★

Crossing the river was the hardest part of leaving Longmarsh. Fred had to find somewhere narrow enough to get across despite the strong currents, but deserted enough to do so unremarked. His first thought was the weir, where he would be able to cross without having to swim, but when he got there he could see insurrectionist forces – or so he assumed – fiddling around with the Archimedes screw turbine that used to provide some of Longmarsh's electricity. Busy with their work, none of them noticed him, and Fred faded back into the trees on the far bank before that could change.

The river was deeper and the currents stronger upstream. Its course would also take him further away from his destination. He decided to go back downstream, below the turbine, and risk being seen. He found a shallow entry point with a pebbled beach and stripped down to his underwear before wading out, his clothes and boots piled together in a bundle and held over his head. The shock of the cold water made him gasp, and encouraged him to half-swim, half-wade across as fast as he could. Not wanting to take the time to dry off and dress, he continued up the bank on the other side

Seeing the technicians working on the turbine was bringing it home to Fred that Devon was lost to him. The days of Spight were over. If Fred wanted to get out before retribution and show trials came into force – as they had after regime changes post-Devolution, and most recently after a challenge to Spight's fourth consecutive term – he would have to move swiftly. He had to get to the fat farm, pick up whatever spare fuel he could and find a vehicle. Thoughts of revenge might have to wait; the instinct for survival was over-riding his need for payback. But he would take the boy as insurance, and the boy would suffer, because the fury Fred was feeling had to have an outlet.

The mixture of river water and sweat coating his skin was attracting horseflies and midges by the dozen. By the time he reached an open area where he could dress he was covered in stings and bites, slapping ferociously at the air and swearing loudly, not caring who might hear. Dressing helped, but a rallying cry must have gone out, because the air above him was thick with swarming insects. His head and neck were still exposed and vulnerable; he broke off a piece of bracken and, waving it manically over his head to swat the bugs away, ran up the hill away from the river. The heavy humidity under the trees made him sweat, and the insect numbers grew.

An hour of hard slogging uphill got him to the road and almost to the fat farm boundary, where he paused for breath and to consider his strategy. He had no way of knowing if the farm was now in enemy hands and had to proceed as if it was. With that in mind he found a break in the bank above the lane and climbed up, rather than approaching openly from the drive. By now he could barely feel the new bites through the torment of those already received, and ignored them.

Dorcas was emerging from the front door as he approached the main building. One of her skinny little helpers was following her out and receiving a tirade of instructions as the Matron climbed into the battered car parked on the drive and started the engine. Mrs Harrow was in the front passenger seat. Perhaps they were doing a runner while they could. Fred stayed in the shadows cast by the hedge. No need to let them know he was there. He was relieved to see Dorcas leave; he knew she wouldn't let him take her prisoner away without a fight, or at least a delay.

The car drove away, belching smoke, and the front door was closed. Once they were out of sight, Fred came out from the cover of the hedge and hurried around the side of the house to the kitchen door. The skinny helper and another girl were inside, preparing food for the evening meal. They looked at him warily. He ignored them and walked on through to the corridor that led to the larder.

The larder was empty, only a rank stench and damp stains on the stone floor showing the prisoner had been held there. Fred stormed back to the kitchen.

'Where is he?' he shouted at the girls, who cowered and said nothing. One of them pointed up at the ceiling 'Upstairs?' he barked at her. She nodded mutely. He turned towards the door and ran for the front hall.

★

They were almost in sight of the main building, which lay on
the other side of the hedge. A car had driven away from the
house as they made their way through the woods, which were
almost as dim in daylight as during their previous night-time
visit. They couldn't see more than glimpses and had no way of
knowing who was driving it but, as the Major said, it had to be
to their advantage that there were now fewer people at the
farm. He said this as he checked the chamber of the revolver
he had been given in Littlemarsh, to see how many bullets it
contained.

'One,' he said glumly. 'Hope we don't need more.'

'Hope we don't need it at all,' Will replied. The resistance
only used guns as a last resort. He had only ever fired one on
the range, in training, and hoped he wouldn't have to now.
The thought of shooting anyone made him queasy, but if it
helped Mal, he would.

There was no way to avoid exposure as they emerged from
the woods. No one was in sight, or visible in any of the
windows facing them, as they made for the open kitchen door.
The place was silent, only the clamour of rooks overhead
disturbing the quiet.

'Do we have a plan?' Will whispered.

'Wave the gun around if we have to, collect Mal, get out of
here and call Merryn.'

'What if he's still really sick?' What if he's dead? Will
wanted to say, but the words stuck in his throat.

'Then we find somewhere safe and protect him until help
comes. We're not alone in this, Will.' The Major clapped him
on the shoulder before he disappeared through the doorway.
But Will felt very alone as he followed him inside.

Two young girls were in the kitchen, rolling pastry and chopping vegetables. They looked at the two intruders in fright. One of them made a small shrieking noise when she saw the gun.

'Are you looking for Fred?' the other one whispered.

Fred? Oh shit.

If the Major was thrown, he didn't show it.

'Yes,' he barked, as if he was still in the militia. 'Where is he?'

As the girl began to speak, the door to the corridor was shoved open and Fred came through, staggering under the weight of Mal, unconscious in his arms. Mal looked ghastly, his skin grey and shiny with sweat, the white t-shirt he was wearing soaked with blood. Fred didn't look much better, his face red with effort, and covered in blotchy insect bites, the toll of carrying Mal evident from his harsh breathing and a stream of vicious swearing, muttered under his breath as he lurched through the door.

★

The crowd had grown until it filled Longmarsh's town square and spilled out onto the ancient and ramshackle high street that ran down to the river. Several hundred people, including most of Spight's key supporters from Bodingleigh, stood in tight clumps speculating as to why they had been summoned. Many carried shopping bags, hoping that this was where their cargo was to be delivered.

Those from the villages had endured a long and muddy walk if they hadn't secured transport by donkey, horse or bicycle. A privileged few from Bodingleigh had arrived in a small fleet of cars; these were mostly the older women Merryn had heard referred to as Knockers, who looked annoyed and impatient and insisted on chairs at the front of the crowd, close to the steps he intended using as a stage. One had accosted him earlier, demanding to see her prisoners, her face looking like it had been ironed, it was so smooth. Flora had intervened, leading her back to her seat and telling her that all would be revealed shortly. He prayed she was right.

It was starting to get dark when his phone rang. A noisy generator that stank of human fat was running to power amplifiers that had been put in front of the steps up to the Civic Hall; he had to cover one ear as he received word that they were all systems go. As Merryn ended the call Flora checked her watch and looked at him expectantly. All they needed now was their speaker.

'It's time?' she asked.

'Yes, time for you to get up there.'

'Me? I'm a covert operative.'

'But most of these people know you,' he pointed out. 'They know you as a Spight. If you tell them they won't like it, but they'll believe it. And then I'll do my thing. Meantime, I'll have your father brought out so people can see him.'

Flora nodded, swallowing hard before she climbed the steps. Below the top flight was a broad landing, where a microphone stand had been placed. Flora took hold of the mic and the whine of feedback snared everyone's attention. Faces turned in concert, like sunflowers, and the buzz of whispered conversations died away. Merryn signalled to an activist that it was time to let Mayor Spight out of the car and bring him to where he could have a good view of the proceedings.

The Mayor's daughter cleared her throat and said, 'Thank you for coming.' Her voice wavered and Merryn willed her on. She took a deep breath, and when she spoke again her voice had steadied. 'I have something important to tell you. Something you won't like hearing, about the way we've been living and who has been paying the price.' She shaded her eyes and looked out over the crowd. 'I'm going to need some help with this. Primrose, are you there?' A young woman pushed through the crowd, not making eye contact with anyone, her posture slightly hunched. One of the older women seated at the front gasped; the young woman cringed away from her but continued up the steps.

While she did so, the Mayor was brought to a reserved chair at the front, escorted by two large men who flanked him when he sat down. Those who saw him murmured among themselves, but they were too intrigued by what his daughter had to tell them to pay him more attention than that.

All except the older woman who had recognised Primrose, now switching her attention between the two, unease gripping her features. She leaned across to the woman sitting next to her and whispered. A wave of agitation passed along the row of Knockers.

★

When he saw Will and the Major, Fred stopped in his tracks and gave an incoherent cry of rage, Mal's head lolling against his chest. The Major said nothing, but brought the gun up until it was aiming at Fred, above Mal.

'Put him down.'

The two girls were looking from Fred to the Major, eyes wide with fright. Will gestured behind him to the back door and they took the hint, fleeing out of the kitchen. Something began to burn on the range cooker.

'You won't shoot.' Fred's voice was contemptuous. He held

Mal higher in his arms, making it harder for the Major to shoot without hitting him. The Major lowered his aim and shot Fred in the foot.

The sound of the shot was deafening in the confined space. Will flinched and his ears rang.

Fred screamed and lurched sideways, dropping Mal who fell like a stone, landing hard on the scuffed boards of the kitchen floor. Fred hopped on one leg, clutching at his foot.

'It's over, Fred.' The Major's voice – seeming to come from a distance – was almost kindly. He was still aiming the gun as if it weren't now empty. Fred cowered a moment then, with obvious effort, drew himself upright, his weight on his uninjured leg. The insect bites now stood out in scarlet welts, in stark contrast to a face gone white with pain and shock.

'Go on then, kill me, you coward,' he gritted out between clenched teeth, fists squeezing closed and knuckles whitening as he braced himself.

*

Primrose gazed out at a sea of faces, their expressions varying from curious to wary to hostile. She saw Dorcas and Mrs Harrow and the terror she was feeling, as she opened her mouth to speak in public for the first time in her life, spiked. The Mayor might be there, but she didn't know him; his presence was a vaguer threat than that of the two women.

Five years in virtual seclusion, with only the Matron and other staff and inmates to talk to had not prepared her for this. But then she recalled the events of the last few days, how she had escaped and helped those children, and stood a little straighter.

Mrs Prendaghast gave her a wave, from where she stood to

one side, and Primrose found the courage to start talking.

'You probably don't recognise me. My name is Primrose.' The mic gave a whine of feedback and she stepped back in shock. Flora smiled at her encouragingly and she stepped forward again. 'Until a couple of days ago I lived at the fat farm, and I was there for five years, since my parents tithed me. I did what I was told – I ate what I was given and I got fat, and then I was farmed so that you – or more likely the Mayor – could drive, or turn on a generator for a few hours. Then I'd be fed so I'd get fat again. When I was out in the village, which hasn't happened for a long time, you weren't grateful, you treated me like shit.'

People were looking at each other. What was going on? This wasn't what they were expecting to hear. Some of them looked restless, like they were thinking of leaving. A few, at the front, did get up and leave. She watched as, one by one, the Knockers left their seats and crept away.

'You despise fat people,' she went on. 'Maybe it's because times are hard, and we get all the extra food, and you're jealous. But I read while I was in the farm. It was just about all I was allowed to do besides eat. I read magazines from before, and people hated fat people back then too. They thought we were lazy and greedy, so they made fun of us and made us feel ashamed. Maybe then people had more choice over what they ate, I don't know. I never did. So I ran away after the last harvest, which left me like this.' She gestured self-consciously at her new, shapely form. 'I found friends and one of them told me I had been made how I am now, so I'd fetch a good price in New Jersey. I was going to be sent there as a breeder, or a whore, so you could keep having your imported fizzy drinks and cheap clothes, and the Mayor could keep his hold over you.'

Her audience was definitely becoming restive. Those closest to the front were looking to the Mayor for corroboration or denial, but he was keeping his head down and could have been asleep for all the notice he was taking. Primrose looked at Flora and nodded; it was time to hand back to her.

'I know you have no reason to trust me. Maybe you should listen to Flora Spight instead, to hear what else was going on in your name.'

*

It was almost full dark. One spotlight was angled over the front of the crowd. Flora's voice was still reaching across the square, but she herself had disappeared into the shadows as she said, 'How many here can say honestly they didn't know what was going on? Didn't know that we – and I include myself in this, because I couldn't bring myself to look too hard either – were selling our own for material gain?' People were looking around at each other to assess how widely spread Spight's secret network had gone, though many of his closest confederates had already left, soon after Flora began corroborating what Primrose had told them about selling breeders, and telling them that a dozen children bound for the Real USA had been rescued that morning.

Dozens of hands went up. Their fingers shone white in the glare of the lamp. 'How many didn't suspect a thing? Who here thought that a new washing machine for a few sacks of spuds was just a really good deal?' A few hands went down. After a moment's hesitation, a few more. 'How many would like us to go away, or prefer not to know what I've just told you?' Nervous laughter and a few hands went back up.

'Maybe that's because I haven't got to the good part yet.' Flora took a deep breath. Now came the tricky bit. 'You see, I haven't just come to tell you about people trafficking, or to make you feel bad. I've come to tell you we have friends here who have been working hard for many years to bring power back into our lives, and to put it in our hands.' People were looking at each other, some looking hopeful, most just confused. Flora beckoned to Merryn, now standing to one side of the crowd, and he climbed up to stand beside her.

'I'm Merryn,' he said. 'I'm what you would call an insurrectionist.' He waited for the cries of shock to die down, and resumed, 'And I'm here to put the lights back on.'

He nodded to a woman standing quietly at the back of the crowd. She slipped away, and Merryn said a prayer.

For a long, anticlimactic moment, nothing happened. Wind could be heard in the trees, over the sound of hundreds of people talking and arguing among themselves. Merryn had a moment of panic. What if the whole plan was rubbish and they had failed? Many of the faces staring at them remained implacably hostile. People who had lived at the heart of Spight's dark empire for so long, and benefited from it, and didn't care to know what they were being told. It was going to take more than words to persuade them, if anything ever would.

As he thought this, the town's streetlights stuttered into life, washing across the heads of the crowd and casting their faces into shadow. Above him, the lights of the Civic Hall came on. The sound system he had plugged in blasted music through the speakers that had been amplifying the PA, making some in the crowd scream with shock. Everything in the abandoned buildings in the town, that had been left on when the power was cut, came on, and the lights dipped as chittering mechanical noises sounded from buildings all around the square. Merryn panicked that the power from the batteries – most of which had only had a day of charge from the solar fields – wouldn't be sufficient; if even one connection failed that would be it, back to darkness. They would be mobbed, over-run and end up on a freighter, shackled to a plough or force-fed in a fat farm. But the power held.

★

'I don't want to kill you, Fred,' the Major said sadly.

Mal stirred at Fred's feet, groaning. Will made a move towards him but the Major held him back, not wanting to give Fred another hostage.

'You shot me! Why should I believe you?' Fred's voice was tight with pain.

'Because you're still alive?'

'Ha! You know the chances of me surviving being shot in the foot? About as good as your friend's, from his infection, and look at him.'

'The infection you're responsible for. You tortured him!' Mal had been coherent enough to tell the others that much, back in the boatshed, while they waited to be taken to Dartmouth.

'This is a war, Major. You forgotten that?'

'It's your war. We're offering everyone the chance to end it and achieve peace. You know Spight is done. I can get you medical attention here within the hour. You might even keep the foot.'

'And then what? Live to watch you take everything that's rightfully mine? My wife, my son, my future?'

'None of it was ever yours Fred. Flora is her own woman,

she was never any more yours than she was mine. You despise my – our– son, by all accounts. If you'd loved him, you couldn't lose him. And no one has a guaranteed future. You never know, you might like the way things turn out. Things are better outside Devon. It's only here that you're stuck in some feudal timewarp. Well, here and a handful of other places.'

The Major was concentrating on what he was saying, trying to reach the man across years of bitterness and jealousy. Without his being aware of it, the gun barrel was dipping, pointing more towards the floor than at Fred. When the other man lunged, throwing himself across the space between them, the Major brought the gun back up, but Fred had hold of it, twisting and managing to wrench it free. He threw himself out of reach, turned the gun, aimed and fired. Nothing happened except a dry click.

Screaming in fury as he realised he had been conned, Fred threw himself forward again, using the gun as a club and aiming for the Major's head. The Major blocked him with one arm, punched him in the face with the other and followed it up with a kick to Fred's good leg. He connected just above the knee and Fred went down, screaming with pain, but managing to throw himself towards Mal.

Will leaped towards his friend to protect him. Fred grabbed a fistful of Will's hair, and he pushed the older man away, crying out as a clump of hair tore from his scalp.

Scrabbling backwards and grabbing Mal by the upper arms, Will dragged him away from the fight.

Once both boys were safely out of Fred's range, the Major decided it was time to stop going easy and unsheathed his knife, restored to him from the cache found on the boat in Dartmouth. He held it in front of him and crouched, looking

for an opening. He still didn't want to kill Fred, but if he really
had to, he would.

★

Some time had passed, without further speeches, to allow the
wonder of the electric lights to be absorbed and the shock to
wear off. The generator that had powered the spotlight and PA
had been turned off and its stink had dispersed. The more
technically minded in the crowd had looked for other, hidden,
generators. Not finding them, they had to concede that the
power was coming from a source they couldn't see, by means
of a cable plugged in to a socket hidden in a recess under the
Civic Hall. They had read of such things in old textbooks. The
less technical were behaving as if the lights were magic,
touching the streetlights and speakers with awed reverence.

A few small fires had started, the result of aged wiring
shorting out, and been put out before they could spread.
Merryn had sent out crews armed with extinguishers to look
for signs of others.

It was time for Stage Three, Part Two. Merryn remounted
the steps and took the mic from Flora. As he did so, a throng of
rainbow-hued and hooded activists came out from the doors of
the Civic Hall and lined up to array themselves on the steps
above him. The crowd backed away nervously. Clearly, they
thought this was when the insurrectionists showed their true
colours. Flora hoped they were right.

'We have another gift for you, and another lie to expose.
All those people you thought you lost to border skirmishes,
over the years we've been carrying out our work, all the
people Spight told you had died at our hands? Well some of
them are here. We took them, yes. We told them the truth, we

gave them a choice, trained those who took it … and now they've come back so they can help you reclaim your home.'

At this, Spight raised his head, looking worried for the first time.

As one, the hoods came off. Revealed were young faces, grinning nervously as they faced out across the crowd. Among them were Tom, Dick and Harriet.

A long silence, then names were being called out as parents recognised children long thought dead or lost. A woman approached the foot of the steps, hands held out beseechingly as she called to her daughter, Martha. Harriet ran down to throw herself into a hug. Within moments, the steps were thronged with families coming together after years apart.

★

Primrose observed everything from shadows cast by the pillars holding up the angular, brutalist building that was Longmarsh's Civic Hall. Her throat was tight as she watched the reunions taking place on the steps and spilling out across the square.

She felt very left out. She could see Alise, who was enjoying being the centre of attention as she told her own tale, but Alise had never been self-conscious about anything, including being fat. She was comfortable in her own skin in a way that Primrose envied.

Mrs Prendaghast was making her way towards her, overlooked by those she passed by. Did any of them know what a heroine this woman was? Did it matter? Why did Primrose feel so flat?

'Well done Primrose, that must have been hard. I'm proud of you.'

The rush of gratitude she felt brought her almost to tears. 'Thank you. They don't seem to think so.' She waved at the people standing around them.

'Of course not, you made them feel bad! But they'll forgive you.' Was Mrs P laughing at her? Again, did it matter? Her old life was over, and if she wanted she could make a new one, but it would be harder if she clung on to old feelings. She had to be brave, fight her own, old, poisonous thoughts. Feeling stronger, she took a deep breath and her heart lightened. Mrs Prendaghast squeezed her arm.

She couldn't see the landing from where she was standing but she heard the man called Merryn resume speaking, and saw everyone turning back towards him, reunited families with arms slung around each other. She and Mrs P craned to see from where they stood at the back.

'Spight sold you a lie. He told you that you, as a community, as individuals and families, are on your own, facing the realities and the changes we all have to make in order to live in a way that permits our descendants to do the same. But you're not alone. Well, except in the metaphysical sense that we're all locked inside our own consciousness.' He waited a beat for a laugh that didn't come. Undaunted, he continued, 'But beyond that, there's a whole world waiting to help. Some of us are a bit further down the road, but we all started from the same place. Where you are now.'

★

Fred was weaving where he stood. Blood was pooling on the floor from the hole in his foot, but he wouldn't give in. He wouldn't give the Major – Paul, for fuck's sake – the satisfaction. Nothing had gone to plan, but there was no way he was going to live in the ghastly sort of future that was being painted for him. If he couldn't be top dog, he'd rather die. It was what he had given his life to: the hope that he could be king of the heap. So what if it was a heap of shit, he'd still be at the top of it.

There were other wounds that were bleeding, where Paul had met his lunges with his blade, cowardly little shit. Streams were running down Fred's forearms, joining the spreading stain at his feet. He was becoming light-headed. He knew he was nearly finished. He slumped.

Paul approached him warily. When Fred did nothing, he came a little closer. Which was when Fred threw himself forward in one last attempt to grab the knife and turn it on his enemy. But he was too slow. Paul saw him coming and stepped back. Fred's good leg gave way and he staggered sideways, through the open doorway that led from the kitchen to the rendering room below. His foot came down on something and slipped, and he felt his balance going. The steep staircase yawned behind him and he knew beyond doubt he was going to fall.

As the shock of this flooded his consciousness, for a long moment that stretched time, he thought through the consequences of that fall, and the futility of what he had been trying to do struck him as hard as would that concrete floor, any moment now.

He would take it all back if he could just regain his balance.

Life was precious and his own rage had thrown it into jeopardy.

His eyes met those of the boy with Paul, wide-eyed with horror as he, too, saw what was going to happen.

Life was precious.

Fred took that new knowledge with him as he fell.

Stone steps met him and stars exploded in his head. Pain shot through his shoulder, and agony ripped through his wounded foot where it struck the wall. His momentum kept him moving downwards, and when he came to rest, it was because his head had struck the steel rim of the table to which he had tied the boy, such a short time ago. His undamaged leg had become entangled with strips of plastic from the makeshift curtain and was pulled straight.

The table scraped across the cellar, colliding with the rendering vat where it lay in the middle of the floor with a dull clang.

White light shot across his vision and he lost consciousness, descending swiftly into darkness.

A LIGHT OF
UNDERSTANDING

The Major's heart sank as he climbed down the steep stone stairs, careful not to step on any of the glistening spots of fat that could send him flying. Fred lay crumpled at the bottom, his face turned towards the ceiling, his body twisted round to one side. He wasn't moving, and his limbs were bent at unnatural angles. It looked as though, despite his best efforts, he had killed the man after all.

Will had followed closely behind, after making sure Mal was lying as comfortably as possible on the kitchen floor, tea towels pillowed beneath his head.

'Is he …?' Will whispered.

'Certainly looks that way,' the Major responded with a sigh.

When they reached him the Major stepped over Fred's body so he could crouch and feel for a pulse. It was there, faint and thready. Blood was flowing freely from a gash in Fred's temple. The stench of rendered fat was making the Major feel ill. Fred had ripped through a fly-curtain made up of plastic strips and many of them lay over him, draped like seaweed after a high tide

The Major stood, groaning as he felt all the effects of the fight. 'He's still alive, just.'

'What do we do now?'

'I'm not sure. We can't move him.' He took his phone out of his pocket. There was no signal, here underground. He handed it to Will. 'Go up and call Merryn, see if he can get a medic team over from Cornwall. It's going to take more than Flora's first-aid kit, they'll have to send a helicopter.'

Perhaps it was the sound of his wife's name, but Fred stirred. The Major crouched back down by his side as Will returned to the kitchen to find a signal.

'Fred, don't move or you could do yourself more damage. I'll get you help.'

Fred's body shook. The Major thought he was in shock; it took him a moment to realise the other man was laughing.

'There's no help for me. It's not so bad, I can't feel a thing.' One of his hands, fingers splayed across a cold stone step, twitched. Moved by an impulse, the Major placed his own hand over it. It was icy.

'You're a tough bastard Fred, it's going to take more than a little tumble to take you out.'

'How about a shot in the foot?' His breath was thready and his voice weak.

'Just a scratch. Will,' he shouted, 'bring him some water when you're done.'

'Trying to drown me now?'

The Major squeezed the hand he was holding. There was no response.

'I'm sorry Fred, I really didn't mean it to come to this.'

'Wuss.' There was the Fred he knew, though it was said wryly and without rancour. Without its customary clutch of anger and disappointment, Fred's face was almost peaceful.

*

Merryn's voice was growing hoarse and he stopped for a gulp of water from his flask before continuing: 'By far the biggest lie you've been told, is that the only way to keep yourselves safe is to be brutal, tough and selfish. That a harsh world demands harsh choices. But who does that really serve? You? Or Spight?' He looked the people in the front rows directly in the eyes, and was encouraged that not every gaze slid away from his. There were some in the crowd who were nodding in agreement.

'The only way we're going to move out of the ecological crisis that still threatens to engulf us is by working together and trusting each other. But we can't force it on you. We're giving you a choice. We're not going to make you do anything. If you want, we'll back off over the borders and leave you alone, offering asylum to anyone who wants to leave. We won't tolerate the sale of human beings, so any further export shipments will be boarded in international waters, and any unwilling guests given safe passage to other parts of the country. Or, you can lower your defences, withdraw the militia and be part of something bigger again. Either way, we'll keep the power on.'

★

Fred hadn't lied. He really couldn't feel a thing. He knew that was bad, as things were measured in his old life, pre-stumble and fall. His present life would likely be very short, measured in minutes or hours rather than days, but he found he didn't care. It was life, and he would live it as long as breath came into his body. So he practised that – breathing. If he did that, the fear that was nibbling at the edges of his mind, the fear that had driven and dictated to him for most of his life, was kept at bay.

He knew Paul had taken hold of his hand. He didn't even mind that. He really must be dying and Hell had frozen over.

'Do you think I'll go to Hell?' he asked in a whisper. He had never been a religious man, but here, at the end of everything, the fear fought for a way in, telling him he would be punished for all the pain he had caused.

'I think we make Hell right here,' Paul replied.

'Pussy,' Fred whispered. Breathe.

★

Will brought a pitcher of water, a glass and a straw he had found, alongside the kind of sippy cups he remembered from childhood. They couldn't move Fred to help him drink, and Will really didn't want to drown him. But he didn't think the man, even as things were, would appreciate a sippy cup. He placed the glass of water in the Major's hand and watched as it was offered. Fred took a couple of sips from the straw but found it difficult to swallow. When it was offered again he closed his mouth tightly, refusing more.

'It's strange,' Fred mumbled.

'What is?' The Major's head was bent close to his old enemy's, his posture protective, intimate. If he hadn't been there, Will would never have known the two men had been fighting minutes before. His scalp, still throbbing from where the clump of his hair had been torn out, testified otherwise. He thought he should be angry with Fred, but just felt sad. What a waste, to have been so angry for so long.

'I'm scared, but it's OK. Dying, I mean. You spend your life avoiding it, and it ain't so bad. Kind of quiet inside, mostly.' Fred tried to cough but choked instead. A thin trickle of blood dribbled out of his mouth. 'OK,' he said a moment later when he could speak again, 'that wasn't so good.'

Will waited for the Major to tell Fred he wasn't dying, but

he said nothing, just held the man's hand.

'I'm ready.' Just before his neck relaxed and his eyes glazed, something lit him up from within, and Fred smiled as if he knew something beautiful. A moment later and he was gone.

★

Knots of people were clustered around the square talking, for the most part in low voices. In one or two groups the voices were louder, argumentative, as people disputed all they had been told, and in particular Merryn's promise and offer. There were no signs of people leaving.

Flora wandered among them, listening, keeping out of the pools of light where possible, but still people recognised and approached her, asking anxiously if they would be punished if they opened up the borders. And, more often, asking where her father was; they wanted to ask him what he and Fred and everyone had been doing, they wanted to visit their anger on him. They wanted her to believe they had known nothing, done nothing, that they were innocent.

Spight had been taken back to the car and locked securely inside, for his own safety, while everyone's attention was diverted by the family reunions. Flora told them they would have a chance to hear from him, but not today while emotions were running high.

Eventually, exhausted, she went to find Merryn. He was sitting on the landing on the Hall steps, observing the people below. From here the buzz of conversation was muted by distance.

'It's a no brainer,' she said as she sat beside him. 'You know they don't believe that we'll keep the power on regardless, and they'll vote accordingly. Is that democracy? Or bribery?'

'We're still in a climate crisis, Flora, even if things are starting to improve and level out. We can't afford to have renegades pumping out methane and carbon as if there's no tomorrow worth protecting.'

'Just saying, Merryn.'

'In the long run, even if they're insincere in their choice, I believe we'll win them around to our way of thinking. After all, we'll be appealing to their finer natures, and I have to believe they will always win through given half a chance. Humans are cooperative animals. The Spights of this world can take advantage of that, corrupt the need to belong and make it inward-looking and tribal, but it's a perversion of who we really are.'

The last of his words were drowned out by a clatter of rotors overhead. A searchlight came stabbing down from the skies, sweeping the square with its harsh glare. People looked up and wailed with fright as the helicopter flew over them, heading west towards Bodingleigh, the whine of its electric motors deafeningly shrill.

'Did you call them in?' she shouted over the noise as she watched it move away. The downdraft blew her hair around her face.

'Yes. Will called. I'm sorry to have to tell you, Fred had an accident. Will wanted you to know Paul did everything in his power to bring about a different outcome. The medics were for him and the boy they went to save.'

Below them, people were still staring after the helicopter. If they had needed further proof of the technological might of the world beyond their friable borders, they had it now. She wondered briefly if Merryn had orchestrated that display deliberately, telling the pilot to go out of his way to fly over the town, before turning to the matter of Fred and her disintegrated family.

She felt sorrow for her husband, but it was dispassionate. For a time after their marriage she had almost thought it might work between them. He had loved her, as far as he could love anyone, but that had never been a great distance. There was a gaping void inside him that nothing could fill, and as her activities for the resistance took her away more often, and necessitated greater levels of secrecy for her own safety and that of other agents – she was under no illusions about what her father would do if he found out what she was up to – she had withdrawn from all of them. And now Hector Jr was missing. No one had seen him since he had run away from Paul at the dockside, and she had sent out word to all the activists she could reach, that they should keep an eye out. She wasn't afraid for her son's physical safety, but sure that he was confused and angry and hated her. What a mess. All around her there was hope for a new and more equitable world, a world she had striven for these last ten years, and her own was falling apart.

★

Craning his neck, Will saw Primrose standing with Mrs P, to one side of the people gathered in the square. He hastened towards them, then hesitated. He and the Major had rushed down from the village as soon as the helicopter had landed safely in the field above the fat farm – guided in by the torches they were waving – and the medics it was carrying had been escorted to Mal.

Now, as Will stood behind Primrose, he felt shy, wondering if she would be pleased to see him or if he was making a fool of himself by feeling so excited to be reunited with her.

Perhaps he should have stayed with Mal, but he had been assured his friend would be fine after proper medical attention at a facility in Saltash, and he could video conference with him in the morning. Both he and the Major had been keen to see what effect the revelations had had, as well as to check on the safety of those they cared about; they had driven back down in the Land Rover as fast as they could. The Major had vanished from Will's side as soon as they had parked. Now here Will stood, summoning courage.

He tapped Primrose on the shoulder. She turned, and a wide smile broke across her face.

'You're safe! I was so worried ...' It looked as though she might be blushing. Mrs P was smiling knowingly at him, then looked away tactfully as they both moved forward into an awkward hug.

Later, when Will's emotions and pulse had calmed, he observed the Major, sitting beside the woman he knew as Mrs Mason, on the stairs above the crowd. The Major must have told her about Fred; her expression was calm but sad. Mrs P poked him in the arm.

'What's up? You look like someone who's lost the day, not won it.'

'How could he just leave her here? If he loved her.'

'You're assuming it was his decision. She made the choice to stay. She knew that if she left the resistance would fizzle out. She made a courageous choice by staying here, having her baby, and especially by marrying Fred. The Major was in Cornwall and didn't know she was married or that he was a dad until after Junior was born. By then, everything had changed.'

'Not sure Junior will ever see it as courageous.' Or Fred, thought Will, but didn't say it, remembering the broken body at the foot of the stairs. Fred no longer cared either way. He pondered again the look on the man's face as he'd teetered on the brink of the fall that killed him, and again as he died. It was as if he had seen something profound, as if a light of understanding had kindled in his eyes before they dimmed.

Mrs P interrupted his musings. 'Yes, it's a shame about Junior. Flora hates herself for not keeping him closer the last few years, but he would have gone straight to his grandfather if he had known what she was up to. We just have to hope it's not too late for him to get his head straight. Or crack open his heart.'

'What about the rest of them? Do you think they'll be glad to be rid of Spight?'

'God yes, people just did what they had to do to keep going, and were grateful someone was in charge. You're too young to remember how bad things were when he became Mayor – how many people were dying of disease and starvation. For a short while he seemed like a godsend. But now, given a better alternative, they'll jump at the chance.'

And it was better, Will knew that, and soon they would see it too. He remembered how he had felt when he first arrived in Saltash and saw the way people lived there, how much happier and freer they were than back in Devon. How angry and cheated he had felt, that this had been denied them in Bodingleigh. How, when he was old enough to become a cadet, he had resolved to do all he could to bring the knowledge he had to the people he had left behind.

And they had done it. His heart swelled, filled with gratitude and love for all the people who had made this possible, putting their own bodies on the line to help bring about much-needed change.

Long live the evolution.

⋆

Hector watched everything from the shadows, out among the fringes of the crowds in the square. He had been there some time, after following people up from the quayside, not knowing what else to do once he emerged from the state of shock precipitated by his clash with Fred. He was tired, hungry and thirsty. Again, he was observing comings and goings and listening to speeches that left him confused and, increasingly, angry.

His mother, the girl from the boat, and a middle-aged man in mud-stained clothes, had told everyone his grandfather had lied to them. That might be true, he thought, but if so it must be for their own good. People were stupid, his grandfather often said so. They needed strong leadership, they needed to be told what to do or there would be anarchy. He wasn't sure what anarchy was, but the way his grandfather talked, it had to be bad.

He was resolute in his defence of his grandfather until his mother started talking about children. He remembered the ones on the boat, so much younger than himself, and felt a chill. Were they really being sold off to strangers? Grown ups was one thing, but little kids? He'd heard whispers about what some grown ups liked to do to little kids. His grandfather had put the fear of that in him after Junior had gone off on his own once when he was younger. It hadn't stopped him going, but it had made him wary of strangers.

Surely it was a lie? But his mother never lied, which made the things she was saying all the harder to hear. But if she'd been a terrorist all his life, and his whole life had been one big fat lie, that meant she could be lying now.

His head hurt and he felt sick. He sat down on the ground.

The rest of the talking passed him by until the streetlights came to life. He heard the collective gasp, then more talking.

The appearance of the helicopter overhead, the noise and the whipping wind of its downdraft, the bright glare of light sweeping across the square, made him cower where he sat. He'd never seen one before and didn't really know what it was, just that it was loud, it was flying, powerful, and it meant these people were way stronger than his grandfather. Hector Sr's reign was over. Hector Jr sat there, feeling numb, while his brain came to terms with all this new information.

Slowly, he came to the most important conclusion of all. Despite all he had done to protect himself he'd been on the wrong side. And not wrong just for selling off kids, but the losing side. Thinking that made him feel angry and scared. What would happen to them all now? What would happen to *him* now? How could he keep himself safe?

He looked over to where his mother had been standing, talking to the crowd, and saw her sitting on the steps in front of the microphone stand. As he watched, the man who had locked Fred in the boat shed, the one Fred had told Junior was his actual father, climbed up the stairs to sit next to her. The man who was sitting on her other side, the one who had been talking to the townspeople, got up and left the two of them together, after a quick clasp and shake of hands.

The two of them sat close together while the man told her something that made her sad. They were close but not touching; again it was obvious to Junior, from the way their heads were angled towards each other, that they knew each other well. He felt sure Fred had not lied to him. This man was his father. There sat his father, and his mother.

His mother. His mother was at the centre of all this. She was important. So, too, was his father. This actual father.

Hector Jr smiled. Whatever happened now, he knew he'd be fine.

★

'Mummy?'

Flora looked up and saw her son standing on the steps below where she and Paul were sitting, looking up at her, face shadowed by the lights behind. Then he came up another step and she could see he was filthy, his clothes torn and his knees bleeding through holes in his trousers and her heart stuttered with anxiety. But from the gleam of his teeth, she could see he was smiling at her. She had been so scared of how he would react to the destruction of everything that he believed to be true about the world, that relief not to see him screaming at her overrode surprise. Beside her, she could feel Paul tensing and withdrawing slightly.

She sped down the steps to her son and gave him a hug that he accepted stiffly. 'Hector darling, I've been so worried about you! Where have you been? Are you alright?' She brought him back up the steps to sit with Paul, who was looking awkward.

'I've been listening.'

'It must be so confusing for you. I have so much to explain.'

'I'm not confused. Grandpa did something wrong, and all these people have come here to put it right. When do we punish him?'

'Um, it's not really that simple. Lots of people did something wrong. We can't punish them all when they were lied to. We have to forgive and move on, give people a chance to change.'

'Even Grandpa?'

'Even him. He might have to face a trial. It's too soon to

say.'

Hector Jr did not look relieved to hear this, and his voice was stony as he asked, 'What about Fred? He did wrong too.'

The clutch of fear was back. How to tell him about Fred? About Paul? Flora reached out to hug him again, but he had sidled away and she couldn't quite reach him.

'I have some bad news to tell you about your ... about Fred.'

'He's not my dad – he told me.' Hector turned towards Paul. 'Fred said you're my dad. Is it true?'

Paul was practically shaking as he said, 'Yes.'

'And you're a hero, right?'

'Er, well ...'

'Yes, he's a hero,' said Flora, putting her hand on Paul's arm briefly.

'OK. Mum, I'm hungry. I've not had anything to eat all day.'

Could it really be so easy? She hoped so. Something didn't feel right, but in the rush of relief and the wish to believe all could be so easily repaired, she found herself setting her doubts aside as she rose, heart swelling to hear that he didn't hate her. Her hand grasped her son's as she said, 'Come on, let's go home and get you something to eat, and then I can tell you about Fred. Paul, maybe we can talk later?'

The Major nodded. 'I'll come and find you in a while. There are things I need to do.'

As she walked down the steps with her son, she could sense his attention was still on Paul, his head craned over his shoulder. She must reassure him he would now be her sole focus, that she wouldn't be rushing into anything. Even if there had never been much warmth between her son and her husband, particularly since that horrid thing with the cat, she was shocked by his rapid acceptance of changes that must be devastating to him. He didn't even know about Fred's death yet.

*

The Major watched Flora and Hector walk away, letting out a pent-up breath. His heart was still pounding. That had been more terrifying than facing down Spight and a whole battallion of his militia.

From the foot of the stairs, Merryn beckoned him down to join him and said, 'We need to decide what we're going to do about Spight. People are demanding to see him, and from what I'm hearing, it isn't for a polite chat.'

'Where is he now?' asked the Major.

'Still in the car. We moved it a couple of streets away to make it less likely he'll be spotted.'

The Major scratched his head and stifled a yawn. 'I suggest we get him across the border to Cornwall as soon as we can. We can bring him back for the trial when everything's calmed down.'

'How can we bring him to trial? Devon declared its independence. They have their own laws now.'

'But surely what he's done is illegal, even here.'

'Not necessarily,' Merryn replied. 'So far as I'm aware from talking to Bob, nothing he's done is against the law, because of the part of the constitution that says "Any citizen of Devon is bound by law to do all in his or her power to promote the security of the county and its people. This consideration shall over-ride all other concerns." Besides that, he's made it law that the actions of the Mayor are above scrutiny or prosecution. Taking him across the border, even holding him now, is probably illegal, because we have no extradition arrangements.'

The Major laughed shortly. 'Great. Didn't we plan for this?'

'We were so caught up in the logistics, not so much. It seemed like tempting fate.'

'What if he asked us to?'

Merryn laughed, 'What, prosecute him?'

'Maybe not that. To give him sanctuary, take him across to Cornwall. We can't leave him here. There will still be people supporting him, quietly at least. People who did well out of their ties to him. It'll be like missing cancer cells and stopping the treatment, if we just let him stay. And, which might be worse, they might decide to lynch him. Not a good start for a new democracy.'

'True. We're not really interested in punishing him, we just need to contain him, for everyone's sake. You got any ideas?'

'I just might.'

★

The electric helicopter had shaken him. He knew technological development had continued apace in the wider world, after a brief but dramatic lull caused by stringent carbon taxes, but he'd had no idea it was so far advanced, or that the Cornish – the *Cornish* for fuck's sake – had access to it. For the first time, Spight had to acknowledge he might lose this war. The only thing he had going for him was that this was a load of wimps keeping him prisoner. They didn't have it in them to do what was necessary to win. The fact he was still alive proved that. If it were him in charge, the first thing he would have done was to find a quiet spot and deliver a bullet to the brain. He'd seen who was under those hoods and masks – had they killed *anyone* in the whole time he'd been fighting them? His own grave sites were full of their fallen. He was the one with the balls to see things through.

He was still talking himself up, in the back of the car he was locked inside – *his* car fuck it – when the locks popped open. The Major opened the driver's door and climbed in. At the same time, the man who had been talking up on the stage got into the front passenger seat. The stranger twisted round to look at him and introduced himself as Merryn while the Major started the engine and began navigating his way through the twisty streets.

Spight ignored Merryn and demanded to know where they were going. Merryn shrugged and turned to face forward.

The Major looked at him in the rearview mirror, then turned his attention back to the road. 'It's late,' he said. 'You're not a young man and it's been a long day. We thought you might appreciate us finding somewhere safe for you to sleep.' They were turning right onto the old bypass and heading downhill. There was no other traffic, but still the Major kept his gaze on the road. No doubt his bleeding heart was worried there could be donkeys.

'Then take me home. It's not far. I'm sure even you could find it.'

'Not a good idea, Mayor, people know where you live.'

What was that supposed to mean? Of course they did, he was their elected representative, had kept them fed. Despite what they had been told this evening, they wouldn't forget that so soon.

The house to which they drove him was down by the river. It was clearly one of their safe houses, spartan and unlived in, but there was food in the cupboard. Merryn made him a cheese salad sandwich and said he'd be keeping him company for the night. The Major left, locking the door behind him and promising he would be back first thing in the morning.

'You know you can't detain me, don't you?' Spight challenged Merryn as he bit into the sandwich.

'Quite right. This is for your own protection, while things calm down. You can do what you like in the morning.'

Mollified, the Mayor took himself and his sandwich off upstairs. The bed, in a small room on the first floor, was a bit damp and musty, but tolerable. On a whim, he tried the bedside light. It worked. They were making good on their promise so far. How could he turn that to his advantage? There must be a way. Schemes and plans chased themselves through his brain until he fell into sleep.

In the morning, he dressed in his suit and returned downstairs to the smell of eggs scrambling. Merryn was cooking them on a small camping gas stove.

'No compunction about that fossil fuel then?' he goaded, in a good temper now he was rested.

'Biogas – carbon neutral,' Merryn replied equably. He served the eggs on to buttered toast and put the plate on the kitchen table. Spight set to with gusto, ignoring his captor until he had polished off the lot. Merryn poured him tea and offered milk.

'So you're going to let me go then?' he demanded.

'Certainly. Where do you want to go?'

'Never you mind. Just unlock that door.'

Merryn took keys out of his pocket, unlocked the front door and returned to the kitchen. Spight thought for a moment. He didn't want to walk far. Even after a night's sleep his bones ached from the activity of the last few days.

'I'll need a phone.' He would summon a minion to come

and get him.

'You can have yours back.' Merryn rummaged in a small canvas rucksack left by the front door and brought out the phone they had confiscated from Spight after his capture. He threw it to the Mayor.

Spight found Fred's number in his contacts list and hit Call. The phone rang a long time but no one answered. Lazy sod. Bob, no answer. Dug. Biff. No answer. He went through every number in the list and not one answered. Merryn watched him, his face impassive, but Spight felt mocked nonetheless. Wrenching open the front door he strode outside into the full glare of day.

The thick stone walls and curtains of the house had kept the heat out. Outside, even at midmorning, the force of the sun was fierce. Hatless, Spight put his hand over his head to protect his scalp, and headed for the shade across the street. He hadn't paid much attention to where they were the night before; now he saw he was a few streets away from the river, in one of the more run-down areas of the town, prone to flooding on spring tides.

He had a choice. He could make his way back to Bodingleigh and his house and wait out this ridiculous farce; sooner or later the Cornish would leave and he could resume control. Or he could go to the quayside and find a boat, get downriver and make his way round the coast to allies in Dorset. Give up, in other words.

No. He would never give up. He stuck by every decision he had ever made. Some people might have come out of it poorly, but the majority had done OK. They wouldn't have forgotten that, or how desperate things had been when he took over. He might not be able to persuade them to continue with the live produce shipments, but he still had his special project to fall back on. Devon could still become a world player.

He turned right, heading for the quickest route home. With any luck, he could find someone to help him before he had to walk all the way.

Within moments he was sweating through his shirt and had to remove his jacket, folding it over his right arm. When the stone struck his left shoulder, there was no wool to cushion its sharp edges, and it hurt. There was a *plink* as it dropped to the pavement behind him. Spight turned, and saw someone ducking back into one of the houses he had passed. For a moment, he considered going back and remonstrating with the stone-thrower. What on earth were they thinking? But it was hot, he wanted to get home not remonstrate with lawless hooligans, so he continued on his way, making a note of the address so he could visit retribution on the occupants once he was back at the reins.

The next stone struck the back of his neck. He yelped. When he turned around there were two young men in the street behind him.

'What do you think you're doing? You could have injured me!' he shouted in outrage.

'Slaver!' one of them shouted back, before stooping to look for more stones. The surface of the street was in disrepair; he wouldn't have to look far.

The other already had a handful of stones and was choosing which to throw. 'Baby raper!' he yelled as he let fly. His aim was good but Spight managed to dodge out of the way, his ankle turning as he leaned backwards and the stone whizzed past his nose.

For the first time, he considered that he might be in actual danger.

The safe house was behind the young men, out of his

reach. He had to continue in the same direction, hurrying now.

At the end of the road was a T-junction. Right would take him further into run-down streets. He turned left, towards the river. Spaces were wider there; he was feeling hemmed in and wanted room in order to think.

The street he entered was short. A quick glance behind told him his pursuers were gaining ground; without making it obvious, he speeded up, but refrained from breaking into a run. As he reached the end of the road he was sure he could hear more footsteps behind him but dared not look again and hurried into a small and overgrown park lined with thick hedges, on the other side of which he could glimpse the river, sunlight flashing from its surface, dazzling him. The quayside was to his right and he angled towards that. Perhaps he might have to find a boat for the short term. He would feel safer on the water.

A pitted and uneven path wound around the perimeter of the park, but he wanted to get to the quay as quickly as possible and made a short cut through knee-high grass to the nearest gap in the hedge. He didn't realise the quayside was packed with townsfolk until he had fought his way through dense hawthorn and blackthorn, becoming festooned with the rotting and water-blighted remains of blossom, emerging scratched and torn.

Spight came to an abrupt halt when he saw the crowds of people ahead. They were standing in long lines that snaked back towards the bridge. Squinting, he saw they were queuing up to approach a flotilla of boats tied up to the wall. The people at the heads of the queues were holding out shopping bags, into which fruit and vegetables, cuts of meat and rounds of cheese were being placed by the crews of the boats.

His cargo. They were giving away *his* cargo. Outraged,

Spight's first impulse was to run out, to start remonstrating with them to give it back, but his instinct for survival backed him into the hedge. Until he felt it shake, as his pursuers started making their way through.

Launching himself forward and out of reach, he turned left and trotted away from everyone, looking for a dinghy with oars. It would take too long to locate one with an outboard and a full tank. With no shade to protect him, caught in the full glare of mid-morning sun bouncing off concrete, he was soon gasping from the heat.

It was only moments before he heard his name being shouted, echoing across the quayside and the water.

'Spight!'

He risked turning to look back and saw that the townspeople at the boats had stopped what they were doing and were now looking in his direction. The two men who had been following him were through the bushes, still in pursuit. When they saw him looking back they stopped, pointed, and one of them roared again, '*SPIGHT!*'

One or two of the townspeople stepped in his direction. Emboldened, others followed them. Spight didn't wait to see what the rest would do but turned and sped away from them as fast as the heat and his aching bones would let him.

The end of the quay was getting close, but he still couldn't see a suitable boat. Besides, they might follow him onto the water. The riverbank continued from the end of the quay, but he would have to make his way across tussocky grass or be cut off, trapped. He decided to go to the left, towards the long marsh that gave the town its name, in the hope he could hide among the willows and reeds until they had gone past. Or he might be able to outpace them, double back the way he had come and sneak into town and from there make his way to

Bodingleigh. Fred would still be an ally, as would Dug and Biff. Thoughts whirling, he dashed to his left, towards the marsh.

★

Spight was showing up as a blue dot on the GPS app on Merryn's laptop, made possible by the location transponder activated in his satellite phone. Stooping over the Cornish agent's shoulder, in the kitchen of the safe house, the Major watched as the dot moved across the park, angled left, sped up a little and then turned left again.

Merryn was on his own phone, receiving reports from their people stationed on the quay, and confirmation that the Mayor was indeed being pursued by angry townsfolk and was now heading for the marsh. He ended the call and dialled another number.

★

The mob chasing him was shouting. Spight was sweating, batting at the biting insects that had descended in swarms as soon as he entered the marsh, holding his jacket over his head to keep them away from his vulnerable skin, and to cover the whiteness of his shirt. He looked up, expecting to see clouds of insects forming a huge arrow, pointing at his head and giving away his position, but the stands of willow were so thick he could barely see the sky. From the cries of sudden pain, he wasn't the only one being attacked. Good. Serve the bastards right.

His strategy seemed to have worked. As he listened, the cries and shouts started to fade, the crowds moving out of the brackish bog and heading for dry ground and better visibility.

'We've got him,' he heard a man say as he crashed through undergrowth twenty metres away from where Spight was cowering. 'All we have to do is spread out and wait. He'll come to us.'

Silence. He was alone. Trapped.

What to do now? That man had been right. Anywhere he emerged, he would be seen and chased. The thought made his stomach clench.

He was too tired to come up with another plan. He was also thirsty and his head ached. He'd had enough.

A shrill whining noise disturbed his misery. At first, he thought it was another insect, a huge mutant coming to finish him off. Then the willow began to sway and bend, wind swept the insects away and he realised it was a helicopter, coming in fast and low. It stopped and hovered above his head.

He looked up, his hair whipping over his bitten scalp.

The side door was opened. He could see someone inside, lowering a harness. The phone in his pocket vibrated as it rang.

He could barely hear the voice on the other end of the line, but he could hear enough to know it was the man who had cooked him breakfast and released him earlier that morning. Merryn.

'This is a one-time offer. Get in the helicopter and we'll take you to safety. Or stay there and take your chances.'

Fury almost sent him deeper into the marsh, but he was nothing if not a pragmatic man. He replaced the phone in his pocket and reached for the harness.

*

For a long moment, after Spight had ended the call, Merryn and the Major looked at each other without speaking. Merryn found himself holding his breath and made an effort to let it out and breathe normally.

His phone rang.

The clatter and whine of the helicopter almost drowned out the pilot's voice as she said, 'We've got him.'

BANISHING THE DARK

Will ended the video call and sat back in his chair. After a week of rest and treatment, Mal had looked almost returned to normal during their chat, although he had tired quickly and they didn't talk for long. He would be released from the hospital in another day or two, and his parents would take him home to St Germans while they decided whether to relocate back to Exeter now the war was over. There would be many such decisions being made over the next few weeks and months.

The referendum had been held swiftly. Given the lack of technology readily available, and the urgency of the need to resolve Devon's future, it had been conducted with an old-fashioned secret ballot adjudicated by some of the younger members of the Door Knockers, keen to demonstrate themselves willing to move on from the Spight days. The result had been a 68-32 per cent split in favour of re-entry into a federated British Isles. So, not everyone was happy to see changes coming, but enough were for the decision to stick. Now came a long process of restorative justice. Mediation, meditation and counselling would be offered to those who found the transition difficult, as well as retraining in low carbon industries, renewable energy installation and regenerative farming for those that wanted it.

It was hot in the kitchen of Mrs P's cottage; she had thrown open curtains, windows and doors in a symbolic act of banishing the dark. In consequence, summer sun was baking the room, but it felt good to feel its warmth against the back of his head as it angled in on its way towards the horizon. He checked his watch. Five o'clock. It was almost time to leave. He hoped Primrose was doing OK and would make it back in time.

★

Will had offered to go with her, but his presence would have been a distraction so she had said she would take Mrs P with her instead. Her parents knew Mrs P, and hopefully she retained the authority inherent in being the village schoolteacher; Primrose hoped they would behave themselves if she were there.

The cottage looked much as she remembered it, if a little less dilapidated, with repaired and newly painted windowframes and front door. The raised vegetable beds looked recently built and the crops neatly tended. Red and black currant bushes were flowering and insects hummed around the remaining late blossom. It looked as though they had done well since sending her away. She tried not to feel resentful. Will had been teaching her calming techniques and she concentrated on the rise and fall of her lungs, bringing herself into the present. It wasn't all she and Will had been practising together, but she couldn't think about that now and keep her breathing steady. She felt herself going red at the memories.

Mrs P gave her an encouraging nudge towards the front door. It was closed and she knocked on it. They had been told she would be coming, but not why, and she wondered if they might have gone out rather than see her. But the front door opened and there stood her mother.

She looked older, more weathered and less well-kept than the house, long greying hair in untidy plaits looped onto the crown of her head; she was wearing a shapeless and faded housedress with a pair of secateurs in the pocket. If she felt any strong emotions at sight of the daughter she hadn't seen for five years, she was keeping them in check.

'Primrose.' No warmth in the familiar voice. 'You'd best come in.' She turned and led the way through the short hallway into the kitchen, where Primrose had spent most of her waking life when she lived at home, spared from work in the fields and helping her mother cook instead. She'd thought at the time it was because she was her mother's favourite, and had found a guilty pleasure in that. Now she thought it was probably so she wouldn't get fit, lose weight and be ineligible for the fat farm. Mrs Prendaghast's hand found hers as she they emerged out of the comparative darkness of the hall and blinked in the light falling through the kitchen windows.

Her father was sitting in his customary place at the head of the worn pine table, his face closed to her, his body gaunt and dressed in muddy work clothes. Her mother moved towards the stove and began fussing with the kettle that lived on a hook above it, pouring in water from a jug and placing it on the hot plate. There was no sign of any of her siblings. She wondered if perhaps they had been sent out so her parents could ensure control of the situation.

'Would you like tea? We have real teabags.' Her mother sounded proud of this.

Mrs Prendaghast accepted for them both, and shoved her towards one of the chairs drawn up to the table, sinking down into another with a sigh. Primrose felt she had been rendered mute, trying to remember why she had come here. What were these people to her, besides a genetic legacy?

Her father broke the silence.

'Well, you're here. What do you want? If it's a home you're looking for now your farm's shut down, we might consider it, but you'll have to earn your keep.' He looked her up and down. 'Or we could marry you off. You're not looking too shabby since they sucked all that weight off.'

Where had he been these last few days? Did he not know that everything had changed? Was this what Will called denial? That some people couldn't see things as they were, had to rewrite everything to fit their idea of how things should be?

'I've come to ask what you were thinking, when you gave me away?' Her voice was shaky, but she got it out, and sat straighter while she waited for a reply.

'We didn't give you away, we traded you, and gave you an easier life, girly.'

Girly. Like he couldn't be bothered to remember her name.

'Easier life? Are you *mad*?' She could barely choke the words out. 'Do you have any idea how I was treated? How much it hurt? Do you know what they were planning to *do* with me?'

Her father was looking at her like she was one of the cattle he herded, with mastitis or some other complaint that might cost him grief from his boss. Like it might be cheaper and less trouble just to cut her throat. 'It was un*comf*ortable, was it?' he sneered. 'Pah! Life hurts, get used to it. You were housed and fed. It was more than we could do at the time.'

Primrose looked towards her mother, but she was busy pouring hot water into a teapot. She looked to Mrs P, who rolled her eyes and shrugged as if to say, what can you do?

The whole conversation suddenly struck her as ludicrous. How could her parents think she wanted to come back to them, to be married off or worked to death? Were they crazy?

She took a deep breath.

'I also came to say goodbye, actually. I hope you get everything you deserve out of a long life, both of you.' Without another word, she got up and headed for the front door.

'Well, it's been a pleasure,' she could hear Mrs Prendaghast saying as she scraped her chair back from the table. 'I can assure you she will be very well taken care of. A brave and resilient girl like that has a wonderful future ahead of her. I know, as her parents, that means a lot to you.'

Neither parent said anything until Primrose and Mrs Prendaghast had reached the door, when they heard Primrose's mother say, annoyed, 'Well, what a waste of tea!'

'Are you sure you won't come with us?'

Now the time had come, Primrose felt bereft at the loss of her friend, and panicky at leaving behind everything she knew. She was travelling with nothing; she had nothing to take besides the clothes she was wearing, again donated by the teacher, far too large and very worn, but received gratefully. She had been assured she wouldn't need anything, that Will's sisters would find her a wardrobe more to her liking, but she was feeling crippled with insecurity.

'Oh, no,' Mrs Prendaghast laughed. 'Or at least not yet. I'll come and visit soon, and you make sure you come back here too, when you can find the time.' The teacher patted her hand through the car's rear window, then straightened with a grunt of effort. 'I'm old and ready for a rest, and then to see how things pan out here. It's going to be interesting – I'm looking forward to designing a new curriculum!' Her eyes sparkled. She looked years younger, despite her protestations.

Merryn was in the driving seat, looking impatient to be off;

he had confided to Primrose that he was missing his littlest
girl's birthday and was keen to get back home. It was just her
and Will in the back seat, with Demelza, an agent she didn't
know in the front passenger seat, catching a ride. The Major
and Flora stood behind Mrs P, waving and smiling; they were
staying in Devon with their son for now. Hector Jr stood
beside Flora with his mother's arm across his shoulders. For
once the boy was actually smiling and sight of it made her
heart lift. If Junior could change, anything was possible.

The electric car was the same one the Major and Will had
borrowed from the safe house near Yealmpton, retrieved from
the outskirts of Dartmouth. It slid away silently as she and Will
waved goodbye out of the open windows, and within thirty
minutes of uncomfortable jouncing on the uneven roads, she
was further away from Bodingleigh than she had ever been
before. Will and the other two activists were talking about
Cornwall and people she didn't know. Primrose listened for a
while but her attention turned inward, even as her gaze took in
the unfamiliar landscape passing by the windows.

She re-ran the conversation with her parents, looking for a
sign of warmth, of love, wondering if it was her fault they
didn't care for her. Why had they had so many children if they
didn't love them? Or was it only her they didn't love? She tried
to remember if there had ever been signs or gestures of
affection when she lived with them. For anyone.

For most of her life before the farm, she remembered her
mother as pregnant, or breast feeding. Then pregnant again.
She might as well have been one of the sows in the farrowing
pen. If Primrose hadn't run away from the fat farm, had been
sent across the sea, that could have been her. With a shock, she
realised her mother had had no more choice over the direction
of her life than Primrose would have if she had been sold to a

baby farm in New Jersey. Her father hadn't been so much better off, even if as a man he had more status. Both of them had been trapped from birth, given roles and responsibities regardless of whether those suited them or not, because that was what benefited the people in charge.

What a relief. She could stop feeling so sorry for herself, as the burden of pity shifted and she found herself feeling sorry for them. She looked up and saw Will watching her, looking worried. A huge smile burst out of her as she looked at his face, grateful to have this chance of a new start.

The car was returned to its owner in Yealmpton, who accepted the keys from Will with a sardonic smile but no reproach, before leading them to the rooms they would stay in overnight and telling them a small party was being held in their honour; information that prompted a mix of social anxiety and delight in Primrose, who had never attended a party before. She worried she was not appropriately dressed, but everyone present in the rather grand dining room was wearing ordinary clothes, and she felt quite at home in Mrs Prendaghast's castoffs. A toast was drunk to the four of them, and she blushed at the attention. It was all delightful, but she was happy to leave them to it after a couple of hours and accompany Will to the room they had been given, where they curled up together in the big bed and fell straight to sleep.

They left early the next morning, walking down a steep and winding path through woods to the river, as the rest of their journey would be made by water. Merryn had explained that Cornwall had been cut off since the Devon militia blew up the road and rail bridges to Saltash and mined the roads. There were good transport links with northern France and the south coast of Wales, but the county had been largely cut off from the mainland since.

'Did us a power of good,' he had said. 'We pooled resources, sorted out our food and energy, without resorting to any of the drastic measures Devon adopted. We're almost self-sufficient now. But having the border open will be a boon, once we've cleared the mines.'

A crossing could be made across the Tamar, but it would be safer for them to sail round to Saltash. Plymouth was having some trouble adjusting to change, and the area was considered too volatile for a river crossing there.

Primrose had never been on the water before. The novelty of climbing on board the dinghy and being rowed out to the boat – which seemed large enough from the riverbank but was dwarfed the moment they left the mooring and headed out midstream – swiftly wore off. There was so much space between her and the horizon, once they emerged from the steep valley that cradled the River Yealm, that she hid below deck until forced back out into the fresh air by seasickness. Will held her close and told her to look at the horizon to keep the nausea at bay. She gulped the air and, as feelings of sickness and panic receded, the exhilaration of moving across water asserted itself, the only sound the creak of ropes and mast.

Fires were burning in Plymouth. Great plumes of black smoke tainted the blue of the sky. Some had been caused by the power grid coming back online. Others had been set by rioters trying to assert control in the power vacuum left by Spight. Merryn told them local SCREW activists were patrolling the streets on behalf of the UN, until the new Devon decided how to handle things.

Her head was nodding as they arrived at the stone dock below the ruins of the old bridges at Saltash. The sun was heading towards the horizon by the time they were done putting the boat to bed, but as the four of them walked up the steep road, there was enough light left in the day for her to look around and wonder at how much difference such a comparatively short journey had made.

The street surface they walked upon was even and flat. The doors of the houses stood open and children ran in and out in gangs, looking cheerful as they shrieked and played; all the children she had known in Bodingleigh had been too tired from chores to do much at the end of the day. Older residents sat on the front doorways of tidy-looking buildings, or weeded windowboxes full of salads and herbs. House and street lights were on, powered no doubt by the solar panels that covered the southerly exposure of every rooftop.

When they reached the top of the street they emerged into a sea of colour from a large garden that occupied the whole of the road, which Will told her was communal. Anyone could help plant or tend vegetables and fruit, and everyone could harvest, regardless of whether they had done any work. Primrose remembered her father beating someone who had snuck in and stolen potatoes from his patch, and the people hanged for taking what didn't belong to them. Such abundance and generosity were shocking to her.

'Where are the cars?' she asked, as they moved along the road. The garden spread out before her as far as she could see. She could even see stands of grain and rows of small trees growing among the vegetables, herbs and flowers A few sheep were tethered in one area of grass, cropping it peacefully.

'We keep them on the outskirts,' Demelza replied. 'We have bikes, rickshaws, scooters, skateboards, all sorts inside our towns. Cars are shared. Will can teach you to drive if you like, so you can book one through the car club if you want to explore, or go visit Mrs P once the roads have been repaired.'

Primrose looked at Will to see if Demelza was joking, and he nodded, amused by her expression. The thought of driving was something she had never considered before. Perhaps learning to ride a bike should come first.

Merryn stopped outside a house. 'This is where I leave you.'

'This is where you live?'

A small face was watching them from inside. It disappeared, and a moment later a girl aged about five had shot out of the open front door and thrown her arms around Merryn's legs. He scooped her up and held her close, nuzzling her hair so she squeaked with delight.

'Yes. Come visit tomorrow and Will and I can show you around the bigger farms, the wind farm and anaerobic digestion plants if you like.' He turned to Demelza. 'You take care now, I'll see you at the Assembly next week.' He hugged them all in turn with his one available arm, said goodbye and went into the house, his daughter chattering her news throughout.

'What's the assembly?' asked Primrose, as the three of them continued onwards.

'It's a general meeting, anyone can come,' Demelza explained. 'It's where we share news, celebrate successes and make decisions. It's fun, you should come. The next one'll be, like, a huge party.'

Demelza left them at the car club at the edge of the town, to collect a vehicle to drive to her home village of Millbrook. The cars were parked neatly in rows under screens of solar panels, heavy black umbilicals leading from the panels to power them. Primrose could see how this would shade them in hot weather, and the panels could be placed where they were needed, without taking up more room than necessary.

She admired the logic, but 'How much further?' she asked, starting to droop.

'Not much, we're just a couple of streets further on.'

Will's house was in the middle of a terrace. Here too, the door was open, light spilling out onto the front step. It was almost full dark now. Primrose hesitated when she heard voices inside. What if his family didn't like her? Will dragged her up the shallow steps, then paused in the doorway. When his eyes met hers, he looked nervous.

'I hope you'll like it here, Prim. I want you to stay.'

She looked at him, incredulous. 'Are you kidding? Where else am I going to go?'

'Anywhere you like. No one's making decisions for you anymore.'

She considered that for a moment. It opened up a freedom that made her feel dizzy with possibilities. The whole world was hers to explore.

'I think this will do fine, for now at least.'

He looked anxious at that, until he saw the smile at the corner of her mouth and kissed it.

'Come on,' he said as he pulled her through the open doorway. 'Come meet my folks.'

ACKNOWLEDGEMENTS

Many thanks to my readers, Jo, Jane, Rebecca and Becks for giving feedback on early drafts, and keeping me going with encouragement. Also thanks to my editor, Lynn Curtis, and to designer Tricia Stubberfield for the awesome cover.

Thanks also to the people inspired me. In particular:
Pete Bethune, of Earthrace Conservation, who sparked this story when I read in an interview that he and his crew each donated a kilo of fat for their first boat. (One kilo = 1 litre fuel, approx. Don't try this at home.)
Polly Higgins and her team, for their campaign to criminalise the destruction of ecosystems and have ecocide recognised as a war crime.
Greenpeace.
Bill McKibben and 350.org.
Greta Thunberg and the school strikers.
Extinction Rebellion.
Everyone who has put their bodies on the line or otherwise dedicated their lives to maintaining a liveable biosphere on our beautiful planet. I salute you.

ABOUT THE AUTHOR

Sophie Galleymore Bird has a varied CV that includes selling audioguides at the Tate and life modelling for the Royal Academy. Her first novel, *Maneater*, was published in 1993, an experience that led to her working in marketing and social activism for the next quarter century. *To See The Light Return* is her first self-published novel.

Sophie lives in a corner of a mock-Gothic manse with a laurel-infested garden, in Devon, with her family, dog, cat, chickens and abundant wildlife.

She is currently working on a trilogy of crime thrillers. To find out more, visit her Facebook author page or find her on Instagram under sophiegorebird.

10% of profits from this book will go towards funding the activities of Transition Town Totnes, part of the Transition Network.

Lightning Source UK Ltd.
Milton Keynes UK
UKHW041902020519
341997UK00001B/233/P